For my sister, Deirdre.
People consider me the weird one. I blame you
and Alice Cooper. Thanks for being a great sis and
friend. We've come a long way together.
Love you always and forever.

Love to my baby girl, Casey, and my beautiful
nieces, Tina, Tasha, Lexy, Ashleigh, and Peggy.
You're amazing young women, each of you unique,
each of you an inspiration. You all enrich my life.
Reach for your dreams— there's nothing
you can't achieve.

—*Terri*

• • • • • • • • •

To all the youth at Rainbow Alley
who boldly live free and true. You are my inspiration.
And to the many youth who remain chained by fear,
may you find strength and community so you
can shed your secrets and simply live.
You're astonishingly beautiful, just as you are.

—*Lynda*

BREAKING UP
is hard to do

*Stories about falling out of love
by four incredible authors*

Written by
Niki Burnham
Terri Clark
Ellen Hopkins
Lynda Sandoval

GRAPHIA

An Imprint of Houghton Mifflin Company
Boston 2008

Last Stand

BY NIKI BURNHAM

CHAPTER ONE

I am, without a doubt, the luckiest guy in the entire West Rollins High School junior class. Here's why:

1. I almost have the 'rents talked into ponying up half the cost of a car.
2. I made the cross-country team.
3. I have an extremely gorgeous girlfriend, Amber.
4. She is also stacked.
5. She's totally into me, quirks and all.
6. I have a shot at becoming first-chair sax. Which means I'd look straight across the room at the first chair clarinet . . . who is almost certainly going to be Amber.
7. I scored Mr. Daniels for Chemistry. Hello, easy A.

Of course, such a list requires clarification. First, I realize that for many people, making a sports team is a given. Not for me. Because participation in sports furthers my quest to maintain a bare minimum level of social acceptance—a tough thing when you're the class brain—this is an event that causes great frivolity and rejoicing. When no one is watching, of course.

And the stacked thing? I understand that this is a totally sexist thing to say. So shoot me. They're THERE. You can't help but notice. If I were really sexist, I'd have put this item first on the list.

I met Amber DeWitt in kindergarten when we were at the same station—the water balloon toss—on field day. I didn't really notice her, but she claims that I told her I thought her striped shoelaces were cool. I'm not so sure. If I did, it would've been because she specifically asked me what I thought. Spontaneously complimenting a girl on her shoelaces isn't something I'd do. Plus, we're talking kindergarten. No way was I more interested in some girl's shoelaces than in the chance to lob water balloons with no repercussions.

The first day I do remember Amber clearly was in second grade. I was at Britton Field, waiting for my Little League game to start. She was sitting in the bleachers watching the end of her younger brother's T-ball game. She hopped off the bleachers, walked over, and leaned against the fence with a hand on her hip, watching me and my friends toss the ball around in the grassy area outside the left-field fence. She had one side of her face all squinched up and her eye was closed.

I asked her if she had something stuck in her eye and wanted us to go find her mom or something. She had bruises on her legs and a couple of scabs like she'd fallen off her bike, so I figured she was a klutz and did something to herself climbing off the bleachers, and was standing there hoping we'd get a grownup to help her with her current injury.

Her face went red; she stopped doing the squinchy thing and mumbled that she was fine. A minute later, she went back to the bleachers and left us alone. I chalked it up to weird girl behavior and didn't think about it again.

Last year, after we'd been together for about seven months and we were sitting in those same bleachers watching her little brother playing shortstop on his traveling team, she admitted to me that she'd been trying to wink at me that day. She said she'd wondered for the longest time whether I'd known what she was doing and was being mean, or if I was simply clueless but nice. She kissed me and told me she was glad to realize I'd just been clueless but nice.

I was a total sappy dork and told her I couldn't believe it took me eight years to get a clue and ask her out. It wasn't like I was asking out tons of other girls—and none at all until about seventh grade, when I learned pretty fast that it's not fun unless you know for a fact they like you already—but that sappy statement earned me an even better kiss later, when we weren't sitting in view of Little League parents.

Now that it's the first day of junior year, and the one-year anniversary of the first time I ever kissed Amber, I'm hoping a little of that sentimental stuff earns me even more mouth-to-mouth gratitude. Not that I'm a scumbag who only wants you-know-what from a girl. So not the case. Amber expects the sap and the kissy stuff that follows. Who am I to deny her?

"Hey, Toby!"

I look over my shoulder, through the crowd in junior hall, trying to see Griff. Griff Osterman's been my best friend since we were seated together in first grade, so I'd recognize his voice anywhere. A moment later, he emerges from behind a knot of seniors with a huge smile on his face. His dark brown hair juts in every direction at once. In an effort to maximize his sleeping time, Griff clocked his morning routine last year. He told me it takes him exactly ten minutes to take a leak, brush his teeth, shave (right), and put on his clothes, and then eight minutes to get from home to school. He gives himself two minutes of cushion when setting his alarm clock, just in case. When I asked him where deodorant and flossing fit into his twenty-minute routine, he shrugged.

Girls don't seem to care, though. He makes disheveled look Calvin Klein–model cool. Jerk.

"I'm wiped, man. Didn't get back from Texas 'til yesterday morning," he says once he reaches me. "My parents were stupid enough to want to drive instead of fly. So how'd cross-country tryouts go?"

"Fine. Hot." I set my sax case down on the floor. Can't wait to get the thing into one of the band lockers so I don't have to schlep it through the halls. "It was in the high nineties all week."

"I meant how'd it go for you, dumbass."

I almost died from heat exhaustion. I shrug. "Made it."

"Sweet." He says it as if it's no big thing. Of course, he made the team without even attending tryouts. He was one of our top runners last year (yes, as a sophomore), so when his mom explained to Coach Jessup that Griff would have to miss tryouts to attend an out-of-state family wedding—and that they'd be gone the entire week—the coach didn't care.

Told him to have a great time and watch out for the bridesmaids.

"How's Amber?" he asks. "I think I saw her maybe twice all summer."

"You're not the only one." I step sideways to let a group of gum-cracking senior girls walk by. "She was working fifty hours a week at Friendly's. More, sometimes. Made good money, though."

Griff looks past me and grins. "Yeah, and she put some of it to good use. Damn, she's smokin' in that shirt. It's gotta be new, 'cause I'd have noticed *that.*"

I turn to see Amber threading her way through the hall, eyes focused right on me. Be still, my heart, 'cause Griff is right. She looks frickin' fabulous. She's wearing a pair of loose, cocoa-colored shorts that hit just above her knees, and a short-sleeved pink T I've never seen before, one that shows off her assets, but in a casual way that makes you wonder if she realizes just how well fitted a top it really is—at least from a guy's perspective. I elbow Griff. "Eyes to yourself."

"Like you could stop me. Catch you at lunch?"

"Sure." He says hi to Amber as he passes her in the hall, then looks back and mouths a "hot damn!" to me. I ignore him.

Junior hall runs along the back of the main building. One side is lined with lockers, and the other with windows that start at waist height and go all the way up to a very high ceiling, so there's tons of sunlight in the morning. As Amber approaches, I decide that the architect must've been thinking of exactly this moment when he designed those windows, because the way the light is streaming in behind her makes her dark hair look like it's ringed with a halo.

Hot damn? Oh, yeah. But not in the do-me-baby way Griff thinks. There's something ethereal and fragile about her, something that makes me want to take care of her, yet at the same time always has me questioning deep down inside if she's for real. That's what makes me think *hot damn.*

She stops a whisper away from me, nearly kicking my sax case. "I have something for you."

"Yeah? I have something for you, too." I lean in to kiss her, but she giggles and pushes on my chest with one hand.

"That's not what I meant, dork boy." She eases her camo backpack off her shoulder, unzips it, then pulls out a gift wrapped in sparkly silver paper. "I know I should wait 'til after school, but I'm dying to see what you think. Happy anniversary."

"You didn't have to get me a present." Even though I got her one. I'm not the total dumbass Griff says I am.

"Open it already!"

I hike my backpack farther up my shoulder and take the gift. I prop it on the windowsill and she cuddles in beside me, watching as I start to unwrap. Within seconds, I see the cover of the book. Correction: The Book. Capital *T*, capital *B.*

"Hour by Hour: The True Story of the Alamo," I read aloud.

"You didn't buy it for yourself already, did you?"

I shake my head. It came out this past Saturday; I know because I've been waiting for it for months.

"Oh, yay!" Her arm is around my back, just at the top of my shorts. I can smell her perfume. Or shampoo. I'm never sure which, but it's delicious. I've missed that smell. Lately, she's reeked of old grilled cheese and dried-up ice cream. Eau de Friendly's.

She says, "I know it's the kind of thing you love—famous last stands and all that. Keira said you'd been talking about getting some Alamo book, and the woman at the bookstore told me this one is brand-new.

The guy won a Pulitzer for his book about Pancho Villa, so I figured that even if this wasn't the right Alamo book, you might like it."

"It's exactly the right Alamo book." I'll have to remember to thank my sister later. I turn so Amber and I are hipbone to hipbone, right there against the row of windows. "Thank you."

"Happy anniversary, Toby."

The warning bell for first period rings, but I just smile at her perfect, freckled face and kiss her. This time she kisses me back.

Yep. I'm officially the luckiest guy in the building.

Someone yells at us to get a room. Amber pulls away, but she's still smiling, and it's the same lovesick-happy grin she had at the beginning of the summer, on the night we almost did it. Capital *I* and *T.* The night before she started her incarceration at Friendly's. "Time for band, I guess."

"Yep. Let's go." She gives me a final kiss, then slides her hand into mine for the walk outside and across the quad to band.

Man, am I glad to be back at school and done with summer. I need my Amber.

• • •

During sixth-period American History, I feel a vibration in my pocket just as Ms. Lewis finishes going over page three of the mind-numbing seventeen-page class syllabus. I wait until her back is turned, then pull out my cell phone. Careful to keep it under the desk, I read the text message from Keira:

know you're in class but stewie sick . . . daycare called . . . need to pick him up then take him to doc. pls pls pls cover for me for hour or so after practice? appt at 4:45 will try to be fast . . . will pay you.

Crap. I'll have to go straight from cross-country to the coffee shop, which means no time for homework if I want to go to Amber's later.

But if Stewart's sick, I gotta help. Mom still doesn't get the difference between a cappuccino and a latte. Plus, Keira feels bad enough about having to live at home; asking Mom or Dad to fill in for her at the coffee shop would border on self-torture. Under the desk, I text back an okay. Between classes, I text Amber to tell her I might not be able to make it over tonight, that my sister needs help.

I slide into seventh period just as the bell rings and hope like mad that Amber's not too pissed.

• • •

"Toby, you so rock," Keira says as she whips off her green Fair Grounds apron. She looks twice as tired as I feel, and I'm fresh off a three-mile run.

I hope I don't look that wiped and old at twenty-two.

"I have ten minutes to pick up Stewart from daycare or they charge me an extra fifty bucks. They can only keep him so long once it's determined that he's running a fever."

"Go." I slip the apron over my head, then wave her toward the door. Thankfully, it's slow at this time of day—just a few people huddled over laptop computers, coffee already in hand—because I haven't showered yet and therefore have no desire to interact with customers. Hopefully the smell of freshly ground coffee beans will disguise my stink until she gets back.

"You're the best," she says, grabbing her car keys and purse from under the register. "I should be back in time to close up at six. It's probably another ear infection. They can diagnose that and get me medicine fast."

"Really, it's no problem." Especially since she promised to pay me, which brings me that much closer to automobile ownership. If it stays quiet, maybe I can get some of my American Lit reading out of the way, start on Trig, and still try to meet Amber. Not that she's acknowledged my earlier text.

I check my text messages one more time. Finally, a reply:

no prob. catch u later . . . A.

Yep. She's pissed. Otherwise, there'd be a "love, A." at the end. I start to dial, then remember that she stayed after school to get a head start on some work for her Model U.N. class. I hang up, deciding it's better to call when I know I can talk to her, not her voice mail, and tell her I think I can get to her place tonight. I should probably bring her something from the coffee shop as an apology gift, just to cover my bases.

Unfortunately, within ten minutes of Keira's departure, I'm over-whelmed by the entire junior varsity volleyball team, who all decided to grab iced coffees post-practice. When Keira shows up at five min-utes after six, with Stewart crying in the crook of her arm, I'm only halfway through wiping up the tables and have read exactly zero pages of *The Great Gatsby*. The volleyball girls left black mystery sludge on the table nearest the TV, and I'm trying to soften it up with a wet rag. Soaking is the solution to all messes, isn't it?

"I can get that, Toby," she says.

"And put Stewart where?"

Keira glances down at Stewie, who nestles in closer. "You have a point."

My nephew loves me like crazy—who wouldn't love good ol' Uncle Toby, the guy who sneaks you pieces of French fry when your mom's not looking?—but when Stewie's sick, he's all about Mommy. He'll scream like mad if she sets him down or hands him off to me now.

I use my fingernail to pick at the edge of the black stuff. Don't those girls care that they made a mess on such nice tables? Keira shopped forever to find them, hoping to give Fair Grounds just the right combination of comfort and class. It hacks me off when people have no respect for others' property.

"So what'd the doctor say? Another ear infection?" The kid's only eighteen months old, and he'd had at least six or seven already.

"Yep. And strep."

I stop working on the table and look at Stewart. His cries have settled down to hiccups now that he knows his mom's going to keep
cuddling him. "Isn't that pretty serious?"

She smoothes his hair back from his forehead and smiles at him.
"Nothing modern drugs can't cure. Problem is, no daycare for a couple of days. They won't take him back until he's fever free for twenty-
four hours so the other kids don't catch it. Of course, daycare's probably where Stewie got it, but whatever."

I go back to chipping away the table gunk. The soaking must've
worked, because it peels off in one big sticky strip, like frozen maple
syrup, leaving the table unmarred. "So what are you going to do about
the shop?"

"Beg one of the morning people to pull a double shift. I can't keep
Stewie here with me, even in his high chair. Don't want to expose customers or staff, you know?"

"What if they can't do it?"

"Close up early." She says it like it's no big deal, but I know it's a
huge deal. She's open from four-thirty in the morning until six in the
evening. She has two people who come in and work the early half of
the day, while she's giving Stewie his breakfast and getting him to daycare, but she's always here from eight 'til six—and all by herself after
two, when the lunch rush ends. If she has to close at two for a few days,
it'll hit her profits hard. The afternoon guys—the ones with the laptops—can nurse one coffee for hours, which is how Keira handles the
shop by herself then with no problems. But boy, do the laptop folks
spend money. They're the ones who buy the fancy coffee mugs, take
home bags of shade-grown organic coffee by the pound, or grab a
dozen muffins on a whim to take back to the office. The stuff with
good profit margins.

I go behind the counter to rinse out the rag in the sink. "I could
try—"

"No, you can't. You have cross-country and homework and other
responsibilities. I'm not so far out of high school that I've forgotten.

I'll swing it." She walks to the door of the shop and flips the sign to indicate the place is closed.

I want to tell her that Pete should be swinging it, too. But they broke up, he joined the Army and went to some post in Georgia, and she's stubborn enough not to accept anything from him. Says she doesn't want a dime, doesn't want to deal. No ties.

She claims she's ecstatic about this arrangement. I've programmed my brain and mouth to issue a "Whatever you say, Keira" auto-responder whenever she tells me this.

I think she doesn't remember what she was like pre-Stewie any-more. She was totally into sports in high school, had lots of friends, and did a decent job on the academic front. She met Pete, who's from Northglenn, at a high school football game and they hit it off. Things were even better when she got to college in Boulder. Pete was there, too. She loved her classes, raved about her professors. She even claimed to love her dorm. But after two years, she was back home again, pregnant and single. She said it was fine, that she'd manage, and promptly used the rest of her college savings to put a down payment on Fair Grounds.

To everyone's surprise, Keira got the place in shape in only three months. Within a week of opening, it became *the* popular place to be, despite the fact she looked like she'd swallowed a basketball at the time. I know she's proud of how Fair Grounds has done and claims she's happy beyond words with her life.

But she's not the same Keira anymore. Always tired, always seri-ous. She doesn't talk about her friends from high school or college, and I don't think she ever sees them, even when they're in town dur-ing school breaks. It's all about Stewie.

Not that it shouldn't be all about Stewie. It just strikes me as a lonely life, no matter what she says.

She grabs the drawer from the cash register and sets it on the counter with one hand, balancing Stewart against her chest with the other. He's completely quiet now; he probably loves the smell of coffee and the relaxed atmosphere of Fair Grounds as much as I do.

I take off my apron and toss it on the counter. "Want me to help tally?"

"Nah. Go do your homework. Don't want to screw things up on the first day of school." She pauses. "Isn't it a big day for you and Amber?"

The one downside of my first-ever kiss with Amber? My sister walked in on us. It's not like we told everyone that today's the one-year anniversary of that event, but since Amber mentioned talking to Keira before buying the Alamo book, I'm guessing Keira put two and two together.

I brandish my cell phone. "I'm going to call her on the walk home."

"That's not good enough, Toby. Girls remember the first kiss. Even if that kiss happens to occur in a garage."

"I bought her a gift, all right?"

"A good one?" Why unromantic Keira focuses on this is beyond me. Females are a mystery, my sister most of all.

"So how's Pete doing these days?" I ask. "Gonna fill him in on Stewie's strep? Guys like to know that kind of thing."

She rolls her eyes and laughs out loud. "Now, was that necessary? You could have just told me to leave it alone, mind my own business."

"Coulda. Didn't." She's so used to me making comments, she doesn't even get annoyed anymore. I grab my backpack from under the counter and ask her one more time if she wants me to tally the receipts. On her assertion that she'd prefer to handle it herself, I tell her I'll see her at home, then slip out the front and down the stairs, holding my cell phone above my head so Keira knows I'll call Amber ASAP.

CHAPTER TWO

I'm dialing Amber's number when I hear her calling my name.

I turn and display my cell phone while she jogs to catch up to me. "I was just calling you."

"Saw the lights still on at Fair Grounds and had Meghan drop me off on the way home to see if I could help you close up. Keira told me you'd just left." Amber's out of breath, but smiling. She weaves her fingers through mine, and we head up the road, toward the gates of Rocky Knolls, the development where we both live. Saying "the gates of Rocky Knolls" makes it sound fancier than it is. They're two generic stone pillars with a sign that says "ocky Knolls"; we lost the "R" my freshman year. It's a source of constant amusement for the kids who don't live in Rocky—or "ocky"—Knolls.

As we walk, I apologize for the text, but she says it's cool, that she'd have done the same thing for Keira and Stewie. We talk a little about Model U.N. She thinks she and her best friend, Meghan, may actually get to be ambassadors this year, which is why they stayed after school to help out. I gather being an ambassador is a good thing, so I say all the appropriate supportive boyfriend stuff. After that, we're quiet, just enjoying each other's company. Eventually, my mind drifts to my homework. How long could it take to read thirty pages of *The Great Gatsby* and do twenty Trig problems?

"You're not going to come over tonight, are you?" Her voice is soft, but there's a pouty undercurrent to her words. She's forgiven me for the text message, but she's unhappy about it jeopardizing our time together. And she knows me well enough to know that when I'm quiet, it's usually because I'm making a mental to-do list instead of thinking about her.

"I'll try to after I shower and eat. I need to see how bad the Trig homework is." I can't screw up the first week. I had a teacher in middle school with a reputation for being super strict. I was so nervous about impressing her that I vomited at my desk on the first day. Not only did my friends tease me for weeks—they still bring it up, so to speak, from time to time—but I swear the teacher held it against me the whole year. Thought of me as the strange vomit kid.

It's never, ever something I'd admit out loud, but I want to make a good impression on my teachers this year. They're the people I'm going to need to write college recommendation letters for me.

I stop walking and tug on Amber's hand to stop her, too. "Think you could stop by my place for a few minutes right now?"

She shakes her head. "I promised Mom I'd get home by six-thirty for dinner."

"Just for a sec? We're nearly to the gates already. You can still get home on time." I have to find a way to give her the necklace today. She's big on celebrating events on the exact day. No party for her on Friday night when her birthday's actually on Thursday, no attending Fourth of July fireworks on any day other than the Fourth.

She turns and starts walking again, but doesn't let go of my hand, so I follow along. When we get to the intersection where I usually go left to my house and she goes right, heading uphill to her family's two-story French colonial, she stops and looks up at me. "You know if I come to your house, I won't make it back by six-thirty and I really need to get home. Just come over later and bring your Trig. All right?"

I know I should say no. Just stay home, wash off the cross-country stink, finish my homework, and then do a lightning-fast run to her place to deliver the necklace before she goes to bed. But I want so, so badly to go to her place, to curl up with her on the basement sofa, like we did before summer and Friendly's got in the way, that my mouth overrides my brain.

"Fine," I tell her. "But we actually have to do homework."

"No problem. I have a bunch, too." She gives me a quickie kiss goodbye, and I tell her I'll try to be there in an hour.

• • •

"You kids all right down here? Need anything else to drink?" Mrs. DeWitt is standing halfway down the basement stairs, leaning over the railing so she can see Amber and me on the sofa in front of the television. I'm sprawled at one end, with my Trig book open, calculator out, and fifteen problems finished. Amber's at the other end, feet tucked under her, reading her American History assignment.

"We're good, thanks," I assure her. Amber adds a "yep."

"Holler if you need anything." She turns and heads upstairs, then shuts the basement door behind her. We listen as her footsteps sound on the hallway floor above us. Seven steps, then the sound deadens as she hits carpet in the family room. Amber looks at me. We both know this is the signal that we're being left alone for the evening, that her mother expects us to keep working on our homework.

We also take it as the signal that we're good for at least an hour if we feel like making out. There will be seven more steps, the sound of the door opening, and five steps down the stairs until she hits the visual danger zone. But she probably won't be back, and Amber's giving me the look.

"How're you doing on that?" I ask, shooting a pointed look at her history book.

"Almost done."

"Me, too. Only five more Trig problems." Of course, I still have to do the *Gatsby* reading. But if I can just finish this—

Amber's feet tangle with mine on the sofa. I move a little closer, trying to focus on the next Trig problem.

No dice.

My papers slide off onto the floor as Amber grabs my ankles. In a matter of seconds, she has her hands beside my knees, then around my waist, and we're lying on the sofa kissing like we haven't kissed in months.

Screw Trig. Screw F. Scott Fitzgerald and impressing teachers.

I want Amber's weight on top of me, my hands in her hair, the warm, fulfilled feeling I get whenever my arms are around her. The headiness of being so close, I can inhale whatever it is that makes her smell like *her*.

Amber's hands slip under my T-shirt, and I'm all too happy to reciprocate, sliding my fingers under the sides of her bra, then slowly forward, feeling the soft curve of flesh right at the edge of the cups. It's our usual routine, her pushing my shirt up and me pushing up hers, so we're skin to skin on the sofa as we kiss, but in a way that allows us to yank our clothing back quickly if there are footsteps in the hallway above.

But tonight, instead of letting her hands continue to explore under my shirt, Amber reaches down and slides her hands along the waistband of my shorts, first on the outside, then along the inside. "One year," she whispers as her lips move toward my ear. "One year since you kissed me in your garage. I thought you never would."

We'd been dancing around our connection for months, becoming friends through marching band, then hanging out together whenever we practiced outdoors. She was going out with Connor Ralston most of the year—one of those superjocks who are good-looking and at ease in every situation—and she started confiding in me about the ups and downs of their relationship. First, in bits and pieces during those outdoor hours in band, then in more depth via IM and late-night cell phone calls when she and Connor had a particularly dramatic day.

In other words, I'd happily relegated myself to the same pitiful role all average, somewhat geeky guys take when they're around a gorgeous, out-of-reach girl: I became her sounding board just so I could spend more time around her. I never in a million years thought I'd be anything more than a friend to her, but neither did I want our symbiotic relationship to be put on hold just because school was out for the summer. So when freshman year ended, I asked her on a whim if she wanted to get together to practice over the summer.

She shocked me and said yes, even though no one really expected us to practice.

When Connor dumped her in early August for a girl from another school, her girlfriends assured Amber she'd get Connor back. It bugged her, she claimed, because she wasn't even sure she wanted Connor back if he wasn't going to treat her the way she deserved to be treated. I told her to ignore her friends and go with her gut, that if she got back with him, fine. But if not, when she was ready she'd find someone better. Someone who'd spoil her.

I even gave her *names*, I was so pathetic. (And I thank God she laughed out loud and said, "Too full of himself!" when I suggested Griff.)

The day before sophomore year started, when her mom took her to pick up new reeds for her clarinet, she called and offered to grab some for my sax. She dropped them off a few hours later as I was sweeping out the garage, trying to earn car money. We flirted a little, talked about band and whether she could possibly make first chair as a sophomore, and then I was kissing her. Just leaned over the push broom and did it without letting myself think about it first.

And it was perfect. At least until Keira walked in with a garbage bag full of dirty diapers, yelled, "Whoa! Um sorry!," dropped the bag on the floor, and hurried back into the house laughing her head off. One year ago today.

I remember the necklace I got for her and whisper, "Hey, I forgot. I have something in my backpack."

"Really?" She eases back, and the grin on her face is downright heartstopping. I forgot how much I like the way she smiles at me while we're kissing and no one else is around. Like I'm the only person in the world who makes her feel this happy.

I reach to the floor and unzip the bag one-handed, keeping my other hand in its comfy location, tucked under the side of her bra, and pull out the box containing the necklace. I slide it so it's on my chest, right between us. "Happy anniversary, Amber."

Twin lines furrow the area between her eyes, like she was expecting something else, but they disappear when she smiles. "You got me a present! Um . . . you want me to open it now?"

"Yeah. Is there a problem?"

"Of course not!" She sits up, letting her rear end slide into the space between my thigh and the back of the sofa, so I push myself upright and pull her onto my lap. She eases a finger under the tape, then peels off the wrapping paper without tearing it.

My heart nearly stops at her sharp intake of breath as she opens the box from the jeweler. "Toby, this is gorgeous!"

"You like?"

She nods, fingering the gold-dipped aspen leaf and the small round opal set in its center.

"I thought you might like something outdoorsy," I explain. "When I saw this one, with your birthstone, it seemed like something you'd wear."

She doesn't say anything. She just stares at the necklace lying against the fuzzy blue velvet inside the box.

"If you don't like it, I can take it back and you can choose something else."

Could I sound like a bigger dweeb? I can just hear Keira's reaction. She'd say, *If she already told you it's gorgeous, why in the world are you offering to return it? Take a girl at her word!*

Amber blinks, then smiles at me. "Never. It's perfect. I'll wear it all the time."

She takes it out of the box and asks me to hold her hair out of the way while she fastens it. Once it's on, she wraps her arms around my neck and kisses me, long and slow and soft. It's quiet; I can't even hear the television upstairs. Just me and Amber and the low hum of the DeWitts' air conditioning. Like no one could ever disturb us down here.

She must have the same feeling, because she slides her hands down my back, then eventually around to the front to play with the button on my shorts again.

I want to stop her, but I don't want to, either. The sensation of her fingernails running along my waist, then lower, just below my belly button, is driving me nearly over the edge. I think I'm going to combust, but in a very, very good way.

I know she can tell, since she's sitting in my lap, but it's not stopping her. I swallow hard and try to think of something else. Cars I might be able to afford. Ms. Lewis's stupid syllabus. Ms. Lewis herself. But nothing's easing the problem.

Then she maneuvers my shorts down a few inches, so they're barely covering me, and pushes me backward on the sofa so she can get them the rest of the way down if she wants.

"Amber, we can't," I tell her between kisses. "If you keep . . . any more and I might come."

She smiles against my lips and moves her body—with her porno mag–worthy breasts—against me. Then she slips her fingers into the waistband of my underwear.

"Really, Amber. We need to stop." I can't believe I'm saying what I'm saying to her—it's bad enough I just used the word *come* in a sentence out loud—but what's my alternative? "If . . . well, it'll make a mess. Your parents are gonna know."

And I don't want to.

When it gets right down to it, no matter how good this feels physically, my brain's telling me it's *wrong.* I can't get a hand job in her parents' basement. It was bad enough that she gave me one at Sophomore Blast last year, when we were hidden away in her tent. Well, *good,* as in how it felt, but bad in the sense that we could have been discovered—by Meghan, who was sharing the tent, by one of the chaperones, by anyone who happened to stumble away from the annual sophomore class lakeside party. And bad in that when I realized what she really wanted then was to have sex, that the hand job wasn't the destination but a prelude to what Amber considered the main event, I squirreled my way out of there before she could say the words. I cut her off mid–*I want to* and told her Griff was going to come looking for me because I'd promised to play on his team in the flag football game.

"We'll figure something out." Her eyes lock on to mine, but her hands stay right where they are. "Toby, it's our anniversary. I . . . I think today should be the day. I've been thinking about it for months, and Toby, we're ready for this. We are."

"So you really . . . ?" I can't say the words, but it's plain from her face that she's planning on way more than a hand job tonight. That in her mind, we're picking up where we left off in the tent.

It felt all out of whack then. It feels out of whack now. Surreal.

"That's a big step," I say.

She's a virgin. Connor pushed her, but she never went all the way with him. I know because she gave me all the details back when I was just her friend, hoping I could give her, in her words, "the guy's perspective." (Like I'd have the slightest insight into a mind like Connor Ralston's. Just because I'm male doesn't mean we're the same species. But I wasn't going to admit that to her.)

A blush creeps across her cheeks. "I, um, actually thought, when you went for your backpack earlier, that you might have a condom in there. Maybe."

No.

"But the necklace was okay," she adds in a rush. "I just thought, after having virtually no time together this summer, and with it being our anniversary, it'd be perfect. I've missed you so much."

"Your parents are upstairs."

She laughs. "You know they won't check on us for a while. Their favorite show's on, and there's no way they're leaving to check on us. We're focusing on homework, remember?"

What I remember is that I'm supposed to be doing my homework instead of my girlfriend.

I reach up with one hand to push her hair back, looping a long strand behind her ear. Man, she looks cute like that, with her hair hanging down on one side of her face and tucked back on the other.

"I really want to, Toby. I think it's time to take our relationship to the next level, don't you?"

I know I should make an excuse, like I did in the tent. Say that the timing's not good since it's nearly nine p.m. on a Tuesday and I have to get home. Point out that I do *not* have a condom, not in my wallet or backpack or even at home in my nightstand.

Tell her I think she's too special to lose her virginity on a basement sofa.

A dozen gentle letdowns run through my head, but what do I say? "No."

CHAPTER THREE

As soon as the word leaves my mouth, I know I'm screwed, and not in the way Amber originally intended.

Her eyes widen for a moment, like she's unsure whether I'm kidding around, then fill with tears as she realizes I mean it.

"I don't believe this," I think she says. It's more to herself than to me, so I'm not sure. She shoves at my shoulder, unable to get off me fast enough.

I sit up and grab her hand to stop her from getting off the sofa. "It's not that I don't want to keep going, Amber. I mean, this is fantastic. I just didn't think tonight . . ." I swear, I must be insane. "I'm not ready."

She glances down at my shorts. "All evidence to the contrary. Unless you mean you're not in love with me enough yet."

I scoot so one of the pillows from the back of the sofa gives me some cover. "It's not that, either. Definitely not that."

I can't imagine being as into someone as I'm into Amber. Who else in the world would tell her friends that it's cute when I describe the hand-to-hand combat that occurred during the sea battle marking the final defeat of Blackbeard? Who else would appreciate how much I want to be first-chair sax? And I can't imagine anyone else calling me at exactly midnight on February 28 to wish me a happy birthday, telling me she's thought of me on this date since she first saw my Leap Day birthday posted on the hall calendar outside my kindergarten classroom and thought it was cool.

I cup her face in my hands, forcing her to look at me, to see how serious I am. "Amber, I love you. I hope you know that." It's not like I haven't told her before.

"Is it . . . is it a protection issue, then?" she asks.

"I don't have any." I can tell from the lift in her expression that she's about to tell me she does, but I don't want the discussion to go down that particular road. I let my hands drop into my lap. "But that's not it, either."

"A religious thing? I mean, I completely understand if that's it." She gives me a lopsided grin. "It didn't stop Keira from doing it, obviously, but she did tell me she doesn't believe in abortion, that it was part of her Catholic upbringing."

"You talked to Keira about us?" Who asks a guy's *sister* about this kind of thing?

"No! I stopped in for coffee on my way to work last week and she mentioned that Stewie loves his new daycare. So I asked if it was hard for her sometimes with a baby, or if she ever worried about how she'd handle it all when she first found out she was pregnant. And she told me not handling it wasn't an option; she knew that she could never have an abortion as a good Catholic—those were her exact words—and said she knew she'd have to find a way to make it work. That's all."

"Oh. For a minute there, I was wondering—"

"No way! I would *not* talk to your sister about sex! Geez." She smiles when she says it, but quickly gets serious again. "I just figured that if Keira feels strongly enough about being Catholic . . . I dunno. But if sex before marriage is out of the question for you, I assume it's something you'd have told me by now. Is . . . is that how you feel?"

There's a look in her eyes I know cold. It's the look that tells me to tell her what she wants to hear, which in this case is along the lines of how I want her bod in the worst way, that I'm tempted beyond words but am worried about going against a deeply ingrained religious principle.

It's the perfect out. If I take it, though, will she think I *never* want to have sex with her? Because I just don't know. Simply having that thought in my head—*sex with Amber DeWitt*—is enough to blur my vision. And even though it's true that I'm Catholic—my parents definitely get me to Mass every Sunday and I pay attention for the most part—I'm not against sex before marriage. So it'd be a lie.

And I can't lie to Amber about who I am and what I believe.

"Amber, it's not any of that. I'm just not ready." I try to think of the best way to explain this to her. I want to say, "It's not you, it's me," but it sounds so clichéd, she'll think I'm hiding something else. Finally, I go with "Look, we've been apart for most of the summer. Let's try to ease—"

"Geez, Toby. Just say it. It's because of me. You're just not that into me." There's a finality to her words, one that scares me.

"No, that's nuts! If anything, it's the opposite. You're—"

She focuses on me, and the hurt in her eyes makes my chest feel like it's being physically crushed. "Just stop, Toby. I know better. Back in June, at Sophomore Blast, we had the whole night together up by the reservoir. There was nothing to stop us; no one would have noticed if you stayed in my tent all night. Meghan knew we were in there, so she'd planned to crash with Christy Daggett or Joely Wiedermeier. And the chaperones were focused on the kids they thought would sneak in alcohol. We were completely under their radar."

Amber's voice gets higher the longer she talks, her tone going from one of mild upset to full-on rage. I'm afraid Mrs. DeWitt's going to hear us and come downstairs, so I try to quiet Amber down by putting a hand on her knee. The gesture only gets her more riled.

"You said you thought it'd be better to wait, to make the night special. To wait until there was no chance Griff would walk in on us to grab you for flag football or whatever. And I believed you. I thought it was just a timing thing. Well, Toby, no one else is around tonight, and what the hell's more special than our anniversary? Than celebrating the fact that I'm done with Friendly's and we've made it to junior year, and the fact that we love each other? Or don't we, really?"

"Are you kidding me? Haven't you heard a word I've said?" I can't believe this. How'd we go from making out to fighting so fast?

"It's all words, Toby."

"You're out of frickin' control, Amber." Anger bubbles up inside me. I know her feelings are hurt, that she's probably lashing out because she's feeling rejected. But my feelings are hurt, too. Does she think I'm stringing her along? Or that I'm like Connor, who—at least in my opinion—didn't respect her enough? "Look, Amber, I told you I loved you. You can believe it or not."

"Then why? It's not like half our friends aren't doing it. And they aren't in relationships nearly as tight as ours." When I don't respond immediately, she adds, "And it's not like we'd be stupid like Keira and not use protection."

How she knows that is beyond me, since I never asked Keira if she and Pete skipped protection, a condom broke, or what. I figured it wasn't my business. But maybe Amber's just tossing it out, trying to convince me.

Or maybe she's bringing my sister into this—and referring to her as stupid—to try to get me to lash out the way she is. It seems like she *wants* to fight. In the calmest voice I can muster, I ask, "Since when did anyone else's relationship become our yardstick?"

She just arches an eyebrow. It's the same thing I've seen her do when she argues with Meghan and knows she's in the right.

Screw this.

I run a hand through my hair. It's still wet. I practically sprinted here when I got out of the shower, so I could give her the time she wanted, and it's pissing me off that I knocked myself out just so she could pick a fight.

I'm afraid if I stay any longer, she's going to get one. And that's not me.

I let out a deep breath, hoping I sound less angry than I feel. "Look, we're arguing and we don't need to be. With all your work hours and the stress of being apart all summer, maybe we've put too much importance on school starting and on the anniversary. You think?"

She stares at me for a few long seconds. I have no idea what she's thinking, so I make an effort to keep a positive expression on my face.

"Maybe you should go home and we can take a break for a day or two," she finally says.

"If that's what you want, sure," I tell her. I don't really want to, but maybe it's better if we talk later when we've both had a little while to settle down.

She stands up, then gathers her books and stacks them on the coffee table.

I take the hint and pick up my Trig papers, shoving them into my backpack. I sling it over my shoulder, then look at her. I move to kiss her goodbye, to ask her if she's all right and tell her again how much I love her, but her arms are crossed over her chest and it's clear that—in her mind—our break is starting now.

"See you in band?" Tryouts are tomorrow during class, so we'll know if the practice time this summer paid off and we each get picked to be first chair in our sections.

She nods, but more to the coffee table than to me.

"I'll be cheering for you," I tell her, then take the stairs in twos. Things will look better in the morning, after she's through her tryout. I'm sure of it.

• • •

Now that eight flute players—going on nine—are through their Grieg solos, I've gone from nervous to downright sick. The clarinets are set to play next.

Amber isn't as serious about school as I am, and that's a good thing. My friends tell me my kind of insanity is certifiable. Still, she's never late for band.

Steve Rickett, who's sitting behind me, pokes me in the back with his trombone. "Your girlfriend sick or something?"

I shrug, keeping my eyes forward. I can't help but fixate on the empty chair in the clarinet section. Wonder if Mr. Beels, the band director, will let her audition later? Or will he just stick her in some preordained spot in the pecking order?

I hope this isn't because of last night.

"She's here," another trombone player replies in a too-loud whisper.

"Saw her talking in the hall with . . . uh, with somebody."

"She's screwed if Beels saw her," Steve hisses back.

I shoot a look over my shoulder while Mr. Beels is focused on one of the flute players. "Shhh."

"Mr. Maitland, is there a problem?"

Shit. I turn to look at the band director. The overhead fluorescents make it easy to see right through his thinning black hair to his scalp. "No, just thought I dropped something."

"Your classmates would appreciate quiet while they're auditioning. I'm sure you'll appreciate their patience while you take your turn?" His voice goes up at the end of the question, meaning he expects a response with an appropriate level of contrition.

At that moment, Amber eases in the door behind Beels. Her face is pink, but not from embarrassment. Some kind of drama's been happening in the hall.

She slides into the row of clarinet players, taking the empty seat. The girl next to her, Annabelle Gatsksowky, hands Amber her clarinet, which she'd apparently put together and tucked on the side of her chair.

So she knew Amber would be late. What the hell is going on?

"Mr. Maitland?"

I realize Beels is still focused on me. "You're right. I'm sorry," I answer, hoping it's heartfelt enough for him without making me look like a total kiss-up to everyone else. "It won't happen again."

He returns his attention to the final flute player, then notices that Amber's arrived. "Miss DeWitt. Kind of you to join us. Please remain for a moment after class."

She tells him it's no problem, as if she has a perfectly legit explanation, but I know better. The minute his back is turned, she gets the same edgy, wiped-out look she used to have whenever too many customers were vying for her attention at work, or when she and Connor were on the verge of a nasty argument.

Which means her tardiness probably *is* about last night.

We've had fights before, but never over how far we will go. It's usually over silly stuff like whether I said "blue" or "two" in answer to a pie-piece question in Trivial Pursuit. The worst was when I forgot to bring coffee to a football game like I'd promised, and she'd been craving it for nearly an hour.

But never the kind of fight to put that look on her face.

Beels moves to the clarinets and asks Amber to go first. She smiles like she doesn't have a care in the world, then plays the first few notes of her solo. Everything's technically correct, but the rich tone and energy she normally has when she plays are missing. The lack of warm-up is hurting her, and it doesn't help my guilty conscience when Steve hits me in the back with his trombone again and whispers, "She's off."

Ten seconds in and Amber finally hits it, the wonderful sound that only she can get a clarinet to produce. She sails through the rest of the piece, and even Beels can't hide his pleasure at her performance.

"Well done, Amber." He makes a few notes on his clipboard, then nods at the next person in the row, who promptly begins the same piece. It's clean, but not the same.

No one's the same.

"Playin' for second," someone down the row whispers. I catch Amber looking at me. I start to give her a thumbs-up, letting her know she nailed it and trying to communicate that I'm sorry if her rocky start was my fault. But she turns to watch the other clarinet players as if she never even noticed me.

That's when I see she's not wearing the necklace.

• • •

As everyone bolts for lunch, I scan the clumps of people jamming up the hallway. I've been waiting at my locker a solid five minutes, and it's slowly dawning on me as the hall gets emptier that she's taking our "break" seriously.

The locker next to mine opens with a clang. "Everything okay, Toby?"

"Sure. Why?" I fake a smile and watch as Ginger Grass empties the contents of her backpack into her locker.

She shrugs, but her casual attitude is as fake as my smile.

I give up on Amber and ask Ginger what she's doing for lunch. We haven't had lunch together in a long time, I realize. Maybe freshman year, even, when we were lab partners in Earth Science.

"I was going to be subversive and eat in the library while I write up my Chemistry report."

This is why I've always liked Ginger.

Well, that and the fact that she doesn't take crap from anyone about her name. What illegal substance her parents were on when they named her is anyone's guess. If my last name were Grass, I sure wouldn't name my kid anything plant- or herblike.

"Want company?" I ask.

"Depends. What'd you bring to eat?"

"Turkey on wheat, applesauce, string cheese. Oh, and a bag of Skittles."

"Okay." She zips her backpack and hefts it over one shoulder. "But only if you actually let me write up my Chemistry. And you share the Skittles."

"Deal." Relieved that I brought lunch today, I fish the brown paper bag and Coke money out of my locker, then walk beside her through junior hall and down the stairs to the library.

Ginger's one of those people you don't much notice at school. She's decent looking, with light brown eyes, clear skin, and brown hair that's usually in a ponytail. She plays basketball during the winter and runs track during the spring, but doesn't stand out at either sport. Her grades are good enough for honor roll, but not top of the class. In other words, she's the kind of person you like to get paired with on a group project because you know she'll have good ideas and will do the part of the assignment she promises to do, but she won't take over and boss everyone around.

You have fun with her when she's around, but she's not someone whose absence you notice right away when she's out.

After we pass the sign at the library entrance that demands no food, no drink, and no headsets, we scoot past the librarian, then through the reference section to see if my favorite table is occupied. It's near the back, behind most of the stacks, so we can hear people approaching long before they see or hear us. Luckily, three of the four seats are empty—Griff's in one, working on the Trig homework he has due in an hour—so we grab two of the empty seats.

Ginger surveys Griff's food, then takes a seat. They joke around while she takes out her notebook, a soynut butter sandwich—she has a serious peanut allergy that resulted in an ambulance ride when we were in fourth grade—and a Diet Coke. We all get to work pretty quickly. I finished everything I have due this afternoon, but figure if I get a head start on *Gatsby,* I can go to Amber's after cross-country and get things back on track.

Twenty minutes in, Ginger excuses herself to go to the restroom. Griff watches her leave, then whispers, "Things screwed up with Amber today?"

I play dumb and pretend to keep reading. "Huh?"

It's not like I eat with Amber every day—she usually eats with her girlfriends—which makes me wonder if I look that obviously upset or if Amber's been talking. Griff isn't the most observant guy on the planet.

"Let's see," he says, putting a finger to his temple like he's straining to think. "You've been moving in slo-mo all day. I haven't seen you two groping in the hallway for at least twenty-four hours, and, hmmmm . . . I saw her talking to Connor Ralston in the hallway before school. Standing about yay close." He holds his thumb and index finger two inches apart.

So he's more observant than I thought.

"He flirts with her whenever he sees her," I tell Griff. "Still wants to own her or something." Both statements are true, but could Connor's timing suck any worse?

"Oh. Well, who wouldn't with that rack?" Griff goes back to his Trig, but the silence between us is uncomfortable.

"What?" I finally ask.

Griff exhales, then puts down his pencil. "Look, I'm telling you this because I'm your friend. But the flirting wasn't one-way."

My ears heat the way they always do when I'm embarrassed, meaning my face is going to be the same stop sign color as the library carpet within seconds.

Griff glances behind me, making sure Ginger's not on her way back yet. "You two having a fight?"

"Sort of."

"About?"

I cannot talk to Griff about this. He might be my best friend, but he's also a horndog, first class.

"She asked you a favor and you said you didn't have time," Griff guesses. "Or you were two minutes late meeting her and she threw a hissy and said you must not love her."

"Give me a break."

"You wanted to do the wild thing after she got you that nerdy history book and she said no." A grin slides over his face and he puts the back of his hand to his forehead. In a mock feminine voice, he adds, "Oh, Toby, baby, I have *such* a headache!"

"Get your mind out of the gutter."

I think Griff's soda's going to come out of his nose, he's trying so hard to keep his laughter under control. When he recovers, he starts to say something else, then pauses, studying me. "Holy shit, Toby. Is that it? Oh, man. I'm sorry I—"

"That's *not* it."

"Your bright red cheeks tell me otherwise, dumbass."

It sucks that he knows me so well. I set down *Gatsby*. Not like I can focus on it, anyway. "All right, fine. But it was the other way around," I whisper after making sure no one's in hearing range. "And keep it to yourself!"

Griff fake-bangs his head against the table. Ginger's going to be back any sec, so I kick him under the table and tell him to cut it out. He looks up at me and rolls his eyes. "Miss D-Cup wanted your scrawny bod—which is shocking enough in itself—and you turn her down? What's wrong with you?"

"Maybe I respect her, all right?"

"It doesn't sound like she wants your respect."

"Griff—"

"Okay, okay. So what happened?"

Now that he's serious, I decide it's safe enough to give him the ten-second rundown. He sighs. "That's rough. But you know, it sounds to me like she just got her ego bruised."

"Well, that's what I thought, too, but then she was ignoring me in band this morning. And what's with her flirting with Connor? *Assuming* that's what she was doing and it wasn't just him, of course."

Griff makes a face. "I can't help you with that. Maybe you should ask Ginger. She can give you the girl perspective. And you know she'll keep it in the vault."

"No way." It's bad enough I mentioned it to Griff, and he's my best friend. Amber would be mortified if I confided in another girl.

"Just ask her. She's coming through the stacks."

I hear footsteps behind me, then Ginger slips into her seat. "Ask me what?"

I glance at Griff, then at Ginger. I gesture toward her notebook. "How long are you planning to make your Chem write-up?"

"Daniels said he wanted three or four pages to answer all the questions." She grins. "I wouldn't bother going longer. You know Daniels, he's an easy A. Hit three pages and you're golden."

"Cool." I wrote five. Not that it's important.

Griff leans back in his chair, just out of Ginger's peripheral vision, and mouths, "Loser!"

CHAPTER FOUR

At three a.m., I pull a pair of mesh shorts on over my boxers and pad down the hall. Stewie's crying and, once again, I'm awake while Keira and my parents snooze in total ignorance. This despite the fact that cross-country kicked my tail today and I stayed up later than usual waiting for Amber to return my call.

Make that two calls and a text message. Not that it's important.

It's a wonder I'm ever alert at school.

I push open the door to his room. He's cuddled in the corner of his crib wearing nothing but a diaper, chewing the arm of his stuffed monkey and staring at his Thomas the Tank Engine nightlight.

"Hey, little guy. What's wrong? You feeling bad?"

When he sees me, he cries harder, like he can't believe he's finally being rescued from his prison. I lean over the edge of the crib and muss his hair, then stroke his forehead. He doesn't feel warm. "It's okay. Tell Uncle Toby."

He snuffles some more—for effect, I think—then manages to tell me he wants out of the crib because he's cold.

"Well, that happens when you yank off your clothes." He's gotten good at unzipping his one-piece footie pajamas and removing them. It's his way of protesting bedtime. It never works, but he keeps trying. Keira says we're lucky he hasn't figured out how to take off the diaper yet. That thought helps me put the perpetual jammie-stripping into perspective. I pick his jammies up from the corner of the crib and realize they're soaked.

Gross.

I toss them toward the door so I'll remember to take them to the wash, then put both hands over the edge of the crib. "C'm'ere."

He stands up and waddles a step closer so I can haul him out. Luckily, he's big enough now that I don't have to wrestle with him on a changing table anymore; he stands still so I can change him right there in the middle of the floor, easing off his old diaper and stuffing it into the Diaper Genie, then taping the tabs on a fresh one.

"Stay right there and I'll get you some clean jammies, okay?"

I pull another pair out of the dresser drawer and turn to put them on him, only to see that he's wandered over to the nightlight and is reaching out to touch the bulb.

"No, Stewie!" I grab for his hand. "That's a big owie."

"Owie!" he giggles, as if he knew it all along and was simply baiting me. Wily kid. At least he's not whining about his ear infection or strep. Keira told me at dinner that he was feeling better already, though he needs to keep taking his antibiotics for several more days.

I wiggle him into the clean pajamas without much trouble, but he's less than enthusiastic about getting back into the crib when I try to put him in there. Balancing him on one hip, I lean over and feel the sheet to make sure it's dry. No dice. I fumble in the drawer for the backup one, then remember he wet the crib last night, too. It's probably still in the wash.

"You wanna sleep with Uncle Toby, kiddo?"

He responds by letting his head fall against my shoulder, then nestling in under my chin.

Keira's going to kill me for bringing him into my bed. She'll say I'm letting him manipulate me, but whatever. He'll fall asleep faster with me than he will in the crib—which I'll have to remake, assuming I can find a clean sheet—and I'm all for taking the path of least resistance, especially if it means more shuteye for me.

I carry Stewie down the hall and put him on top of my bedspread, making sure he has plenty of space, then spread pillows between him and the edge of the bed to keep him from rolling off. He never has, but I worry. The kid sleeps in a crib for a reason. He needs to be caged.

"I have exactly the thing to put you to sleep," I tell him, sliding in next to him as I reach for the book on my nightstand. "Let's learn about Davy Crockett and Jim Bowie. They were brave men who fought in a famous battle a long time ago."

I smile to myself, picturing Griff hiding his face from Ginger while calling me a loser. Maybe sometimes being a loser is the honorable—the *right*—thing.

• • •

"You did a great job yesterday."

Amber jumps at the sound of my voice coming from behind her, just as I knew she would. It's quarter after seven Thursday morning, and the halls are virtually empty since school doesn't start for another twenty minutes. Normally, Amber doesn't get to school this early—she tends to cut it almost as close as Griff does—but I figured if she wanted to avoid me, she'd get her things out of her locker and escape junior hall before I got here.

Today, I'm not letting her hide. Somewhere around four a.m., I had an epiphany.

"Toby!" she says on an exhale. "You surprised me."

"Sorry." I won't tell her I didn't mean to, since I did. "I read the book."

She blinks. "The Alamo book? *All* of it?"

"All four hundred and twenty-two pages." The book put Stewie to sleep, but not me. I couldn't stop turning the pages. When I finally read the last paragraph and closed the book, I lay in bed, wide awake, listening to Stewie's even breathing and thinking.

I make sure Amber's totally focused on me, then say what I've been mentally rehearsing for hours. "Anyone who knows me well enough to buy that book as a gift should know that when I tell her I love her, I mean it. And she should know that when I say no it doesn't mean I don't want her."

"Toby . . ." She crosses her arms over her stomach, then looks down at the floor. Since when did I make her uncomfortable? She only ever

LAST STAND 💔 35

got this way with me when she talked about Connor, in the days before the two of us hooked up. And usually it was when she was too embarrassed to tell me about something that'd happened between them. Some dumb fight over who she'd been hanging out with after school, or about when he was supposed to call her.

"I know you're upset about the other night, Amber. But . . . I don't understand why you're *this* upset." So upset she might've been confiding in Connor about me before band yesterday.

Yikes. There's an awful thought. Where the hell did that come from?

"Look, Toby, it's not you. It's me."

It occurs to me that this is the exact phrase I avoided using night before last, specifically because I knew it'd upset her if I said it. Before I can respond, she meets my gaze, and any hesitancy she might've had before, when I first approached her, is gone. "I just need some time to figure things out."

The trickle of people behind me is turning into a stream, their chatter about classes and parties and sports increasing in volume. I hate that we're discussing this here, where even our body language is likely to generate gossip. It's simply the way of things at West Rollins. On the other hand, I sense that if I let her walk away now, she could be gone for good, and I don't think either of us wants that.

"I'll give you whatever time you need." I lean in, so my mouth is closer to her ear. "But it would be a lot easier if I had a clue why. We've been together a long time. I didn't realize you still had things to figure out at this point."

Someone brushes my shoulder while passing by, presumably on the way to his locker. Amber shifts, her gaze taking in who's who behind me. "I'm supposed to be meeting Christy Daggett to go over our German assignment. If I don't go now, she's going to wonder what's up and come looking for me. Plus Beels will murder me if I'm late to band twice in a row. Can we meet up after school?"

"Sure."

"Parking lot, right after. I have to do some research for Model

U.N., but I left all my materials in Meghan's car. We can talk while I grab them. Meet you by the doors in senior hall?"

I nod, then give her a quick kiss. She kisses me back before hurrying off, so I take that as a good sign. Even better, I see Christy walking toward her, carrying a notebook and looking flustered. At least I know she was early for a reason, not simply to avoid me.

This'll blow over. I know it. No more drama, everything back to normal.

The hand on the oversize clock hanging from the ceiling jumps from 7:25 to 7:26 as I head toward my own locker.

Who am I kidding?

Amber's always been a drama queen. Independent, smart, and a hell of a clarinet player, but a drama queen. Never about me—not before this—but judging by all the drama she had with Connor, and the way she revels in telling me all the details about what's going on with each of her friends, well, there's no telling if it'll blow over.

For the first time, it occurs to me that maybe it's okay if it *doesn't* blow over. I love her like mad, but the way we were last year. When we were going through the day-to-day routine at school. Cuddling at football games, hanging out and playing Trivial Pursuit with our friends like the dorks that we are. Before Sophomore Blast. Before Friendly's, before our anniversary.

When I get to my locker, Ginger's standing at hers, hanging up her coat. I smile hello, empty the contents of my backpack into the locker, then grab my books for second-period Spanish so I can go straight there after band.

"Work things out?"

I pause and frown around my locker door at Ginger. I almost didn't hear her over the clanging locker doors and the knot of girls standing nearby gushing over someone's new purse.

She shuts her locker and takes a step closer to me. Her hair's clipped back over both ears today. Cute. "With Amber," she clarifies. "I assume everything's okay?"

"Griff's voice carries, huh?"

One side of her mouth quirks into a grin. "Yep. No one else heard, though. The stacks were empty other than the three of us."

"That's a relief." I play with the strap on my backpack, but stop when I realize it probably makes it look like I'm not so relieved about what's going on with Amber. "Doesn't matter though. Everything's fine."

"Good. Didn't mean to butt into your business by asking, but you're a nice guy. Don't want ot see you hurt or anything."

I smile and thank her, but I have to wonder: When girls say this, do they realize it's *not* a compliment? No guy wants to be told he's "nice" because it translates to "You're worthy of my friendship, but not cute enough to be going-out material." It's doubly bad when it comes from someone who's pretty average herself, like Ginger Grass, because if she thinks I'm a "nice guy" it means I'm pretty much invisible to girls who occupy the higher social strata.

She starts to walk past me, to join the current of people navigating the hallway, but pauses to say, "Don't forget that you still owe me some Skittles. Doesn't matter how nice you are, I still want 'em."

"No problem." I never did open the bag yesterday when we were having lunch in the library. I lean down and snag them from the side pocket of my backpack to toss them to her, but when I look up, she's gone.

During band, I keep my focus on my sheet music, making sure to avoid direct eye contact with Amber. I have no idea what to say to her later, no idea what to expect, and I don't want to telegraph anything she'll take the wrong way.

It pisses me off that I'm spending an entire hour feeling like I have to *not* look at her.

• • •

It occurs to me when Griff and I are midway through the lunch line that if I meet Amber, I'm going to be late to cross-country. I must've been in a complete brain fog this morning not to realize it.

"Stromboli," Griff groans. Just the thing to top off my day. It's called "Special Italian Stromboli" on the school lunch menu. Sadly, it is neither special nor Italian (the land of Julius Caesar, Michelangelo, and Enrico Fermi would never claim this lump of bad pastry and mystery meat). Since I've never tried stromboli anywhere but the West Rollins High School cafeteria, I question whether it's even stromboli. But I take one anyway, add a salad, then scan the room as Griff and I walk to an open table.

I don't see Amber anywhere in the caf, so I assume she went somewhere with Meghan and Christy, her usual partners in crime. In between bites of salad, I text her asking if we can meet up later, either at my house or hers. Coach Jessup doesn't accept absences unless you're so sick you missed school, you're hurt and running will aggravate the injury, or you have a death in the family. Unless your name is Griff Osterman, of course. In that case, as long as you drag your sorry carcass to practice more often than not and make it to the meets to earn points for the team, you're golden. If I miss cross-country, I'm screwed.

But when the last bell rings and I check my cell, there's still no reply from Amber.

• • •

By the time I spot Amber in the parking lot, I've worked my way from mild annoyance to flat-out pissed-offedness. I don't care if *pissedoffedness* isn't a word, I'm so pissed. She's standing next to the open rear door of Meghan's red Dodge, flipping through a pile of papers. As I make my way across the asphalt, she stuffs a few of the papers in her backpack, grabs a file off the back seat, then closes the door and starts to walk away from me, toward the front entrance of the school.

I jog and catch up with her a few cars past Meghan's, at the edge of the lot.

"Hey, where were you?" I ask. "I was waiting by the senior hall doors."

She stops walking and frowns. "I said I would be at Meghan's car."

"How am I supposed to know where Meghan parked her car?"

She gives a one-shouldered shrug. "Why didn't you ask?"

"Because you said to meet by the doors to senior hall!"

"Toby, geez. So there was some miscommunication. Why are your boxers in such a twist?"

I am sorely tempted to walk away. Cross-country starts in less than ten minutes, which means if I go now, I might still be able to change and get there on time. Does she not have the ability to say she's sorry? Could she truly have forgotten she told me to meet her in senior hall?

And does she not realize there are still people in the lot, so that when she raises her voice on the phrase *boxers in such a twist,* everyone looks in our direction?

I study her face, trying to figure her out. But as I take in her confused expression, the familiar pattern of freckles across the bridge of her nose, and her hair tucked behind one ear the way I love, I figure that maybe after a year together, I owe it to her to cut her some slack.

I take a deep, slow breath and start again.

"I sent you a text at lunch asking if we could meet later, at home, so I don't miss cross-country," I explain, sounding remarkably composed, given how I feel. "You never answered it. And then I couldn't find you in senior hall, and I got frustrated. But at this point, it doesn't matter. Let's just talk, all right?"

She visibly relaxes. "Okay."

"You said you needed to figure things out?"

"Yeah."

I wait. Nothing. "And . . . ?"

She shrugs. "I guess, well, I just don't *get* you, Toby. You say you love me, and you sure seem to like being with me. I don't think you've got hang-ups about your body or anything. So I'm trying to guess why you don't feel ready." She makes quotes in the air with her fingers as she says the last word. "If you're not ready now, and it's not a matter of religion or worrying about getting pregnant . . . I mean, come on! It's the next logical step in our relationship, and if we're not moving forward, then . . ." She waves a hand in exasperation. "Are you afraid that if we sleep together, then we break up at some point, you'll regret having done it with me?"

Since the odds are that, yes, at some point we will break up, I want to say, *What do you think?* Instead I ask, "Well, how do you think you'd feel about it now if you'd slept with Connor?"

She starts to answer, to say our relationship's not like hers with Connor, but her words catch.

In that instant, I know. And she knows I know it, too.

I let my backpack slide to the ground, then lean against the light post behind me. I can't even begin to respond. Even though it must've happened a long time ago—presumably when Amber was a freshman, or else the summer between freshman and sophomore year—I feel like my gut's being ripped out with a dirty fork. I feel like it happened today.

Amber had sex with Connor Ralston.

"Okay, so maybe you *don't* have regrets," I say. "Though you obviously felt awkward enough about it that you didn't tell me." God knows she told me everything else about their relationship, in minute detail. I've heard more word-for-word accounts of random conversations between Amber and Connor than I ever care to remember.

"I don't regret it," Amber says. "And the only thing that's awkward, the only thing that upsets me, is that I've done it with him and not with you. And you're the one I care about more."

She takes a step forward and grabs my hand, pulling it into hers. Other students are still hanging around the lot, talking or rummaging around in the trunks of their cars for forgotten cleats, running shoes, or socks before heading to the athletic fields for practice. As I watch them, I know I should go. Just put this whole thing with Amber out of my mind for now and haul ass to cross-country. Talk to her again when no one's around. But my feet won't move; I'm numb.

She slept with him, he dumped her for someone else, and she has no regrets?

Funny. Now *I'm* the one who has to figure things out.

"I've been wondering," Amber says quietly, "if it's just that you're worried I'll get pregnant like Keira? I won't."

"You know, Amber, my brain wasn't even at that point yet."

If she was sleeping with Connor, does that mean she's on the pill? Would she still be on it now, or is it the kind of thing you start and stop?

Has she been mentally preparing to have sex with me the whole time we've been going out? She *has* always been the one to instigate things, at least after the first kiss. It was Amber who first took our relationship public by telling friends. Amber who started the makeout sessions in her parents' basement. Amber who grabbed my hand and directed it up her shirt the first time.

"I don't know how you *wouldn't* be thinking about it." Amber's voice is placating, soft. "I've seen how you take care of Stewart and how you worry about Keira. I think it's sweet. And I like that you'd worry about me getting in the same situation. But *I'm* not worried."

If we actually had sex, I sure would be. Nothing's a hundred percent effective. But that's not the point, and I tell her so.

All it does is annoy her.

"Then what's your problem?" she asks. "Because one thing I did learn from Connor, if a guy is into you, it's at least crossing his mind now and then. And more likely, he's thinking about it all the time."

"It's not that it hasn't *crossed* my mind. It just hasn't crossed my mind in the sense of actually doing it. More of a late-at-night, nice-thing-to-fantasize-about-as-I'm-falling-asleep thing. Does that make any sense to you?" I feel like I'm pleading with her to understand what I'm saying. But I've finally put my finger on why I'm uneasy about going any further with her—why I felt so wrong about what happened at Sophomore Blast, and why I bolted night before last. "The truth is, if we sleep together, it really has to mean something."

"It will—"

"No, it has to be something I know I'd never, ever regret."

She's smiling like she's scored a victory. "Toby, you won't! And neither will I. Your sister told me once she would do it all over again with Pete, and it's not something she was saying because she loves Stewie. And even though Connor drove me crazy, if I knew then what I know now, I don't think my choices would've changed. Neither of those relationships worked out, but neither of those relationships was *us*. With us, it'll be different. *We're* different."

"You're right," I shoot back. "We are different."

I let go of her hand, because I have a feeling she'll break my fingers in a sec if I don't. "Remember the other night when I said we couldn't use other people's relationships as a yardstick for ours? It's because every relationship's different. We can't compare ourselves to anyone else and decide, hey, they did it, and it worked out all right, so we'll definitely be okay because we're a better couple.

"The thing is, I'm not wired the way you are." I point back and forth between the two of us. "I'm not wired the way Keira is, either. If the two of us are ever together that way, it won't just mean *something* to me. What I should've said is that it'll mean *everything* to me. I can't do what Keira did without regrets. And I can't do what *you* did, either."

Amber's face turns bright red and she clutches her Model U.N. papers tighter to her chest.

I step back, my jaw locking as I prepare for an onslaught. If I'd been smart, I'd have just moved my frickin' feet and gone to cross-country. Insisted on talking about this tonight, at home. But nope.

And now that I've gone too far, I can't help firing off a final shot. "And I wish you'd stop pressuring me."

CHAPTER FIVE

"Are you judging me?" Her voice is loud. Too loud. The entire parking lot seems to pause, waiting to hear what's next.

"Of course I'm not," I tell her, hoping she'll follow my cue and lower her voice. "Like I said, we're all wired in different ways, and that's fine. But—"

"I can't believe you!"

My throat seizes up because I sense what's coming, even though I've never seen her this way. She's going to lose it like she did in her basement the other night, and worse.

"You're calling me a slut, and that's just wrong. You can go to hell, Toby Maitland!"

I manage to get out an even-toned "Amber, you can break up with me over this. I think it's stupid, but you know, it's your prerogative. I'd really appreciate it if you wouldn't yell it out to the entire school, though."

She snorts, affronted, then leans in and hisses, "Fine. Then I'll *not* yell this: You can rationalize this breakup—and it *is* a breakup—all you want. The problem's not mine, it's yours. You don't have the balls to go through with it, and you can't admit it. Even to yourself."

She turns, her hair swinging out behind her, then walks toward the school doors. People have their heads down as if they're minding their own business, but they sneak peeks as she passes. Then they glance at me.

All I can do is stand here, wondering what in the world just happened.

And *the balls to go through with it?*

Isn't there something wrong with the idea that the decision of whether or not to have sex with someone hinges on bravery? Not that Amber would listen if I pointed that out. She just accused me of calling her a slut, something I'd never, ever call a girl. Not that some girls aren't. Guys, too; not that there's a word for it. But once you've heard the term applied to your sister—even by adults—and see the hurt that results, you find it's not a word that pops out of your mouth. Amber *knows* I feel this way, so what the hell? Did some demon take over my girlfriend's—or *ex*-girlfriend's—body when I wasn't looking?

A dark blue Corolla pulls up to the curb, so I step out of the way. There's the hum of a side window going down. I'm sure so someone can tell me what an ass I am. Great.

"Need a ride home?"

The feminine voice isn't unfriendly, so I bend down to peek in the car. Ginger's in the driver's seat, leaning over and waving for me to hop in. No one else is in the vehicle.

I check my watch and realize I'm way late for cross-country. The group is off on the trail, long gone. I could still show up with an excuse, tell the coach I had to finish up a project after class, but I can't bring myself to work up the energy.

I reach for the door handle and climb inside. "Thanks."

After I'm buckled, she circles so we're headed out of the lot. I don't have to look in the side-view mirror to know we're being watched. I've no doubt dirt's being dished about the identity of my ride.

"You're in Ocky Knolls, right?"

"That's the place. You know how to get to Indian Paintbrush Drive?"

She shakes her head. "Just tell me when to turn and I'll get you there."

We're quiet for a couple of minutes. I don't know whether I should say anything about what happened with Amber. I don't want Ginger thinking I called Amber a slut. I don't want *anyone* thinking I called Amber a slut. But maybe it's better to let it go unless Ginger brings it up first.

With any luck, she was already in her car when Amber went ballistic and didn't hear that part.

To distract myself, I study the car's interior. It's completely clean. No empty soda cans, no straw wrappers, no scattered papers. There's not even dirt on the floor. It's how I'll keep a car when I (someday) own one. There's a crystal hanging from the rearview mirror, though—something I'd never have—and there's another one, larger, sitting in the coin cubby.

Ginger rolls her eyes when she catches me looking. "Those are from my mother. I have a zillion more at home. They're not me at all, but if I keep a couple on display it makes her feel appreciated."

Ohh-kay. Me, I'd tell my mom to save her money.

We slow down for a yield sign, and she glances my way. "You promise not to laugh if I tell you something?"

"Not if it's really funny." Who can promise not to laugh?

"Then at least promise to keep it to yourself." When I agree, she tells me, "My middle name is Crystal. That's why my mom keeps buying them for me. It'd really hurt her feelings if I told her to knock it off."

I manage not to crack up, even though I'm dying to. Instead, I go for the joke and make a show of sniffing the air. "Does she buy you ginger, too?"

"No. No ginger." She laughs—which is a relief—then steals another peek at me before focusing on the road again. "But you have to wonder if a drunken fortuneteller somewhere convinced my parents Ginger Crystal Grass would be a good name for a kid. When I go to college, I'm going to tell everyone my name's Gin and let people think it's short for Virginia."

Virginia Grass isn't much better than Ginger Grass, but that's a thought I decide to keep to myself.

We're halfway home when I remember that Stewie's out of daycare again today and Keira was begging the morning staff for a volunteer to pull a double shift. I tell Ginger not to take me all the way to Rocky Knolls (or Ocky Knolls), but to drop me at Fair Grounds so I can see if whoever's on duty needs a hand. May as well, I figure, since I'm not at cross-country.

I point out an empty spot at the end of the street so she can pull in, rather than trying to double-park in front of the shop to let me out. I'm about to thank her for the ride when she says, "That's really generous of you to help your sister. You could be hanging out with friends, finishing homework, whatever."

I shrug. "No big deal. She needs the help. She pays me, too."

"Really? That's cool of her." I'm reaching to open the door when Ginger adds, "Some people would take advantage of a nice guy like you in that situation."

I turn in the seat to face her. "That's the second time today you've called me a nice guy and implied that it's a bad thing."

"Toby, it's a *great* thing!" Ginger laughs, but it doesn't feel like it's at me. More with me. "You're the kind of person other people like to be around. That's rare. Who else do you know at WRHS with no enemies?"

Amber might be an enemy now, not that I'm going to point it out. "So why do I feel like there's a big 'but' that comes after your nice-guy statement?"

"Oh, probably because there is." She shrugs. "I'm not sure being the nice guy always makes *you* happy. I bet you'd help Keira even if she didn't pay you."

"She's my sister."

"Doesn't matter. Remember back when we were in fourth grade together?"

"Yeah. So?" Her peanut episode will ensure I never forget fourth grade.

"You were always the first person to volunteer to help the teacher with stuff. Or to help other kids with their assignments. You're a pleaser."

"Gee, thanks, Dr. Phil."

"Eww. Now you're not being nice at all!" She shudders. "What I'm saying, though, is that you help out no matter what. It's just who you are. Keira's lucky to have you for a brother, and you're lucky she never takes advantage of that. A lot of girls would take advantage of a guy like you. Especially girls who are serious attention junkies. They know you're the guy who's going to give them their fix, and that makes you a target."

"Can I go now, or do you get to berate me a little longer as payment for the ride?" I can't help but grin at her. Ginger Grass, amateur psychologist. Who knew?

She swoops a hand toward the sidewalk. "You're free to go. Just lookin' out for you is all."

I flick the ribbon that holds the crystal on her rearview mirror. "You keep it quiet that I'm a nice guy, I'll keep it quiet that you have the world's most hideous name."

"Deal."

I thank her for the ride, then hop out of the car. She pulls a quick U-turn, and I wave as she heads off, presumably toward her own house. I wonder where she lives. Not Rocky Knolls, since she was never on my bus when we were kids. Funny that she knew I lived there. Huh.

My cell phone pings in my pocket. I pull it out, wondering if Amber's going to do a one-eighty and apologize, or if she's calling to rant at me some more. Instead, it's a text from Griff:

hey toby where r u . . . u missed c-c

I text back that I had to skip—I'll give him the details later—and that I'm standing in front of Fair Grounds. A few seconds later, I have a reply:

stay put . . . getting ride

I let him know I'll be inside. I open the door to the shop, expecting to see one of the morning girls, but Keira's manning the counter alone, just as she would on any other weekday afternoon.

"Where's Stewie?" I ask after she finishes with a customer.

"Home napping. Mom told me she'd cover." At my look of surprise, Keira adds, "I know, I know. But she insisted. I figured just this once I could accept her help."

"Speaking of which—"

"Go home, Toby!" She grabs a large bag of coffee beans and refills the grinder. "Isn't it enough that you got up in the middle of the night with Stewie? I swear, he yelps, you run. That boy's no dummy; he knows who'll bend over backward to make him happy."

Did I just have this conversation with Ginger, or what?

"He was wet," I argue.

She reseals the coffee bag and puts it away. "I figured that much out when I saw his pajamas. But you could've gotten me when you heard him cry. And you definitely didn't need to take him to your room when he pulled his fussy routine on you."

"How'd you know he was in my room?" I put the kid back in his room just before Keira got out of bed. I was wide awake, so I decided to remake the crib.

"When I got him this morning, he said"—she waves her arms in reenactment—"Mama, Mama, I sleep Unnca Tobeeeeee!"

Busted.

"Go home," Keira tells me. "Take a nap, do your homework. You've helped me enough for one day. Want a coffee for the road?"

I tell her I need to wait for Griff, but I'll take an iced coffee with milk. As she preps it, I take a seat alongside the counter and ask, "Has it ever occurred to you that you never want to accept help from anyone, yet I'm constantly trying to help everyone?"

She takes the milk out of the fridge, then talks to me over her shoulder while she adds some to my coffee. "Put us together and we might balance out to one normal person."

"I guess."

Griff walks up, as if on cue, and tells me that while Keira has hopes of normalcy, I'm a lost cause. He orders an iced coffee for himself, then we walk back toward Rocky Knolls as we drink. He's still in his running gear, though he usually changes and showers at school before heading home.

"So, you know you're in trouble with Coach Jessup," he says once we're out of earshot of the coffee shop.

I nod. "Amber. Long story, and I don't want to talk about it."

"Just grovel appropriately tomorrow, all right? I don't want you to lose your spot on the team." When I assure him there will be an abundance of groveling, he asks if I want to blow off homework for a while and come over to his house to play video games. "It's an anti-Amber treatment," he assures me.

I shrug and follow him home. For once, I don't feel like being responsible.

CHAPTER SIX

I think every single person at West Rollins hates me. As I walk out of second period and head toward my locker, people either steal peeks at me or turn away and whisper back and forth about how I look—am I angry? sad? happy?

Do they think they're being subtle?

Being the center of attention makes me twitchy.

"No need to tell me that long Amber story," Griff mutters in my ear as he strolls next to me. "If you couldn't guess from all the stares you got during Spanish, Amber's been telling her own story."

"She didn't have to," I reply, careful to keep my voice down and a grin on my face, like Griff and I are talking about some great joke we just heard. "She ensured she had plenty of witnesses yesterday."

"Sucks, man. It'll blow over soon." When we get to my locker, he asks if I want to meet up for lunch.

"You pack one?"

He shakes his head. "Hit the snooze button this morning and had to run. Gotta buy."

"Me, too," I admit. Slept in to make up for the night I spent up with Stewie and reading the Alamo book. I realized on the way to school, however, that I should've taken the extra minute or two to pack a lunch so I could avoid the fishbowl of the cafeteria. "I may just buy a sandwich and scoot to the library, though. Don't feel like eating in the caf today."

"Good plan. Meet me here at the lockers and I'll run the gauntlet with you."

• • •

Griff's his usual laid-back self when we get into line for lunch, doing a great job of making it look like the two of us are oblivious to what's happening around us.

"Not so bad," he says, discreetly surveying the room. "No one's paying much attention to you. They're all looking at Little Miss He Done Me Wrong."

My back's to Amber, but I saw her when I came in. Couldn't miss her. She's wearing her favorite purple V-neck top, the one I once told her makes her look fabulous. I meant her eyes at the time, since I was kissing her when I said it. But it also highlights her other assets. Big time. So to speak. And she knows it. "Holding court, huh?"

"Yep. The usual minions are gathered at her table. Meghan, Christy, the whole group. And Annabelle Gatsksowky is at the front of the line waving for them to save her a seat. She has another girl with her. Another band type, I think."

"Hmmm, wonder what they could all be talking about." Yep, that was sarcasm in my voice.

Griff smiles, then adds, "Oh, and don't look now, but Connor Ralston and a couple of his friends are sitting down at the table behind her. She's pretending not to notice."

"Great." I wonder if part of her hooking up with me was to get back at Connor. For someone with no regrets, she sure doesn't seem to have him out of her system. I bet Griff's right. The flirting before band was probably two-way.

Griff mutters, "For a girl with a broken heart, she sure seems to be loving all the drama and attention."

I shake my head, because that's when it hits me. Serious déjà vu.

"What?" Griff asks, catching my eye. There's concern in his voice, but to his credit, he still looks like he's Mr. Casual. "What'd you see?"

"Nothing." I wave him off. "Just realized that you've been right all along whenever you've called me dumbass."

"Well, of course. I'm always right."

The first time I had lunch with Amber was this week, last year. We'd just gotten together, and everyone in school was speculating about us. Connor was seated a few tables away. Since the two of them had broken up over the summer, most people hadn't heard about it. Not until school started and Amber sat with her new boyfriend at lunch and the gossip began.

She'd been happy and giggly that day, smiling like I hadn't seen her smile in months. I'd thought it was because she was happy to be with me, that she'd totally forgotten that Connor left her for some other girl. Now I'm thinking she was happy for the attention. What was the term Ginger used?

Attention junkie.

Guess it should be capital *A*, capital *J*. Like a syndrome.

We get to the front of the line, skipping the trays and hot food choices in favor of pre-made, wrapped sandwiches, apples, granola bars, and sodas we can carry out. I'm about to pay when the basket of candy calls to me. I grab myself a Snickers, then toss it back in favor of a Twix—no peanuts in Twix—and add a bag of Skittles.

Griff oinks behind me.

"I owe Ginger some Skittles from lunch yesterday. I'll give 'em to her at her locker later," I explain.

I toss the food in my backpack, then Griff and I make a beeline out of the caf. I hear Amber's cheery laughter as we pass near her table—she's not laughing at me, but it's definitely meant for my ears—and decide that Ginger was dead-on. Amber wanted me for the attention and the attention only. It's probably why she was so insistent about sex. If the relationship didn't escalate—if I couldn't meet her demand for increasing doses to feel the high—it meant she wasn't getting her fix.

If she really wanted *me,* she wouldn't have thrown her public fit. And she'd wanted it to be public. Otherwise, she'd have answered my text asking her to meet me at home so I wouldn't miss cross-country. I know she got it; she's obsessive about checking between classes.

Of course, if I'd have ignored one of her texts for hours, she'd have been pouty. I wasn't paying attention to her. I didn't *love* her if I didn't jump to answer right away.

"You know, Amber was a lot of work," I tell Griff once we're safely out of the cafeteria.

"You're just now figuring that out?" In a girly voice, he adds, "Toooh-beeee, you're going to walk me home, aren't you? Oh, Toooh-beeee, why didn't you answer my IM?"

"No kidding."

How often did I do things with—or for—Amber because she expected me to, rather than because I really wanted to?

Or worse—spending so much on the necklace I got her for our anniversary. I could've added that money to my car fund, but now the necklace is probably sitting in a drawer in her bedroom, never to be worn.

"So how come you never said anything?" I ask Griff.

"Maybe 'cause you wouldn't have listened? You were blinded, man." Griff cracks up. "Probably by her boobs."

"Gee, thanks." Good thing the hall's empty except for the two of us.

"Don't mention it."

We enter the library, give the librarian a friendly wave as we pass her desk—Eat in the library? Who, us?—then make our way to the table at the back of the stacks.

Ginger's already there. She looks up from her notebook as we approach and raises an eyebrow. "You two officially stalking me?"

"No way. I was here first yesterday, and the two of you barged in on me," Griff says. He jerks a thumb in my direction. "And he brought you Skittles. Not stalker behavior."

"Pay up and I'll consider letting you sit."

I drop my backpack into one of the empty chairs, locate the Skittles, then toss them to her. She catches the bag in one hand and sets them in front of her on the table, then reaches down to the floor to pick up the Diet Coke she hid as we came through the stacks.

"Can't be too careful," she says as Griff and I sit. "So how's your morning been, Toby?"

"Haven't you heard?" Griff's voice is filled with snark, which garners him a smile from Ginger.

"Some." She leans back in her chair and fixes her ponytail. She catches my eye, and it's clear to me that she not only heard the gossip, but heard everything that went down in the parking lot—including Amber's "slut" comment—loud and clear.

"She actually witnessed it," I tell Griff as he spreads out his lunch. "My most glorious moment."

"Came riding in on my white horse to rescue his ass."

"Well, a blue Toyota," I explain to Griff. "She gave me a ride to Fair Grounds."

"That's how you got there at Mach speed," he says between bites of his cafeteria-bought ham and cheese. "I knew you couldn't run that fast."

I fake punch him. He smirks, then asks Ginger, "So was it gory? Amber beat the crap out of him and leave him for dead?"

"Just about." Ginger's eyes are lit in amusement. "I swear, it was like watching Custer ride across the prairie. He went into the situation with no battle plan and no knowledge whatsoever of the strength of his enemy."

Griff elbows me. "You'd think a history freak like you would know better."

"Well, he got out alive and acted with honor," Ginger says. "Better than Custer did, on both counts."

How much do I like her right now? Not just that she called me honorable, but that she knows about the Battle of the Little Bighorn?

"You guys realize I'm sitting right here while you talk about me, right?"

"Yup," they reply together.

I crack up, then pull *Gatsby* out of my backpack. Have to read the last few pages before class. I haven't been called on yet, which means I'm due. Just what I need on a day where everyone's talking about me.

Somehow, though, kicking back alongside Griff and Ginger, I'm feeling no pain. Like I'm looking back at my relationship with Amber from a decade in the future and seeing that I've lived and learned.

Griff leans over to two-point his wadded-up sandwich wrapper in the trash can. As he shoots, Ginger winks at me. No squinching, no posing against a fence with a hand on her hip. Just a straight-up wink.

"So you live to fight another day," she says.

I smile at her, then reach across the table to steal back a Skittle from the open bag. "You think?"

She yanks the bag away before I can get one, but her lips curve into a smile. "Positive."

Don't Mind Me

BY TERRI CLARK

● ● ● ● ● ● ● ● ● ● ● ●

CHAPTER ONE

Virginity is highly overrated.

I mean, really, what is it?

It's not some identifiable body part you can give away, like, say, your hair or a kidney. Those you'd miss. And, yeah, before you go uttering that icky word—*hymen* (which sounds like "Hi, men! Aim right *here*")—let me just say I'm pretty sure my brother's bike busted that when I fell on the crossbar. Yeowch!

That said, what've I got to lose?

Nothing, right? Which is why I've decided tonight—two days before the start of our senior year—is the night.

Rick Travers and I have been dating for three months and I'm head over combat boots in love with him. And if you'd told me back in May that I, Dee Delaney, otherwise known as Dark Dee, would be dating *the* "A" number one football jock at Rocky Ridge High, I would've told you to lay off the absinthe. But I believe that saying "Once you go black, you never go back" refers to Goths, because Rick seems to like this freak just fine and tonight I intend to let him impale me.

Here's hoping he knows how to wield his stake.

● ● ●

"That frickin' rocked," Rick hollered. "All that blood and you totally screamed."

"Did not!" Miffed, I folded my arms over my chest and scowled. "It was more like a gasp."

"Yeah, right." He snort laughed. "And you covered your eyes." Taking one hand off the steering wheel, he mimicked the way I'd peeked between my fingers.

"Just when her skin peeled off," I excused. "Now keep your baby blues on the road. It's foggy as hell out here."

"Perfect post–horror movie weather." He leered at me with a bug-eyed, evil grin and made creepy *oooh-wee-oooh* sound effects. "It's black as night, we're surrounded by a thick mist, and there's probably a backwoods butcher somewhere in those woods. Waiting. *For you.*"

I rolled my eyes at his dramatics.

"Don't worry, darlin'," he said in a gruff macho voice as he flexed his impressive guns. "I'll protect you. Come 'ere."

Laughing, I unsnapped my seat belt and scooted across the cab of his truck. When he wrapped his arm across my shoulders, I snuggled into his side.

"And to think they call you Dark Dee?" he scoffed. He loved to needle me about my softer side, the one few people saw. That he knew I had one, and could tease me about it, made me feel especially close to him.

"Hey, now," I said, playfully swatting his belly. "Just because I'm alternative doesn't mean I'm impervious to gore. Eli Roth is a sick director who knows how to make his audience squirm."

Rick tickled me under my chin. "I know how to make you squirm."

"Stop," I shrieked and batted his hand away.

"Or what?"

"Or I'll make *you* squirm," I threatened in a throaty voice.

He raised his eyebrows at me. "Really? How you gonna do that?"

"Mmm," I murmured into his ear. "I've got a few ideas."

"Such as?"

Rising up on my knees I started to kiss his neck. "Like a little of this," I whispered, then nipped at his earlobe with my teeth. "And some of this." My hand slid up his thigh and over his crotch. "And a whole lot of *that*," I breathed.

"Dee?" he asked in a strained voice.

I smiled in the shadows and confessed, "You've won my wary heart, Rick, and I'm ready."

His hands tightened on the steering wheel.

"You sure?"

I unsnapped the button at his waist. "My family's gone." Unzip. "Take me." I cupped him through his underwear. "Home."

This was a big moment between us. Not only was I going to give him my virginity, I intended to whisper those . . . three . . . little . . . words . . . when I did.

Tonight would change everything.

Licking his ear, I started to stroke him.

I wish I knew what you're thinking, I thought as he moaned.

Suddenly, the truck swerved. Rick swore. I flew forward. Something cracked. And everything went dark.

• • •

The crack?

My head.

Against the windshield.

I have no idea how long I was unconscious. I only know I woke up, sprawled across the seat, hearing Rick say, "Holy shit, she's dead!"

I tried to assure him I wasn't, but only managed an incoherent moan.

"Thank God," he said. "Maybe I can still get laid."

What?!? Did he REALLY just say that?

I groaned again. My skull pounded as if someone had whacked

me with a mace. Raising a shaky hand to my forehead I felt sticky wetness.

"You okay?" my boyfriend asked.

Opening my eyes I saw two of him.

"Man," he said, "she looks like that chick in the movie."

That's not good. I blinked a couple times to get Rick in focus.

"Dee?" Yanking his Denver Broncos T-shirt over his head, he used it to wipe my face and apply pressure to my head. "Say something."

"Do I really look that bad?" I croaked, taking the shirt from him and holding it to my gash. My eyes slid closed against the pain in my head.

"Should I lie?" I heard him ask.

"Tell me the truth," I muttered. Why did he keep talking like I couldn't hear him?

"Uh." He hesitated. "You hit the windshield and cracked your skull."

That would explain the blood and throbbing agony.

"Broke my frickin' window, too."

I opened my eyes and glared at him. "Gee, sorry my busted head broke your frickin' window."

He gave me a funny look. "No worries," he rushed to say, "let's just get you home." *Maybe I can patch her up and still win this part of the bet.*

Whoa. I'd heard him say that last bit, though his lips never moved. What the hell?

I shook my head to clear the craziness. Bad mistake—EXPLO-SIVE KILL-ME-NOW PAIN!—I rolled over on the seat and barfed my popcorn and soda all over the floor of Rick's truck.

"What the fuck!" he screamed.

I wiped my mouth with his shirt. "Sorry," I whimpered, closing my eyes against another wave of nausea. "I feel like shit."

"Great, just frickin' great"—he flounced back against his seat and smacked his hand on the steering wheel—"my truck's smashed up,

Ghoul Girl's smashed up, and it smells like puke in here."

With great pain and concentration I pulled myself into a sitting position and looked at him. "*What* did you call me?" I asked in a low, shocked voice. Surely I'd heard him wrong. He'd never debase me like that.

He looked confused. "Dee?"

"You called me Ghoul Girl," I accused.

Shaking his head he argued, "No, I didn't."

"You said 'My truck's smashed up, Ghoul Girl's smashed up, and it smells like puke in here.'"

He flinched. "Did I say that out loud?"

"Obviously," I said, raising my voice. "How *could* you?"

He raised his hands in a placating manner. "I'm sorry. I'm upset. I wasn't thinking."

I reached for the door handle and, mindful of the putrid puddle on the floor, stumbled out of his truck. My legs wobbled on the uneven gravel, and the gliding, low-lying fog gave me a trippy sense of motion sickness. Woozy, I held on to the door frame until I caught my balance.

"Be careful," he warned, rushing around the back of the truck, pants still unzipped. "I don't want you passing out." Then he yanked me into his arms. "Dee, I'm sorry I called you that. It's just the adrenaline and fear talking. I thought you were dead."

He sounded genuinely contrite. And, come on, who hasn't said something hurtful when they're upset? "It's okay." I sighed and hugged him back, pressing my face to his bare chest. "Are you hurt?"

"Not a scratch," he said and I pulled back to confirm it. Yup, still hot and hard-bodied.

"Seat belt," he explained with a shrug.

That's right; *I'd* stupidly taken mine off to get closer to him. Note to self: Don't ever be a crash test dummy.

Still a bit wobbly, I shut the car door. "What'd we crash into?"

Rick pointed to the front of the truck. Branches and leaves from a blue spruce covered the hood, and the bumper had a trunk-size dent in it, but the tree itself stood mockingly solid.

"Whoa, we're lucky," I said and looked at Rick. "It could've been a lot worse."

Easy for you to say. It's not your truck.

Again, I heard his words, but his lips never moved. Instead, when he did speak out loud, he said, "Let's hope she still runs."

"Rick," I said in a tremulous voice, raking my hands through my hair, "I think there's something wrong with my head."

Great, he said snidely, *she's lost it. Must've damaged some brain cells.* But to my face he asked, "What do you mean?" with careful concern.

Massaging my temples, I looked at him suspiciously. "Is this some kind of joke?"

I'm sure as hell not laughing. I was this close, this frickin' close, to FINALLY sealing the deal and being able to scratch the Goth off my list. Then, in an exasperated tone he said out loud, "Sorry, Dee. You ain't being Punk'd."

Holy Houdini!

I was *hearing* his thoughts. And they nowhere near matched the words coming out of his mouth. How could this be?

"Rick?" I asked hesitantly. "What's three hundred and forty-seven times two divided by four?"

Huh. Well, three hundred times two is six hundred and then I gotta times the . . . What the hell— "What the hell—"

I shook my head. "Never mind." Shock and suspicion rushed through me like an icy IV solution. "About tonight . . ."

"Yeah," he said, sounding like an eager puppy. *Maybe I can still nail her.*

I hid my wince and gave him a coy look. "You want me, don't you?"

"Yeah." *Hell yeah, I wanna see if you're as freaky in bed as you are outta it. I wouldn't have been so damn patient otherwise. But if you're a real twisted sister, that could make this whole bet worthwhile.*

"Bet?" I said under my breath. Never mind the insulting freaky-twisted-sister part, that was the second time he'd said, er, thought the word *bet*. I had to figure out what was going on. I had to know if I really was brain damaged or if I could actually hear—

"What'd you say?" Rick interrupted my thoughts. Both his face and his body had gone rigid.

I looked at him through narrowed eyes. "Bet. I said bet."

He looked away. Boils and bats! I *had* heard his thoughts. Was that guilt on his face or frustration?

Aw, hell, he swore in his inner voice. *Does she know? Phil and I have been so careful.*

That answered that question. And Phil? What did his best friend have to do with any of this? Feeling like Alice in Wonderland, I wondered what rabbit hole I was about to trip into. And did I want to know? Yes, yes, I did, because something felt really wrong here. Really. Wrong.

"I know about you and Phil," I bluffed.

"Shit," he muttered, tugging at his spiky hair. "How'd you find out?"

"Doesn't matter."

"Listen," he said, taking me by the shoulders, "no harm, no foul, 'kay?"

I didn't say anything. I didn't know *what* to say.

"I'm sure you think I'm just an asshole out to get some T and A, but it's more than that. We're conducting valuable research," he said with self-importance.

My spine stiffened. I was part of some kind of research? Not understanding, and desperate to put puzzle pieces together, I thought back through his previous comments. "And, um, I'm the Goth you need to scratch off your list?"

"Exactly," he said, huffing out a relieved breath as if elated I understood. "So, whaddya say? Are you game?" *Please, oh, please, oh, please.*

Dread knotted my stomach and I hugged my arms around

myself. "About this research . . ." I hedged.

"It started as a bet," he said, "but then we saw the potential for more. Now it's a bet *and* research."

"Research?"

"For our book."

WTF? The words *research, book,* and *Rick Travers* have never been uttered in one sentence before. Yes, he was my boyfriend, but he was still a jock. Big on brawn, not on brains. However, I'd thought, *believed,* he had a huge heart and an open mind. Now I was beginning to think—

"We're calling it *The Guy's Guide to Getting ANY Girl,*" he interrupted. His cocky grin said he expected me to appreciate his title.

"Catchy," I said, "and your research involves—"

"Girls," he said, in a like-duh tone. "Both of us have to get a chick from each clique—"

"'Get'?" I whispered in horror.

"You *know,*" Rick said, as if *I* was the imbecile, "but she's gotta say 'I love you.' That, more then anything, proves you've really won her. And then the first one to get the girl—from whatever group we're working on—wins the side bet."

"And you're writing a book to teach other guys to—"

"Our tag line is 'Be Who They Want You to Be.'"

"So you pretended to be who I wanted you to be?" I asked in an anguish-choked voice.

"Yeah, isn't it brilliant?" he brayed, oblivious to my withering heart.

Man, I can't believe how cool she's being about this, I heard him think.

"What about Dark at Heart?" I asked. "You said you loved it."

"Hated it," he sneered. "Stupid fem Victorian club."

"The Sixty-nine Eyes?"

"Freaks. Who calls themselves the Helsinki Vampires?"

I pointed to his kohl-lined eyes. "Eyeliner?"

"Gay."

"Black nail polish?"

"Gayer."

"Horror movies?"

"Those, I like."

"Me?" I asked, tears running down my cheeks.

Finally, he seemed to notice my upset.

"Oh, hey, you're all right."

I sobbed/laughed, choking on my own waterworks. "All right," I repeated. "ALL RIGHT!" I screamed.

"Yo, Dee," he said, taking two steps back, his hands held before him. "I thought you were cool with this."

"You thought I was cool with finding out my BOYFRIEND has lied to me about *everything* for three months so he could get laid and scratch the Goth girl off his frickin' to-do list."

"It's not about the sex—"

"Oh, that's right," I said as I slapped myself on the forehead and then cried out in pain. "How could I forget? You also need an oath of love. Then what?"

Huh. "What what?" he asked, a Cro-Magnon look of befuddlement on his face.

"After you've gotten loved *and* laid, what do you do?"

Uh-oh. Better make some shit—

"Don't you dare"—I poked him in the chest—"make some shit up. You intended to dump me as soon as you got what you wanted, didn't you?"

You can say that again, crazy witch. "Of course not. Dee, baby, you're making a mountain out of a mole."

"It's molehill, you moron. And the only thing I'm doing is dumping your ass."

"What? Here?" he asked incredulously.

I started walking back to the road.

"You're gonna walk home in the fog with the butcher in the woods?" he taunted.

"Bring him on," I said. "I'll tell him where to find you."

"Freak!"

"Fraud!"

He got in his truck and I heard the *rrrr-rr-rrrr* of a motor that wouldn't turn over. "Foiled again," I yelled back to him, cackling like a maniac in the dark.

And to think I almost pledged my love and gave my virginity to that conniving, manipulative, low-down con man with a jock for brains.

Thank Goth I didn't.

CHAPTER TWO

"What's with the 911 text?" Pixie asked as she barged through my bedroom door with her usual pigtails and piercings. "Hellfire!" she hollered as she stopped dead in her tracks. "What happened to your head?"

Gingerly I raised my hand to the lump on my forehead. Last night's gash had looked worse than it was, but I'd woken up with a raging headache. A couple of pain pills chased by two cups of coffee had numbed the worst of it. "Looks pretty bad?" I asked self-consciously.

"Um." She hesitated. "The black and purple goes quite well with the black and pink streaks in your hair."

"Gee, thanks." I patted a place next to me on the bed.

She sat and lowered her zebra-striped glasses to take a closer look at me. "You've been crying. You *never* cry." Reaching out to touch my goose egg, she thought twice and lowered her hand. "Does it hurt that bad?" she asked with a sympathetic wince.

I waved away her worry. "No and that's not why I called you. Think of a number between one and a million."

She crinkled her studded nose. "You called me here to pick a number?"

Arching my eyebrow, I gave her a get-on-with-it look.

"Ooo-kay," she said and closed her eyes.

"Nineteen hundred and eighty-nine," I blurted.

"Whoa—" Her green eyes widened. "How'd you—?"

"Now concentrate on a crush, one I don't know about."

"Dee—"

"Please," I begged. "You have to do this or you'll never believe me." She quirked her mouth to the side and gave me a nod.

"Ew," I said in the next second, "sweaty Coach Crandall?"

"What?" she asked hotly. "He's gorgeous."

I caught her thinking about his tight buns and sweat-glistening chest. Not bothering to argue I said, "Last test, think about a secret."

"Dee, stop it," she fussed. "Tell me what's—"

"Think," I said.

She flopped back on the bed. "But you know everything."

"Surely not," I said. "I didn't know about Coach."

She shook her head, but a quick thought flashed through her brain.

"Malice Alice," I gasped. "You *took* my doll?"

"Mindfreak!" Pixie yelled and scrambled off the bed, looking wildly around the room. "Where's Criss Angel?"

"Pix, why'd you take her?" I asked, genuinely shocked. "All this time, I thought I'd lost her."

"I'm sorry," she said, her face tight with misery. "I wanted one so badly for my twelfth birthday. It was the only thing I asked for and when you got her and I didn't—" *I'm a horrible, terrible friend.*

I stood and pulled her into a hug. "You're not a horrible, terrible friend, you're my bestie."

She pulled back, her eyes brimming with tears. "I've felt so guilty and rotten, for so long. I wanted to give her back, but the longer I waited the harder it became."

"Do you still have her?"

She nodded and swiped at her eyes under her glasses. "She's in perfect condition. I couldn't bring myself to play with her. You'll have her back today." *I'll do anything so you don't hate me.*

I gave one of her brown pigtails an affectionate tug. "I could never, ever hate you."

"Dee." She gave me a shake. "You're creeping me out. *How* can you read my mind?"

Grabbing her by the hand, I pulled her down onto the floor where we leaned our backs against the bed.

"Last night I broke up with Rick."

"Tears," she said with a sage nod. "What happened? I thought last night was the point of no return?"

"I thought so too, but then we got into a car wreck."

"Head," she said. "That explains two out of three. And the mentalism?"

I shrugged. "Head against windshield, I think."

"Tell," Pixie said.

"Everything was going great. We saw *Slaughter Shack*—"

Ooh, wonder how it was.

"It was amazing," I answered her thoughts, "everything was perfect, we were driving home, cuddling and teasing and—"

"Teasing?" she asked. "As in ha-ha teasing or as in he should've kept his hands on the wheel teasing?"

"Um, well"—I plucked at the shag carpet—"his hands were on the wheel, mine weren't."

"Crash," Pixie said knowingly. *Note to self: Heavy petting while driving is dangerous.*

I burst out laughing. "I'll make a note of that, too."

Pixie shook her head. "I am SO going to have to watch what I think around you."

"At least your thoughts match who you are," I said.

"Meaning?" she asked, a confused look on her face.

"Pix, he lied to me about everything." The tears I thought I'd spent started again. "He was using me."

Between sobs and swears I told her the whole sordid tale. When I finished she simply said, "Stupid ass."

"He's not the only one." I sniffled and scrubbed at my swollen eyes. "I fell for every lie he told with his artificially sweetened tongue."

Pixie laid her head on my shoulder. "You couldn't know. And, believe me, you're not the only girl who's fallen for a great pretender."

I blew out a frustrated breath and tucked my head against hers. "I suppose. I don't even know if I was the first girl on his list."

"Probably," she assured me. "That kind of thing would get around. How could it not? And now that you know about his point-

and-clique scheme, I'm sure he'll take a sabbatical from sleaze."

I peered down at her. "Guess I'll find out soon enough."

"School," Pixie sighed. "Tomorrow."

"Sucks," I finished.

Wonder what I should wear, Pixie thought.

"Your new black-and-white houndstooth skirt with the big buckle belt and your kick-ass Nana Black books."

Pix bumped her head against mine.

"Oops!" I covered my mouth. "Invasion of privacy. Sorry. Guess I need to figure out how, or *if*, I can tune things out."

Pixie pulled away and pivoted to better face me. "I don't mind you reading my mind, but what's it going to be like in a building with over a thousand brains?"

I blanched. "I'll become schizophrenic!"

"Easy," Pixie soothed. "You just need to learn how to tune out the voices in your head."

"I've been telling her that for years," a snarky voice interrupted.

I grabbed a black pillow off my bed and threw it at Braden. "Get out!"

He ducked, then leaned against the doorway. "You know, there's meds for that," he said with a smirk.

The world considered my fourteen-year-old brother athletic, adorable, and amusing. I considered him a royal pain in my—

"What do you want?" I barked.

"Mom told me you got wrecked. I just came to—"

"I'm fine. Now get out."

"I see the brain damage didn't improve your personality," he snapped, closing the door behind him. *Sheesh, guess a guy can't check on his sister.*

"Braden!" I shouted, feeling bad when I realized he was being sincere.

He peeked through the door. "What?" he huffed, to hide his hurt.

"Sorry. I'm okay." I gestured to my head. "I just got a lump and a headache. Thanks for asking," I said.

He nodded as he closed the door and I heard him think, *Thank God she's all right.*

"Huh," I said.

"Huh?" Pixie repeated.

I pointed to the door. "Maybe he's not such an ogre."

"And the miracles keep happening," Pixie joked. She retrieved the missile I'd thrown, stretched out on the floor, and tucked the pillow under her head. "Now let's practice tuning in and tuning out."

"Like a radio?"

"Exactly. Hopefully with enough practice you can scan to the channels you want and ignore those you don't."

"And if I can't?"

She rolled over on her tummy and looked at me. "You might consider a lobotomy."

"Gee, thanks."

"A traveling carnival or circus is another option," she said with a cheeky grin that emphasized her dimples.

"And what?" I asked with contempt. "Be part of the freak show?"

"You could be"—she held up her hands as if reading a billboard—"Dynamic Dee. Maybe you'll become so famous they'll post a sign that reads: Centennial, Colorado. Home of the Great Deedini."

I rolled my eyes and gave her a shove. "As long as I don't become Demented Dee."

"Too late," Pixie chirped.

"Hardy har har," I said, not feeling like joking. "Seriously, Pix, this is scary." Distracted, I drew patterns into the carpet with my finger.

And cool.

"Yeah, cool too," I said, acknowledging her thought, "but weird. Is this temporary or something I'll have to live with the rest of my life?"

I don't know. You just have to deal with it while you've got it.

"You're right."

But you're going to have to be careful.

"I know."

Do you?

"Yeah." I automatically answered.

"Then the first thing you have to do is *quit* responding to people's thoughts. We just had an entire conversation and I never said a word. If you do that with anyone else, you're going to be locked in a rubber room or a laboratory."

I gave her a stricken look. "Hell's bells, I didn't even realize. How am I going to make it through school?"

"Mind over matter." She frowned. "Or would that be mind over mind?"

"I don't know, but the worst thing about tomorrow will be seeing Rick again."

"Forget him. Maybe the butcher in the woods found him."

I laughed. "We can always hope."

"Think about it, Dee," she said excitedly. "Tomorrow is the first day of our *senior year.* That's colossal. Nothing—not a fleabag ex or a mind-reading ability—is going to ruin this year for us."

"You're right! And maybe," I said with a wicked grin, "we can use my new superpower to our advantage."

Pixie rubbed her hands together and, giving her best Igor impression, asked, "What do you have in mind, Master?"

"I don't know. Yet. But they don't call me Dark Dee for nothing."

CHAPTER THREE

In actuality, they—they being every pom and prep at Rocky Ridge—called me Dark Dee because of my affinity for black leather and lace, spikes and studs. It was annoying, but predictable. Truth be told, I liked standing out. Normal was boring. But at times I realized my feral fashion sense not only set me apart—it also alienated others. People tended to give me a wide berth.

I looked down at myself. Frankly, I didn't see what was so frightening about black and pink highlights in blond hair, or a black satin bustier with black cherry earrings. I suspected they thought I might put a hex on them, but I was more spiritual than satanic. Yeah, I liked to tip my toe into the darker side of things—horror movies, Gothic rock, vampire fiction—but I also believed in a higher power and the strength of positive thinking. Boo. Scary. Don't you think?

For me it's all about dark romanticism. Seeing beauty in blackness. Too many people are afraid to seek the shadows and therefore never see the whole picture. Life is both light and dark, and I live to understand that balance. But as I stepped into the halls of my high school, on the first day of school, I realized I wasn't as enlightened as I believed myself to be.

. . .

"So far, so good?" Pixie whispered, clutching my arm. She'd taken my advice and worn the houndstooth skirt. Her hair was arranged in a series of knobs all over her head and today's glasses were hand-painted with skull and crossbones. As usual, she looked positively adorable.

"It sounds like I have a mosquito buzzing in my head," I said in a low voice. "I want to swat myself."

Pixie grinned, flashing me double dimples. "Well, a buzz is better than a riot of voices. Right?"

"True enough," I agreed. "Practice makes perfect. I'll get this dull roar turned down eventually."

Opening my locker, I stashed my messenger bag and took out a spiral and pen.

Pixie leaned against a neighboring locker and looked around.

"We still have a few minutes, tap into your telepathy. I'm dying to know what people are thinking."

I tried to object. "Pix—"

"Meegan Myers, A-list dance pom bitch." She nodded to a brunette Barbie in Tory Burch. "What's she thinking?"

Curious, despite feeling a bit like an intruder, I tuned in. " 'I'd kill for some carbs,' " I said and Pixie giggled.

Then she nodded her head to the left. "Derek Standish, D-list skater dude with curls I'd love to run my fingers through."

I studied the guy in his Hurley tee and beanie.

" 'Pixie looks hot!' "

"Oh no he didn't," she said, smacking me.

"Oh yes he did."

She gave me an appreciative look. "You could *so* come in handy."

"And you could *so* get me in trouble."

"What about her?" Pixie motioned to Sexy Lexy, captain of the cheerleading squad. "Is she chanting two-four-six-eight in her head?"

" 'God, I so don't want to see him,' " I quoted. " 'I feel beyond stupid.' "

"Uh-oh," Pixie said, a frown creasing the bridge of her nose. "That's not good. Wonder who she's—?"

"Wait," I told Pixie, grabbing her arm. "She just thought, 'Crap, there he is.' "

We both looked around. Coming up the hall, strutting like he owned the world, was Rick Travers.

A combination of nausea and longing rocked my stomach.

Pixie squeaked. "You don't think—?"

I shushed her, concentrating on Lexy's thoughts. *Rick the Prick,* she thought snidely, but I also sensed her crushing pain. A pain I shared. *Bet he doesn't even talk to me.*

And he didn't.

But he *did* talk to me.

"Like the look, Dee," he said with an arrogant wink, pressing his forearm against my locker door to cage me in.

I tried to be immune to his nearness, but a part of me desperately wanted to step into his arms like I had the last three months. He smelled the same (soap and musk deodorant) and looked the same (bad-boy bravado and tight denim), but gone was his dusky charm (faked) and soulful sensitivity (faked). He was a gloating, goading illusion.

"Care to change your mind about me and you? Look." He pointed down the hall where Phil was talking to Desiree McFay. "He's got himself a ghoulfriend."

Suddenly, I didn't want him near me at all. "I'd rather bash my head in again," I sneered.

He raised his hand to touch the lump on my forehead and I jerked out of his reach.

Unfazed, he said, "I see it's turning a lovely shade of pea green and piss yellow." Then he chuckled and turned his attention to Pixie. "Maybe I can interest your fairy friend here."

"It's Pixie," she spat. "And I'd rather shove bamboo shoots under my nails before hooking up with a louse like you."

"Ooh," he said with a lecherous grin. "Kinky. I'm willing to try anything once."

"You're vile," I told him and shoved his chest. "Take a walk. The tribe has spoken."

"No prob, I've already *Goth* another prospect." He snorted. "Get it, Goth?"

I clenched my jaw. "You're still—"

"Conducting research?" he asked. "You know it. Surely you didn't think you were the only one?"

"No, just the first—"

"Far from, baby." He chucked me under the chin. "You're just the one who got away."

I scooted farther away and peered over his shoulder at Lexy.

Maybe I should warn her, she thought.

"Riiick," I said, laying on the saccharine, "does anyone else know about your little book project?"

"Nope, just me, you, Fairy, and Phil." He shook his head. "I still can't figure out how you knew."

"Funny thing, Rick." I pressed my finger into my cheek in an oh-so-innocent gesture. "The best-kept secrets have a way of getting out."

"Is that a threat?" he hooted, his eyes showing anything but worry. "What're you gonna do, tell everyone? Who'd believe ghoul girl over golden boy?"

I didn't say anything.

"No one"—he aimed a dazzling smile my way—"that's who."

I hated that dazzling smile. He'd used dental-perfect deceit to disarm me and I had an overwhelming urge to take a Louisville Slugger to every damn tooth.

"Haven't you ever watched a Western?" he asked. "The bad guy always wears black." He held his hands up and stepped away. "That'd be you"—he gave my outfit a telling once-over—"not me." Then he walked over to Casey Summers's locker and, after tossing me a knowing look, proceeded to seduce Goth number two.

• • •

Turns out Rick wasn't only stringing Casey along, he was also gunning for Ashleigh Masters, a sk8r chick in my Spanish class. Who knew if there was another girl on the line? He was obviously speed dating. Chances are he felt threatened I knew what was going on or he felt patience didn't pay off. Maybe both. Regardless, he was a gigolo on a mission.

I oscillated between being green with jealousy, black with rage, and blue with despair. I was a walking, talking emotional bruise and I wanted to cover up and hide. When he was little, Braden took great pleasure in poking my bruises and asking, "Does that hurt?" knowing full well it did. Rick played that game now.

As we waited for the starting bell to ring, I watched him sidle up to Ashleigh and start a convo. I had to hand it to the guy. He did his research. He actually talked intelligently about nollies and pop-shuvits. You'd think he could grind with the greatest. And Ashleigh fell for his spiel heelflip, lipslide, and stalefish.

I felt like I was witnessing a tragic accident in slo-mo. I knew what was coming. I wanted to stop it. And all I could do was watch in mute horror. *Nooooooo!* I cried in my head. *Dooooooon't do it, Aaaaaaash.*

Too late. They had a date.

When Señor Bailey stepped to the front of the class and called for *atención,* Rick headed to his desk in the back of the room, but not before whispering "Damn, I'm good" as he walked by me.

In that moment I swore to squash his Conquer the Cliques plan. I didn't know how, but I couldn't sit idly by while he wreaked havoc.

Save the Girls, Spare the World became my new motto.

CHAPTER FOUR

"I'll have shirts made up," Pixie said. "Your motto has a certain *je ne sais quoi* I think will really catch on."

We sat at a cement table in the outdoor quad during lunch. It was nice to get away from Rick's constant crowing presence.

I gave an inelegant snort to Pixie's suggestion. "You really think people will wear 'Save the Girls, Spare the World' across their chests?"

"Once we get done with our grassroots campaign."

"Grassroots campaign?"

"Yes, you can't stop them alone." She took a sandwich from her brown paper bag and proceeded to pick it apart. "You need an alliance."

"I have an ally. She's sitting across from me, throwing her ham into the grass."

She peered at me over her glasses. "While I am your bestie, and everyone else is just the restie, you do need to pull some of the others in on your plan to take Rick and Phil down."

"Why?" I asked, eating a spoonful of yogurt. I probably sounded peevish, but I didn't want to become the poster child for stupid girls. Heartbreak was painful enough without adding humiliation.

"Because, much as I hate to admit it, Rick made a valid point earlier."

I pursed my lips in irritation. "You mean when he said no one would take my word over his?"

"'Fraid so. He *is* the golden boy and we—in case you were unaware—are considered freaks."

I gasped. "No, say it ain't so."

"Therefore," she said as if I'd never overdramatized, "people may be hesitant to listen to us. This assignment—should you choose to accept it—is going to require you to step out of your social pentagram and cross clique lines."

I pretended to tremble. "Oh, no. What should I arm myself with? Garlic, crosses, holy water?"

She took her glasses off, put one of the arms in her mouth, and gave me a serious, scholarly look. "I'd start with a cheerleader."

"Say what?" I asked, pointing my spoon at her. "Have you gone mental?"

"Come on," she said, while munching her cheese sandwich. "It's not so shocking. Buffy was a cheerleader."

"So you've found someone who's going to kick Rick's demon ass?"

"No"—she waved her sandwich at me—"*you've* found someone who can help you cross clique lines."

"You mean Lexy?"

"Yes, I think it's fairly obvious she's fallen prey to the great pretender."

I had to agree and I wasn't sure who I felt worse for, her or me. "And how exactly am I supposed to approach her? 'Excuse me, Lexy. I was reading your mind and discovered that you, too, have been screwed by Rick the Prick. What do you say we team up to take him down?'"

"Close"—Pixie held up her finger—"but not quite. We don't want to frighten her unduly. As it is, your approach is going to create immediate alarm."

"Gee, thanks," I sneered. "You sure know how to stroke my ego."

She shook her head, dismissing the diss. "You are a Goth. She's a cheer. Never the twain shall meet. Besides, the whole 'screw' metaphor, I'd stay away from it. Methinks while it's a figurative expression for you, she was not so lucky."

"Yeah." I hung my head, knowing who I felt worse for. "I'm afraid he pulled an SOS."

"That doesn't stand for Save Our Ship, does it?"

"Sex. Once. Scram."

Pixie winced. "Don't share that abbreviation with Rick. I'm certain he'd use it in his book."

"There's *not* going to be any book," I asserted. "Not if I can help it."

"So you accept your mission?" she asked, her green eyes alight with excitement.

"I have to," I moaned. "I just don't know what to do. I mean, even if I were to approach Lexy right now, then what?"

Pixie gave it some thought. "You could stand on one of the tables out here and disgrace Rick. It works in the movies."

"Not quite." I shook my head and absently rubbed the bump on my noggin. "He'd just call us scorned women and then we'd come off looking pathetic."

"True, unless"—she held up her hand—"there were more than two of you."

"Even still, do you really think any of his victims—however many there are—would want to stand up and publicly admit they fell for his sleazy seduction?" I pointed to myself. "I wouldn't want to do that. This is embarrassing."

"Right," she said, plucking off pieces of her bread crust and tossing them to the ground. "We want to embarrass *him*. Not the other way around."

"Exactly," I agreed. "We want to tattle-tale without exposing anyone other than Rick and Phil."

Pixie tapped her chin thoughtfully. "Tattle-tale, tattle-tale, tattle-tale," she murmured. "By Bauhaus, I think I've got it."

"Spill!" I said, leaning across the table. "I see the wicked gleam in your eyes."

"Turnabout is fair play, my dear."

"Yes . . . and?"

"And you"—she jabbed her finger at me—"are going to beat him to the publishing line."

Perplexed, I frowned. "I'm going to write a book about Rick?"

"No, a tattle-tale tabloid," she said with smug satisfaction. "You and your pissed-off posse can tell all and remain incognito."

"You mean, instead of a school newspaper we'll publish a gossip rag?"

"All about Tweedle Dee and Tweedle Dum."

I let the idea play out in my mind. "Pixie, you are bloody brilliant."

"I am," she said, huffing a breath on her fingernails and then rubbing them on her shirt. "Behind these piratical specs is a brainiac with a penchant for evil masterminding."

"And *that*," I told her, "is why I can't possibly do this without you."

"I'm in," she easily agreed. "I want to see them crushed like the rodents they are. The first thing you have to do is put together your staff."

I lowered my head to the table. "That's what I was afraid you'd say."

"You, afraid?" she scoffed. "Not in this lifetime, the previous one, or the next."

I lifted my head. "Okay, *afraid* may be too strong a word. How about *dread*? I'm dreading it."

She gave me a quizzical look. "Are you concerned about ridicule, snobbery, or possibly being burned at the stake?"

"All of the above."

"Don't worry your pretty striped head," she assured me. "It's all in the approach."

I raised my eyebrows. "I'll take your word for it, but here's another question for you . . . WHO do we approach?"

"There is that," she said thoughtfully. "We know about Lexy, Ashleigh, and Casey. That's not enough. We also have to scout out the other fall gals."

"How?"

"Why, with your handy-dandy, built-in listening device."

"What?" I shook my head. "You just expect me to go around eavesdropping on the entire student body and hope I find a few people thinking about what a jerk Rick is?"

She grimaced. "Well, when you put it that way . . . I guess that might take a while."

"You think?" I stood and threw my trash in a nearby can.

"Hmm, this bears more thinking. Maybe we can also do some old-fashioned sleuthing and divide up the cliques, although I must say I feel quite disadvantaged compared to you."

"Okay, Nancy Drew," I said, sitting back down. "You really think we can infiltrate the cliques? Won't we look a little out of place?"

"Dee Devlin," she scolded. "You're not even trying. All you have to do is *talk* to people. It doesn't have to be that hard."

"All right, all right," I caved. "How do you want to do this?"

"Since you're so uncomfortable with this, I'll be nice and let you take the skaters. They're not too far removed from our ilk."

I rolled my eyes. Only Pixie would use the word *ilk*.

"But," she went on, "you have to do the cheers and poms."

I groaned.

"Do you want jocks or preps?" she asked and I felt like I was in some surreal game of *Man*opoly.

"Um, preps."

"Okay, I'll do the jocks, brainiacs, band geeks, and gangstas. That leaves you with the Goths and the drama/choir kids."

"Preps, cheers, poms, alts, thespians, and Idol wannabes," I said, ticking them off on my fingers. "Got it." Then the realization of what I was tackling hit me. "Pixie, what in the world are we doing?"

She smiled. "Deconstructing the social strata."

"Committing social suicide," I countered.

"Naw," she said, "we're Goth. Everyone already considers us dead."

I closed my eyes for a few moments. "This is too bizarre. I never thought I'd start my senior year as an activist against assholes."

Pixie shrugged. "When you find a worthy cause, you must rally ho."

And so it went. That afternoon, Operation Expose the Poseur was born.

CHAPTER FIVE

"What'cha doin'?"

"Thinking."

"For realz?" my brother asked in wonder. "Maybe that bump on your brain had some effect after all."

"Could be."

I'd been lying on my bed, staring at the ceiling. My emotions alternated between anger and despair. How could Rick be so cavalier with my heart? And how would I get over him? One minute he was my dark prince and the next he was Satan's son of a bitch. Although my heart was battered by his betrayal, I couldn't move from love to hate in 0 to 60 seconds.

I eyed Braden in my doorway. For once, he was a welcome distraction. "I'm fantasizing about ways to torture you," I teased.

He quirked a single eyebrow. "Black magic? Voodoo? Blood sacrifice?"

"Worse," I hissed. "Humiliation." Wait for it. "In front of a girl."

He shuddered. "Harsh. You're truly evil."

"You have no idea," I said in my best vampire accent.

He crossed his arms over his chest and gave me a cocky grin. "And *you* have no idea who I'd be most humiliated in front of."

I gave him my best wide-eyed innocent look then batted my eyelashes. "You mean Jamie Hargrove?"

His jaw dropped. "How'd you—?"

"I have my ways," I said mysteriously, then patted the spot next to me. He lay down and stared at the ceiling, too.

She's never invited me in here. I've always wanted her to.

I felt bad. Sure, he was Abercrombie and Fitch to my Emily the Strange, but at some point Braden had grown up, quit being a nuisance, and turned into a cool kid. Yet I'd never noticed.

"Let me ask you something," I said. "You've got cliques in your middle school, right?"

"Yeah."

I rolled sideways to better look at him. "Would someone like me ever talk to someone like you?"

"By someone like me, do you mean—?"

"Prep."

He shook his head. "No, probably not." *But I wish they would.*

"Would you want them to?" I asked knowingly.

"Yeah, I mean, I think you're cool."

My heart swelled. "You do?" I asked with a smile.

He turned his head to look at me. "I admire your whole noncon-formity thing."

"For real?"

"Yeah." He tucked his hands behind his head. "I couldn't pull it off. It's not me, but I admire people who are different. They're inter-esting."

"Are you calling me interesting?" I razzed.

"No way, you're just deranged," he said.

I laughed. "So, hypothetically speaking, if someone like me approached you in school, you wouldn't immediately blow them off? Not even to save face in front of others?"

He thought about it for a sec. "No, I'd be cautious, but I wouldn't blow them off."

"Suspicious?"

"Yeah, maybe, but I'd still listen to what they had to say."

"And if it struck a note of truth?"

"Then I'd give them the benefit of the doubt." He rolled toward me. "Dee, this is a weird convo. What's up?" He frowned. "Does this have to do with that jock you're dating?"

"Were," I corrected and commanded myself not to cry.

He raised his eyebrows. "You broke up?"

"Yup, dumped him."

He nodded his acceptance of this fact. "And now you're interested in a prep?"

"Not quite." I took a deep breath and looked him in the eye. "Braden, I'm about to do something I've never done before. I'm going to confide in you."

Holy cow. That bump did change her. Who is this girl and what has she done with my sister?

"So you think this"—I pointed to my goose egg—"changed me, huh?"

He gave me a weird look. "Um, it's just—"

"Pick a number between one and a million," I directed him, and then I gave him the same psych test I ran Pixie through. Once I'd convinced him of my mind-reading ability—and he stopped repeating "Holy shit" over and over again—he said, "Okay, I think I've wrapped my brain around this whole psychic thing, but what does that have to do with preps?"

"I am about to cross clique lines and I was hoping you'd give me some insight since you're in a different crowd."

"What're you trying to do?"

"I guess maybe I should also tell you *why* I dumped Rick." I lowered my gaze. "But it's humiliating."

He listened and never made a smart-ass remark. When I was done, I looked at him, worried he'd think less of me.

"Dee," he finally said, "you're like the coolest chick ever."

I blinked.

"This guy totally hoses you and, instead of pretending it didn't happen, you're out to save the girls and spare the world from him." Braden gave my shoulder a companionable punch. "You kick ass!"

"I do?"

"Totally. And don't be afraid to step out of your comfort zone."

"Why?"

"Because, you and them, not so different."

"No?"

"Come on," he said, "how have you always defended yourself whenever someone says something about the way you look? When

Grandma Tilly says, 'She'd be so beautiful if only'—?"

"I say, 'Real beauty is on the inside.'"

"And?"

I shrugged.

He thumped his chest. "People are the same at their core."

"Dude," I breathed in astonishment, "you like *actually* listen to me."

"We'll pretend that's not the case later on," he joked.

"So you're saying—"

"Everyone's got the same insecurities and worries. That's what you taught me. You and these girls share something in common. Maybe it's shitty, but it binds you. Just let them know they're not alone."

"Appeal to their sisterhood?"

"Naw, appeal to their thirst for revenge, but use sisterhood to get your boot in the door."

I laughed. "You're not so bad, bro. Thanks for your help."

"No prob, but tomorrow I'm bringing Jamie over after school so you can tell me if she likes me."

I grinned. "I can do that, just don't tell anyone about my—"

"Woo-woo, voodoo," he said, wiggling his fingers for effect.

"Something like that."

"No worries," he said, getting off the bed and walking toward the door. "Your secret is safe with me, but it will require hush payments now and then."

"I don't entertain at parties."

"Gambling tips?"

"No."

"Spying?"

"No."

"But you'll give me a thumbs up or down on Jamie?"

"Yes."

"It's a start." He leaned against my door. "I'll persuade you on the other stuff," he added, waggling his eyebrows.

"Good luck with that," I said sarcastically.

"And good luck tomorrow," he said sincerely. "I know you can do it."

I was touched by his faith in me, but a sudden sweep of nerves weakened my confidence. "Do you think I need to dress different?"

"No, just be you." *Anything else might really scare them.*

"I heard that."

"But it's true, if you become Preppy Dee people will wig."

"Plus then I'm just a great pretender, too."

"Totally. Who knows," he said, lifting one of his shoulders in a half-shrug, "maybe you'll be surprised."

"And maybe tomorrow you'll friend a freak."

"I think I will," he said. "And for what it's worth, I'd like to kill that creep on your behalf."

"Thanks."

"No prob. The right guy will come along."

"I'm not so sure," I said in a small voice.

"I am."

"I think from now on I'll administer lie-detector tests."

He grinned. "Good thing you've got an internal polygraph then."

"Guess I do," I said with a laugh as I watched him walk out the door. "Hey, Braden."

He stopped and looked back. "Yeah?"

"Thanks."

"That's what brothers are for."

He turned away.

"Hey, Braden."

"Yeah?"

"I love you, too," I said, answering the sentiment I'd heard him whisper in his head.

He was right, I realized. I had changed. Still was changing. I always thought I looked at the full picture. Light and dark. But I'd actually shoved my own brother into a far corner and never looked at him. Now that I had, it made me wonder what else I was missing.

Tomorrow could be incredibly enlightening . . .

. . . or massively disastrous.

CHAPTER SIX

"Just go over there and talk to her," Pixie whispered.

"What am I supposed to say?" I asked. It was between periods and Lexy was standing at her locker in her intimidating cheer uniform and a perky ponytail. Now was as good a time as any to approach her, but I was dragging my Converse.

"I know!" Pixie said. "Warn her like she thought about warning you."

I considered it. "That's not a bad idea."

"Of course it's not," Pixie said. "It's *my* idea."

I thought of Braden and pulled myself up with steely determination. "All right, here goes nothing."

"A cheer and Goth confab," Pixie marveled. "Let's hope the earth doesn't stop spinning on its axis."

My heart beat in my ears like a tribal drum as I crossed the hallway.

"Lex—?" I cleared the squeak out of my voice and tried again. "Lexy?"

Her back was turned to me, but I saw her stiffen, obviously recognizing my voice. Slowly she turned. *Does she know about Rick?* ribboned through her mind. "Yes?" she asked politely, her expression revealing none of her apprehension.

I relaxed a little knowing I wasn't the only one afraid.

"Could I speak to you?" I asked.

"Sure." She held her books in front of her like a shield. "What's up?"

"Um, well"—I looked around to make sure no one was paying attention—"I sort of noticed you looking at Rick Travers and well, I, uh—"

"You should stay away from him," she blurted.

I pulled back. "That's what I was going to say to *you.*"

What? "You mean you're not dating him?" she asked.

I shook my head. "Not anymore."

Oh, no. "Not you, too," she said, sympathy sweetening her voice. "Afraid so."

"So he, um"—*screwed you*—"and then dumped you?" she asked, unable to say the words she thought.

"No," I said quietly, my heart going out to her. "I figured out what he was up to and dropped him first."

"Lucky you," she said and I could tell she meant it. *Unlucky me,* she chastised herself.

I wanted to say she shouldn't berate herself, but I couldn't let on that I could read her mind. And, unfortunately, I was about to make things worse.

"Lexy, I, um . . ." I fiddled with the latch on her locker.

Damn, Rick. I didn't want to do this. Didn't want to hurt her any more than he already had. But she needed to know. I blew out a big breath.

"There's something else," I finally said. "Something you're not going to like." Then I told her about the *Guy's Guide.*

She paled and her eyes brimmed with tears. "He's going to write about us? Me?" *OhMyGod.*

"That's their intention."

How could he do this? It was my first time. And it was all a big joke to him. But it wasn't to me. It wasn't to ME, she cried to herself.

My throat tightened and I did something totally shocking. Something completely against my nature. Something that, had it been noticed, could've rocked the foundation of the school.

I hugged her.

GASP!

It was only for a second, but I couldn't help myself. Apparently I had a need to nurture. Who knew?

I pulled away and glanced around to make sure no one had witnessed my . . . inexplicable impulse. No one lay passed out on the floor. No alarms sounded. And Marilyn Manson wasn't clawing his eyes out. All was good.

"I think we can stop them," I told her.

"What do you have in mind?" she asked quietly.

"Beating them to the punch."

I briefly explained my plan for the tattle-tale.

She tilted her head to the side in contemplation. "And we'll remain anonymous?"

"Yes, the only ones who'll be exposed are Rick and Phil."

"Okay." *I want to hurt him, like he hurt me.* "What do you need me to do?"

"Do you know anyone else who's fallen for one of the great pretenders?"

"Not for sure," she said, then bit her lip. "But now that I know the whole story, I suspect Phil may have gone after Peggy Nolan."

"The prep?"

She nodded.

"Do you know her well enough to talk to her?"

"Yeah, better than you know me." She smiled to assure me there was no bite in her words. "If you can approach me, I can approach her."

"Okay, we're going to have our first tattle-tale meeting at my house on Friday at five p.m. If she's willing, bring her along. And if you discover anyone else—"

"I'll recruit them too."

"Great." And just like that, things felt awkward again so I turned to walk away. "See you."

"Dee," she called and I looked back. "Thank you."

I raised my hand to acknowledge her gratitude. "We've got to stick together. It's one man against many pissed-off chicks."

Finally she smiled. "He doesn't stand a chance." She closed her locker. "By the way, I've always wanted to tell you how much I love your hair." *I wish I could get away with that. She's got such a fun and funky style.*

I was so surprised and flattered, I didn't say anything. I just watched her walk away. Pixie wasn't so subtle. She stumbled and crashed loudly against a wall, knocking her hot pink glasses askew.

"*What* was that about?" I asked crossly.

"The earth *did* stop on its axis," she said in awe, shoving her specs back up.

"Shut up, Pix." I started to walk to class. "It didn't stop, it just—evolved—a little more."

Dogging my footsteps she said, "Before you know it, preps will be friends with gangstas and cheers will be friends with nerds." She threw her arms in the air. "It'll be anarchy," she yelled.

I rolled my eyes. "Would that be so bad?"

Clasping her hands to her chest she recited:

"And something's odd—within—

"That person that I *was*—

"And this one—do not feel the same—

"Could it be madness—this?"

"Emily Dickinson?" I guessed.

"Naturally."

I frowned. "Are you implying I've gone crazy?"

"No, I'm implying that this little coalition may change you."

I thought about it and decided she was right. "Yeah, but maybe I won't be the only one."

"You won't," she said with utter confidence. "I predict you upset the balance of the entire school. It's going to be a bea-u-tiful thing."

I narrowed my eyes at her. "You're enjoying this entirely too much."

She shrugged. "It's not every day you get to witness the start of world peace."

"World peace?" I laughed. "You're suffering delusions of grandeur."

"Admittedly, this is just a microcosm, but we'll start in our little fishbowl and then attack the world at large."

I hooked my arm through hers. "You know, Pixie, your positivity is magnanimous. If anyone can achieve world peace, it'll be you."

"One day, *mon amie,* one day," she said, giving me a squeeze. "For now, we'll just continue to bust down barriers like a pair of enlightened Charlie's Angels."

I let go of her and mimicked one of their classic poses.

She gave me her double dimples in return. "There is something so wrong and yet so right about you doing that in a 'Dead' T-shirt and argyle Converse."

I grinned back at her.

"Today is the dawn of a new day," she proclaimed.

"While I appreciate your enthusiasm," I told her, "we still have classes and I need to talk to Ashleigh after school."

"Good luck," she said and flashed me a peace sign before walking into her creative writing class. "May the Goddesses be with you."

Unfortunately, Pixie's blessing did me no good. Trying to convince Ashleigh her new boyfriend wasn't who he said he was . . . yeah, didn't go so well.

• • •

"You're just jealous," she spat at me.

She wore low-slung jeans and a Henley with thumbholes. Her long blond hair was tucked beneath a billed beanie. I pegged her immediately as a tomboy who didn't realize just how pretty she really was. And if her flushed face was any indication, she was also *really* flaming mad.

"No, Ashleigh, I'm not. I'm just trying to warn you."

Yeah, right, bitch.

I gritted my teeth. "Listen, I understand why you might be skeptical—"

"Skeptical," she scoffed. "I don't believe a word you say."

Patience, patience, patience, I chanted to myself. I'd stopped her and her brother on the cement stairs outside the school's front doors.

Fortunately, almost everyone had already left so we weren't creating too much of a scene.

"Okay," I said in the soothing kind of voice hostage negotiators and lion tamers use. "Scratch skeptical. You don't know me—"

And never want to.

I bit my tongue for a second. "But I know how he is."

I studied her brother, hoping he'd feel protective enough to listen, even if she wouldn't. He looked just like her. Blond hair, blue eyes, brilliant smile. A gorgeous guy without an ugly ego. "Trust me," I said, locking my gaze with his. "I know Rick says and does all the right things. Only he's a total fake."

Ashleigh jumped into my line of vision. "You're full of—"

"Maybe you should listen to her, Ash."

I could've thrown my arms around her bro at that moment.

"Stay out of this, Jensen," she barked.

"No." He leaned against the stair railing, arms wrapped around the pole. "She doesn't look like she's doing this out of spite."

"Are you kidding me?" she asked with disdain, then pointed at me. "*Look* at her. She's a freak. She probably has a crush on Rick and he won't have anything to do with her."

"Actually," I said stiffly, "he had plenty to do with me, and he'll try to do plenty with you."

Jensen straightened in alarm. "What do you mean?"

I looked from him to her and back again. "He's out for one thing and one thing only. Then he's gone."

Ashleigh stepped toe-to-toe with me. "Get on your broom and take flight."

"Ash!" Jensen snapped.

"Fine, then I'm outta here," she said and stormed down the stairs.

Jensen shoved his hands in his pockets and gave me an uncomfortable look. "Uh, I'm sorry about my sister."

I waved off his apology. "It's okay. I kinda thought it might go that way."

"No," he argued. "It's really not okay. I appreciate what you did. And I'm sorry he, uh—"

"Oh! Oh!" I gasped, realizing what he thought. My cheeks grew uncomfortably warm. "Um, yeah, he didn't get that far. At least not with me."

His brow furrowed. "There are others?"

I sat down on the steps. "Yeah. We're starting a club."

He sat next to me. "Serious?"

"Sort of." I chewed on one of my fingernails. "Let's just say we're planning to deflate Rick the Prick."

He laughed and the rich sound resonated through me.

"Care to elaborate?" he asked.

"Not really." I ducked my head. "Sorry, but I don't want our plans to get around."

"Understood. To capture your prey you need silence and stealth."

"Something like that." I didn't know why he'd stuck around, but while I had his attention I figured I better press my point. "Listen, I'm serious. Watch out for Ashleigh."

He gave me a grim nod. "I will, and if she comes around—"

I pulled a piece of paper and pen from my backpack and scribbled my e-mail address. "You can reach me here."

He gave me a thoughtful look. "Most people wouldn't do what you are."

"Exact revenge?"

His lips twitched. "No, watch out for others."

"Yeah, well, someone's got to stop him and there's safety in numbers."

"Don't discredit yourself, Dee," he said quietly. "I have a feeling you could handle all this on your own if you had to."

"Are you kidding me?" I rebuffed his compliment. "I wouldn't even be in this situation if I hadn't been so stupid."

"There you go again," he said, shaking his head. "Everyone makes mistakes. It's how we choose to deal with them that makes us or breaks us. You"—he pointed at me—"you're going to make it."

I looked at him in disbelief. "You just met me. How could you possibly know that?"

He gave me a wink and fairies took flight in my tummy.

"I've got good instincts," he said. "And there's one quote I always stand by, 'It's choice—not chance—that determines your destiny.' You've obviously made your choice to make it."

I sighed. "Too bad your sister wasn't as easy to convince as you were."

"I'm a little more—"

"Tolerant of Goths?"

"I was going to say open-minded." He scratched his chin. "Ash isn't so bad. Rick's just her first real boyfriend and she's a little—"

"Gaga," I finished. "I get it. The first time is always the biggest fall. I'd have been pretty pissed if someone tried to tell me my boyfriend was a sleaze."

He smiled and stood. "I'll talk to her."

"Okay, well, thanks for . . ." For what, exactly? Apologizing for your sister? Not shunning me? A pep talk? "Thanks."

"Anytime," he said, offering his hand.

I let him pull me up, savoring his gentlemanly gesture and the warmth of his palm. Maybe it was my imagination, or just sappy romance-novel envy, but I could swear energy sparked where we touched.

"I appreciate your honesty and now I feel there's something *you* should know."

My pulse lurched.

"Some guys actually mean what they say."

I smiled; I couldn't help it, even if I wasn't ready to believe what he said. "I'll keep that in mind, Jensen."

Only when I walked away did I realize I'd never heard his inner voice. He really *had* meant every word he said.

CHAPTER SEVEN

Later that night I logged onto the computer in my bedroom to pow-wow with Pixie.

DixiePixie: How'd it go?

GossamerGoth: Don't ask. U?

DixiePixie: 2 new recruits. Tina Orwitz, jock. Leiann Cornwell, ner—brainiac.

I smiled. I loved the way Pixie refused to call anyone a nerd. We both knew it was because she was a geeky Goth.

GossamerGoth: WTG! Lexy e-mailed me. She got Peggy & 1 other girl.

DixiePixie: We're off 2 a good start.

GossamerGoth: And we still have 3 days till the mtg.

DixiePixie: UR going 2 have a full house.

GossamerGoth: Can U believe it?

DixiePixie: Unfortunately w/ Rick the Prick. 2 bad about Ash.

GossamerGoth: She was MAAAAAAD.

DixiePixie: ☹

GossamerGoth: But her bro was really nice.

Don't you hate it when you type something, hit send, then immediately wish you could delete it? I banged my head against my desk. Why had I said that to Pix?

DixiePixie: Reeeeeally. U <3 him?

I could practically see her salivating with excitement in her bedroom. She'd be practicing her matchmaking mojo if I wasn't careful.

GossamerGoth: W/E. Not his type.

DixiePixie: U never know. Is he a QT?

Another IM message pinged open on my desktop. OhmyGoth! It was *him*.

GossamerGoth: I plead the fifth, but I think he's msging me. BRB.

• • •

ImNotLostRU: Dee?

GossamerGoth: Yes.

ImNotLostRU: This is Jensen.

GossamerGoth: Nice screen name. Tolkien fan or hiker?

ImNotLostRU: Both! ☺

GossamerGoth: Cool. What's up?

ImNotLostRU: Ashleigh got burned just like U said.

GossamerGoth: ☹ *She ok?*

ImNotLostRU: Nothing happened—luckily—but she believes U now. I totally want to go kick his ass, but I thought I'd see what your plan was.

GossamerGoth: Meeting's @ my house. Friday @ 5.

ImNotLostRU: Not even a hint?

GossamerGoth: Nope. Just don't be L8.

ImNotLostRU: Thanks. We'll CYA then.

GossamerGoth: Sure. BTW, I looked up that thing U said about choices.

ImNotLostRU: ?

GossamerGoth: You quoted Jean Nidetch. She's the inventor of Weight Watchers!!!

ImNotLostRU: LOL. True, but a good quote's a good quote.

GossamerGoth: LOL. Tru enuf. TTYL.

I closed the IM window feeling inexplicably happy . . .

• • •

DixiePixie: Well? What up?

She'd been impatiently IMing me the entire time I was talking with Jensen. *Yoohoo! Hullo. R U There? Anyone home?* And, of course, the snoozing emoticon. *ZZZZZZ.*

GossamerGoth: Sheesh! A little patience Pixie.

DixiePixie: Took U freakin' long enuf! So?

GossamerGoth: Got another 1.

DixiePixie: Ashleigh?

GossamerGoth: Yep. But she got away in time.

DixiePixie: Good work. And?

GossamerGoth: ?

DixiePixie: Did he ask U out?

GossamerGoth: No! We just met like five hours ago.

DixiePixie: That's time enuf. ☹ Too bad, but maybe he'll come to the mtg.

GossamerGoth: He's going to, but I'm telling U I'm not his type.

DixiePixie: What type is he?

I thought about that. I honestly didn't know. I couldn't peg him. Goth? No. Prep? Not really. Jock? Not unless hiking counted. Nerd? No way. He was just . . . Jensen.

GossamerGoth: I don't know.

DixiePixie: Then he's perfect! We're breaking down clique lines and UV found urself a guy who doesn't belong 2 a clique.

I shook my head. My little pixie pal was always very astute, an old soul in a tiny teen body.

GossamerGoth: UV always got all the answers, don't U?

DixiePixie: Natch. ☺

GossamerGoth: TTYT, oh wise one.

DixiePixie: CYA. XOXO.

As I logged off our IM, I wondered if there was any truth to Pixie's theory. Was Jensen an indefinable loner? And did I need to label him? Here I'd been feeling quite cosmo for tackling tribe lines, but it seemed as if he'd already done just that. And why did he rattle me so? Was it just a once-burned, twice-shy hesitancy? Before I could sort out my thoughts another IM pinged in.

QrtrBkSnk: Dee?

I stared at the screen, my heart mamboing in my ears. Rick and I used to IM for hours, but all that was pretend . . . wasted time . . . What could he possibly want now? To rub my raw wounds? Rave about his conquests? Finish staking my heart?

My fingers hovered over the keyboard. Should I ignore him? Despite my better judgment, I answered.

GossamerGoth: What?

QrtrBkSnk: I saw U were on. Thought I'd say hi.

GossamerGoth: Why?

QrtrBkSnk: I don't know. I miss U.

I blinked to clear the tears from my eyes. Lies, all lies. I wanted to believe him, but . . .

GossamerGoth: I'm not helping w/ ur research.

QrtrBkSnk: 2 bad. Ur loss.

So much for missing me. I clenched my teeth, typed two words my mom would've soaped my mouth for, then shut down my computer.

Crawling into bed that night I realized something—once I was done crying—while I had full access to other people's thoughts, I was actually learning more about my own.

Maybe it's true that "not all who wander are lost."

CHAPTER EIGHT

"I'd like to call this meeting to order," I said. No doubt my voice quavered; my hands were certainly shaking. Nineteen girls, and one guy, gave me their undivided attention, and once again I asked myself how I'd become president of this little culture club. "I know this is a little weird and awkward," I began, ignoring several internal you-can-say-that-again thoughts, "but we all have something in common." Laying my hand over my heart, I wondered if anyone noticed my conservative attire. I thought the oversize black business shirt belted at the waist gave me a little more credibility. "I, like you," I said to the group, "fell for a guy's lies and manipulations."

"Fake," someone muttered and I hoped they were talking about him and not me.

"Unfortunately, there's more to this than just two boys trying to get laid. Rick and Phil are planning to write a book called *The Guy's Guide to Getting ANY Girl.*"

There were murmurs of shock and a lot of unspoken, but loudly heard (by me), swears.

"Rick confessed that they're singling out girls from each clique, pretending to—"

"Their motto is Be Who They Want You to Be," Pixie sneered from where she slouched in my dad's recliner.

"Yeah," I said, "and then they—"

"Screw them," Ashleigh said. *Dickwads,* she sniped in her head. She sat on the carpet, looking emotionally battered and equally pissed.

I gave her a sympathetic smile. "Yes, but it's even worse." I hated this part, but it's exactly why I was the one leading this insane assemblage. Sometimes being in the know isn't a good thing. Pixie gave me a thumbs-up for support. "The rules of their 'research,'" I continued, "dictate that they get laid *and* get an 'I love you.'"

"Are you serious?" Casey (Goth) asked in outrage. *That's low. Cold.*

I nodded bleakly. "According to them it's easy enough to find a willing slut to sleep with them. It's much harder to find a girl who'll give them sex *and* sentiment. That is the ultimate prize and proves they did, indeed, get the girl."

Everyone looked around at each other. Anger, betrayal, embarrassment, humiliation, and pain rippled through the group, and my head buzzed with too many emotionally wrought thoughts. I closed my eyes for a second and massaged my temples, concentrating on turning down the volume.

"We gots t' hunt 'em down and kill those muthas," Jen (gangsta) yelled.

Back in control I opened my eyes. "If it weren't for the whole jail thing, I'd be right there with you," I told her. "But I have a better idea. Let's beat them at their own game. Pix"—I waved her to the front— "this is your cue."

She bounced toward me wearing jeans that laced up the crotch and a vibrant purple, off-the-shoulder peasant blouse. Obviously, like me, my BFF had dressed to impress.

"Hi all. I'm Pixie Willows. I didn't get conned by either one of those troglodytes, but I'm here on behalf of Dee and all of you. The idea here is to publish a tell-all tabloid magazine exposing Tricky Rick and Fibbing Phil." She held up a handful of grocery store scandal sheets before passing them around. "These are our inspiration."

"I don't get it," Peggy (prep) said.

"They think they're going to write a book about their sexploits," I said, "but we're going to expose them first. Once everyone knows how despicable they are, they'll be unable to conduct any more"—I made air quotes—"'research' and they wouldn't dare try to publish anything because they'd look that much worse."

"A taste of their own medicine. I like it," Lexy said simply. "It's delightfully devious. Where do we start?"

"We need pictures," Pixie said.

A negative buzz abused my ears.

"No way," Tina (jock) said. "I thought we were going to remain anonymous."

"You are," I assured them, and the assault on my ears stopped.

"Pixie is a genius at altering photos. You'll be completely unidentifiable, but to prove they're actually doing this we need physical evidence. We need pics of them with various clique girls." I held up a picture Pixie had doctored of me and Rick together. My face had been blocked out, but you were able to see Rick in full eyeliner and black nail polish glory. "Obviously you can tell I'm Goth by my clothes, but it could be me or ten other girls at our school."

"We're also going to have a little fun at their expense," Pixie added. "You know those online tabloids like Perez Hilton, where they take the picture and—"

"Make snarky comments and draw fake mustaches or cocaine lines on their faces?" Tasha (choir) asked.

"Bingo." Pixie touched her nose and pointed to her. "We're going to show the world what they're really like."

Everyone applauded.

"So gather up your photos and ideas and be back here tomorrow at eleven a.m.," I instructed. "If you've got a laptop, bring it. The plan is to get this done over the weekend and plaster it all over the school come Monday."

Like on Noah's ark, everyone left two by two, matched up with their own kind. Only Ashleigh and Jensen stayed behind.

"Um, Dee," she said, twisting the ends of her long hair, "I just want to say I'm sorry for being such a bitch."

I smiled. "Apology accepted."

"It's really cool what you're doing." Her eyes burned with unshed tears. "I'm glad those jerks will be shut down."

"Me, too, but credit for Operation Expose the Poseur goes to Pixie. It was her idea."

Ash nodded an acknowledgment to Pix. "I guess I'll see you guys tomorrow. Thanks."

She headed for the door, but Jensen stayed behind.

His smile was sweet and secretive. "I like your style, Dee."

Even though I knew he wasn't talking about my fashion sense,

I said, "Thanks, I've been told it grows on people."

He laughed and I found myself happy I'd tickled his funny bone.

"Is it all right if I help out with this project?" he asked. "Or is it girls only?"

"You can help," I said, giving him a questioning look. "But why would you want to?"

"It's for a good cause," he said with a wink. *And I want to get to know you.*

I took a step back. Whoa, I hadn't expected that. I mean I'd sensed a . . . certain something between us, but his thoughts were frank and forward.

"Um, th-thanks," I stammered. "We can use all the help we can get."

"Consider me yours, then," he said with a bow.

The sexy gesture and his choice of words made me shiver. I stood frozen as he walked out the door.

"He is *so* into you," Pixie said, nudging me in the ribs with her elbow.

"I don't think I'm ready for that," I said, picking up empty pop cans and other trash. "Not after Rick."

"Rick was a fake," Pixie said. "Jensen's the real deal."

I looked at the door. "He seems to be, but I'm going to be wary for a while."

Pixie nibbled at a cheese doodle. "No need to be wary when you can just read his mind. What did you hear?"

I sucked on my lip. "He wants to get to know me."

She smiled. "No harm there."

"I suppose not."

But this time, this time, I'd make sure the guy was exactly who he said he was.

• • •

The next day everyone came armed with their pics, ideas, and laptops. I put them into five groups of four. Each team was responsible for creating a mockup page. They drew their layouts on notebook paper and typed the text, while Pixie scanned and uploaded their photos. The tabloid would be an eight-page bi-fold newspaper. She and I were preparing the cover and last two pages. Page seven would be a spoof of the want ads usually found on the last pages of a tabloid, and the back cover was going to be our masthead with faux names like Ms. D. Meanor, Amanda Love, Bess Twishes, Rita Booke, Dane Geruss, and Ferris Faire. Once everyone started brainstorming, barriers and differences fell by the wayside. I supplied the staff with junk food and drinks before settling into my group with Jensen, Ashleigh, Tasha, and Leiann.

"How's it going?" I asked.

Ashleigh spun the notebook paper around. "What do you think?"

The headline read "10 Things We Hate About You."

I laughed. "I love it! It's perfect."

"So far we have 'Ten: Your brain is in your pants; Nine: You're a liar and a cheat; Eight: You're so fake you don't even know who you are; Seven: You don't realize the value of love; Six: You thought no one would find out.' What else should we add?" Leiann asked me.

I thought about it. "How about 'You didn't care who you hurt'?"

"Good." She typed it into her laptop. "What else?"

" 'You never meant what you said.' "

"I don't think he ever spoke a true word," Tasha agreed. *Like when he told me he loved me.*

"No, I don't think so either," I said. "Will you excuse me for a minute?"

I stepped into the kitchen to get hold of my emotions. Anger and hurt burbled inside me like a bad case of indigestion, but I refused to let Rick and Phil get away with their poisonous ploy.

A hand settled on my shoulder and I whirled around.

"Sorry," Jensen said. "You okay?"

"Ye-yeah," I stammered. "This is just—"

"Hard."

"Yes and no," I said. I refused to cry again, especially in front of Jensen. "Obviously I'm not alone and I'm really over him," I explained, "but it's been difficult to learn that people aren't always what they seem."

"I'm sorry he hurt you." He reached out and took my hand. Giving it a soft squeeze, he said, "But it's obvious you're not over him."

"I am too," I said, tugging out of his grip. "It would be stupid to be stuck on a guy who did"—I waved my hand to encompass the convened meeting—"all of this."

"Not stupid. Human. You can't turn emotions off like a faucet."

"Well, I want to let go. Not hang on."

"I might be able to help with that, if you let me."

I laughed nervously. "Are you suggesting therapy?"

"I'm suggesting you go out with me and give me a chance."

"I—I have to do the tattle-tale. Help them." I nodded to the girls in the other room. "I can't think about another relationship. About you. Not yet."

"No hurry. When you really let Rick go, I'll be waiting."

I didn't know what to say to that.

"There's something else going on, too. Want to talk about it?"

Startled, I looked at him. "How'd you—it's just, I've always been judged by the way I look. I never thought I did that. Now, I think maybe I have. I'm realizing our self-perception and the way others perceive us can be very different." I pointed toward the living room. "I never got to know those girls in there, any more than they got to know me. I just made the assumption that they wouldn't want to know me because of the way I look, so I never bothered with them. I was labeling them as much as they were labeling me."

"I've never understood why our society feels the need to attach labels."

"I do. It's comfort. If something, *someone*, has a brand, then we can better understand who or what they are." I pointed to him. "Take you, for instance. I've been trying to place you and I can't. Is he this, is he that? I finally quit trying."

He grinned. "Good, because I'm just me, a guy who thinks Rick is the biggest ass in the world. Not just because of what he did to everyone here, but because he won your heart and then trashed it. You strike me as someone who doesn't love easily."

I hugged myself at his words. "I didn't and I won't."

"That's okay; the right guy will be smart enough to wait."

"Are you saying you're him?"

"No, I'm saying I'd like to find out. But I know you need some time. When you realize I say what I mean, you know where to find me."

And with that he went back to the group while I stood there trying to see past the darkness I suddenly found myself in.

CHAPTER NINE

We put the paper to bed at seven p.m. Sunday. Everyone was tired but humming with anticipation. Tomorrow was D-day and we were more than ready. The entire group agreed our final product was ingenious—a full-color, witty, revealing, they'll-never-see-what's-coming bitch-slap.

Ka-pow!

When the last tabloid was folded and stapled, I handed stacks of twenty to each person. The plan was for everyone to arrive at school uber-early and blanket the campus with our trash mag.

Monday could not get here soon enough.

Tricky Rick and Fibbing Phil were going doooown.

As everyone gathered their stuff to leave my house, proudly armed with their collective creation, I noticed something different. They weren't rushing off in pairs like before. Jen was teaching Lexy some tight new dance moves. Leiann was offering to tutor Tasha in math. Ashleigh was inviting Casey to a skate tournament, and Pixie was standing in a corner crying.

I rushed over to her. "What's wrong?"

"Didn't I tell you it would be beautiful." She sniffled.

"What's beautiful?" I asked, wondering if the ink fumes had gotten to her.

"Anarchy," she said, gesturing to everyone. *It's all so perfect. I can't stand it.*

I laughed and gave her a hug. "Yes, it's beautiful. Think it'll last?"

Pixie removed her glasses and dried her eyes. "I do. I really do. First the fishbowl, then the world."

I raised my fist in the air and hollered, "Pixie power!"

The other girls echoed my salute and that got Pixie blubbering again.

"Hey, Dee," Braden, who'd been helping us all out, said. "Can I keep one of the papers?"

"Sure, but why?"

"Jamie wants to see a copy."

"You mean your *girlfriend?*" I teased. She *had* liked him and that had given him all the courage he needed to ask her out.

"Yeah." He laughed. "Her."

I shook my finger at him. "Just remember to be a good boyfriend."

He gave me his scout's honor.

"What if I make that kind of pledge?" Jensen asked.

I gave him a searching look. "You don't give up easy, do you?"

"I don't give up." *Not on you.*

"Why me?" I asked, genuinely needing to know.

He stroked the side of my cheek. "Because you're beautiful, brave, and bighearted."

"No one's *ever* seen me that way before," I whispered, falling into his ocean blue eyes.

"Then they weren't looking."

"I . . ." I didn't know what to say.

"I'm wearing you down, aren't I?" he asked with a smug grin.

"Maybe," I answered with a smile.

He leaned close to my ear and whispered, "I know they say no one likes a tattle-tale, but, boy, were they wrong."

I laughed.

How could I not?

When everyone left, Braden came up to me.

"I don't need your woo-woo voodoo to know that guy's totally into you."

I raised my eyebrows. "Yeah?"

He rolled his eyes. "He's got it bad and I just have one thing to say."

"And that would be?"

"I told you so."

I scrunched up my nose. "What do you mean?"

"I said the right guy would come along."
"You really think—"
"Sis," he said impatiently, "I'm a guy. Trust me."
Trust him. Trust Jensen. Could I? Was I ready?
Could I put Rick to rest like I had the tattle-tale?
My mind swirled as I put myself to bed.

CHAPTER TEN

D-day dawned early, with bright-eyed girls plastering scandal sheets all over the school. Lockers, bulletin boards, bathroom stalls, cafeteria tables. No surface was left untouched. Giggles punctuated the quiet halls and a tangible expectation filled the air. I should've felt . . . something. I thought I'd feel vindicated. Happy. That I'd be swept into the mayhem and mischief the other girls were so clearly enjoying. Instead, I felt a void.

I didn't want revenge.

I wanted what had been taken from me.

I wanted to trust someone with my heart.

And I wanted him to treasure it.

"Can you believe this?" Pixie said. "The poseurs are going to arrive any moment now." She lifted her digital camera to her eye. "Paper: twenty-five dollars. Ink: seventy-five dollars. The look on their faces: priceless."

"Yeah," I mumbled.

Pixie lowered the camera. "Dee? You okay?"

"Sure. Fine."

Someone hollered that they needed more copies and I handed Pixie my stacks. I had absolutely no desire to post them. With a worried look on her face, she rushed off to replenish the courier.

"What's wrong?" a concerned voice asked from behind me.

I whirled around.

Jensen.

My heart lifted. *He* was the missing piece.

"Make the pledge," I blurted.

He gave me a long look and I thought maybe he didn't know what I was talking about. Then he raised his hand in a three-finger salute. "I hereby pledge to be good to you and say what I mean."

With that, he leaned in and kissed me. Just a soft, sweet brush of his lips against mine, but I let him.

"What are you thinking?" I asked him slyly.

I could kiss her all day.

"I could kiss you all day."

I giggled.

"What's so funny?" he asked.

"Don't mind me," I said, then kissed him again. *Really* kissed him.

Lucky for me, it seems some guys *do* say what they mean.

And, so, what began as a story about a Goth and a jock became a love story about a girl and a guy.

Just Plain Lisa

BY ELLEN HOPKINS

MY NAME IS LISA

Not Alyssa, Alicia, or Aleighsha.
Not Elise, Liza, or Leeza.
Not even Leesa.

Just

Lisa. My mother wasn't
clever enough to come up
with a more stylish name. Or
maybe, considering neither she
nor Dad is exactly what you
might call a hottie, she decided
to give her firstborn a

plain

name, to fit what she figured
the baby would grow into.
I'm not much to look at, okay?
Not totally hideous, at least
I don't think so. I mean, my eyes
are located in approximately
the right position, and my ears
mostly match. But I really
would have a hard time living
up to a more elegant name than

Lisa.

I'M REALLY NOT HIDEOUS

But I'll never make cheerleader,
never become a model. I'm tall
enough, but thick—not fat, not really.

Mom calls it "big bone structure."
Big enough so my grade school
nickname was Elsie the Cow.

Big enough to affect my nose.
It isn't humungous, but the bridge
has a major hump, made even more

noticeable by the freckles playing
tag across it. Oh yes, and the more
than occasional zit taking up

residence just above it. I could use
braces, and my rat brown hair hangs
to my shoulders in straight, thin strings.

Only my eyebrows, in a matching
shade of rodent, are thick. I tried
plucking them once, and ended up

with two skinny question marks
delineating my glasses. That's right.
Along with everything else, I inherited

astigmatism. My eyeglass frames are
cute enough, but through the lenses,
my irises look like huge brown marbles.

Okay, truth is, I avoid the mirror
whenever possible. It only serves
as affirmation of what I already know.

I'm homely as a horny toad. Barring
head-to-toe plastic surgery, a total
Lisa makeover, I will never be pretty.

Get the picture?

NONE OF THAT

Would be so bad, but we happen
to live in Palm Springs. Not in the
Las Palmas section, of course. Our
neighbors   aren't movie
stars or   billionaires.
Still, if you   go to Palm
Springs High,   home of the
Indians, and   want to fit in
with a desirable crowd, you'd
better wear
designer
clothes,
drive a late-
model BMW.
                    Personally,
          even if I could
      find size-fifteen
   Dior, I'd have
   to work two
    jobs to pay
     for clothes
       I'd look bad
         in, anyway.
           So I guess for
             me it's Target
               and Jackie
               Smith, my all-
           time fave bargain
       basement fashion
   designer queen.

AS FOR BEAMERS

My dad sells them. The highlight
of his day is taking someone for
a test drive, because the rules
state the salesperson has to drive
a car off the lot, and Dad actually
gets to spend a few minutes behind
the wheel. To and from work,
my father can be seen in a fairly
new Toyota Camry. White.

Mom has a well-used minivan.
White. She needs lots of room
for carting kids (meaning my two
little brothers and their irritating
friends) to soccer and football
and Boy Scout meetings.
Mom is pack leader. Khaki
is definitely not her color.

And me? Oh yeah, I have a car.
I got a beater Kia, white, for my
seventeenth birthday. Someday I'll have
it painted. White cars advertise dirt.
I work at Jumping Java to pay
for gas and insurance, and have
developed quite the latte habit.
Def not great for the thighs,
but work positively jets by.

WISH I COULD SAY THE SAME

About school. I'll be going
into my senior year, so I know

    it's not forever. Just two more
    achingly slow semesters. I don't mind

        schoolwork. It has never been
        a real focus for me, but it's never

            been all that hard, either. No,
            it's not the work I dread. It's all

        that social drama. You know, proms
        and games and peppy pep rallies.

    Pep-less things that do nothing but
    hurt if you have to do them solo.

So instead you invent any excuse
that might work not to do them.

    No use stressing about it now.
        School doesn't start for two months.

            Who knows? Maybe by then this ugly
            duckling will blossom into a swan.

            Wonder if a homely swan could
            attract a goose. Turkey? Emu?

MOM KEEPS SAYING

Don't worry, Lisa. The right
young man will come along

eventually. Anyway, what's
the rush? Where's the fire?

Easy for her to say. Not that
I like to think about the logistics,

but she's got someone to put out
her fire. I mean, at seventeen,

I'm still fantasizing about that
first kiss. The one I read about.

The one I see in movies, on TV.
Girls half my age get pregnant!

Okay, a slight exaggeration.
And I'm not aching for *that* event.

Mom's my best reminder:
Nineteen hours of labor with you.

I kept screaming for an epidural,
but it was dedicated c-section day.

By the time the anesthesiologist
arrived, so had my little Lisa,

all nine pounds, two ounces of you.
It was the best day of my life.

YEAH, RIGHT

Sounds like it, huh? Anyway,
I have zero desire
for such a wonderful day.

And not a lot of desire for the thing
that might lead to
nine extra pounds in my belly, not

to mention even bigger boobs—
I'm 38D—that leak milk
in public, sag when they go dry.

All I want is someone to call
mine. Someone who'll
send me Valentines, and flowers

on my birthday. Someone who
will take my hands, pull
me into his arms, lift me gently

to meet his lips with mine, show
me what a real kiss is.
Someone who totally cares for me,

who believes that true beauty is
found on the inside,
'cause that's where I'll look for *his*.

PLENTY OF GUYS

Sift in and out of Jumping Java.
Early in the day, they're mostly
guys in business suits. Some of
them are def fine, despite a few
too many worries worn in delicate
webs at the corners of their eyes.

Midmorning, here come skaters,
a few jocks, and lots of artsy types.
JuJa (dumb nickname, but there
it is) is a regular pickup palace.
I watch girls with nothing better
to do than prick tease do exactly that.

And those testosterone-drenched
dimwads, wearing gorgeous faces
over brain-deprived skulls, fall
all over themselves to get teased.
I swear, if I ever decide to tease
a prick, it will slink off happy.

Afternoons bring married guys,
leaving work early to hopefully
hook up with their Internet dates.
Don't know what it is about
online dating, but no one ever
seems to get what they're expecting.

It's kind of funny to watch, really.
One or the other comes in first,
orders straight coffee, sits in back,

pretending to read or write. Soon,
the other half of the not-so-dynamic
duo comes in, glances furtively around.

Nope, no one resembling whatever
photo promised whatever. But their
watch decrees it's the designated
meet time. Finally, with only one
other person in the store,
a cautious approach is initiated.

I used to pretend to clean tables.
But now I don't have to listen
in to interpret the conversation.
He: *Hello. Do you happen to be . . . ?*
His eyes fall straight to her cleavage.
She: *Um. Yes. You aren't . . . ?*

She checks out the bad hairpiece.
Then they sit and chat for fifteen
minutes, each wondering why
the other was less than forthright.
Usually, they exit separately,
shaking their heads in disgust.

Once in a while, I suppose, they
actually do hook up, each figuring:
*What the hell? I'm not getting any
at home. Maybe he/she will be better
than nothing if I keep my eyes closed.*
Nightmare hookups? Not for me.

TODAY THE STORE

Is a little slow. It's just after lunch,
a bit early for the Internet scene.
A couple of the girls have gone off
to smoke, so I'm manning the counter.

About the time I think I'll have to take
up smoking myself or go crazy from
boredom, the door opens and a couple
of guys come in. I've seen them around.

Blake Mayberry is pretty cute. He's on
the swim team, and looks like he's been
swimming a lot this summer. He's tan
and the body under his tank is lean. Hard.

His sidekick is the antithesis of everything
Blake. Chet Burgess reminds me a little
of a koala bear, with round dark eyes,
a prominent nose, and obvious ears.

As far as I know or can imagine, Chet
has never played sports. If I had to guess,
I'd say he was a member of the chess
club, if he's a member of any club at all.

Not sure why he and Blake are tight. Hot
guys usually hang with other hot guys.
The only thing hot about Chet is the soles
of his Nikes. It's way over a hundred outside.

IN FACT, THE GUYS LEAK SWEAT

When they saunter up to the counter.
Somehow it doesn't smell that bad.

> Blake doesn't even smile. *Mega-grande*
> *iced chai.* No "please," either. Wiener.

> Chet offers a goofy grin like it's a gold
> medal. *Um, I'll have a, um . . .*

OMG. He's one of those can't-decide-
between-cappuccino-and-latte guys.

> *An iced triple decaf nonfat vanilla*
> *mocha, double whipped cream. Please.*

Double OMG. Caffeine-less espresso.
Nonfat in the cup, extra fat on top.

Whatever. At least he said please. I start
their drinks as Miranda and Cassie

come back from their nicotine sucking.
Both pounce immediately on Blake,

cracking inappropriate jokes and giggling
wildly, even though they're not the least

bit funny. Still, Blake finally cracks a grin
as he takes a seat, derriere pointed in my direction.

WHICH PUTS CHET

Facing me as Jumping Java
        finally starts jumping. Cassie
takes the register (she's the cute
        one and the tip jar fills faster
for her pouty little smile) while
        Miranda and I grind, steam, and pour.

Every now and again, my
        attention wanders and I scan
 the busy room. The weird
        thing is, when my eyes happen
to land on Blake and Chet's
        table, the koala is looking at me.

Guys hardly ever look at me,
        and when they do I'm usually
sure they're measuring me with
        their ugly meters. This is def
different. If I didn't know better,
        I'd say Chet is checking me out.

Maybe I've got something in my
        teeth, or hanging out of my nose.
I turn away, excuse myself, go
        into the bathroom, take a chance
on the mirror. Nothing unusual.
        Just regular uncheckoutable me.

WHEN I RETURN

The guys are gone. Cassie
and Miranda huddle, giggling,
behind the bakery items.

Only this time, instead of tittering
at their own stupid jokes, I'm
pretty sure they're laughing at me.

Nothing new, I know, but still
my face ignites until I feel
the tips of my ears go scarlet.

     As I start past them toward
     the register, Cassie snorts,
     Hey, Lisa, expect a call.

          Yes, agrees Miranda in
          Latina-tinged English, *that*
          Blake, he asked for your number.

I fight to keep my mouth from
falling open. Through clenched
jaws, I manage, "Yeah, right."

     Cassie grins like an opossum.
     No, really. He did. Hope you
     don't mind that we gave it to him.

I SERIOUSLY

Have no clue what to say,
let alone what to think
about such an

                unlikely

event. Of course,
considering the source,
it's not exactly

                impossible

that they're lying to me.
But with so little to gain,
I can't imagine

                why,

any more than I can guess
the reason for Blake's
possible request. I really
don't know what to

                think.

I stumble through the rest
of the afternoon, trying
to push it away and not fret

                about

it. But, through the p.m.
rush of online hopefuls and
caffeine fanatics, a slender
thread of possibility weaves
in and out of my brain.

                What if . . .

WHAT IF

Cassie and Miranda are
telling the absolute truth?

Yeah, but what if they're
absolutely not?

What if Blake doesn't think
I'm as plain as I think I am?

Yeah, but what if he thinks
I'm just plain ugly?

What if he doesn't care
about looks at all?

Then why does he have
a hundred-dollar haircut?

What if intelligence and
wit matter more to him?

Puh-lease. Blake is so not
looking for Ms. Mensa.

What will I say if he
actually does call me?

If he actually calls me,
I'll stutter like an idiot.

I WORRY

About that all evening.
All through dinner, dessert.
All through *American Idol*.

I'm so focused, in fact,
that I don't even cheer for
Barry, my all-time fave.

> *Earth to Lisa,* Dad finally
> says. *Exactly what planet
> are you on tonight?*

I can't confess that my brain
is wrapped around Blake
Mayberry. "Uh, what?"

> *Uranus,* cracks my brother
> Brian, in his half-bass, half-
> tenor thirteen-year-old voice.

> *Is that anything like Angus?*
> asks Paul, who at ten has just
> learned why that's funny.

Inane chatter, but I don't
care. At least I don't have
to explain why I'm not here.

The boys continue their banter.
I ignore them and finally tune
in to *Idol.* I'm locked on Katie,

who is doing a tolerable job
of recreating a Janis Joplin
ballad, when the phone rings.

Mom goes to pick up and
I'm shocked when she calls,
Lisa! It's for you. And . . .

She saunters into the room,
phone extended like a gift.
She whispers, *It's a boy.*

So you know the old saying
My heart leaped into my throat?
Well, I totally get it now, except

the verb is all wrong. My heart
doesn't leap. It rockets into my
throat. I'll stutter for sure.

MY HAND TREMBLES

As I reach for the phone.
"Huh . . . hello?" I croak.

The whole family is staring.
A boy calling? A definite first.

I'm so flustered, I completely
miss the first part of his sentence.

> . . . *uh, and I was wondering*
> *if you'd like to go along.*

Wait! "What? I'm sorry, my
little brothers were yelling . . ."

(Lie, and their grimaces
let me know they heard it.)

"Could you please start over?"
This isn't going so well.

> He laughs. *I said, Blake and I*
> *are going up to Lake Arrowhead . . .*

Blake and I? It isn't Blake
on the other end. It's Chet.

> *Marissa Scott is going and I*
> *thought you might like to go, too.*

Marissa is on the dive team.
She and Blake must have a thing.

Disappointment stings.
But I'm not exactly sure why.

Not like I really believed
Blake would ask me out.

        Chet babbles on about Jet Skis
        and dinner on the way home.

And suddenly all I can see is me
and a koala, tandem on Jet Skis.

"Hey, Chet," I interrupt, "my
dad needs me. Can I call you

right back? Okay, give me your
number." I scribble it loudly

on a ratty piece of paper
taking up space on the end

table, fully intending to eighty-six
it after I hang up the phone.

EVERYONE IS STILL GAWKING

In fact, except for the ones on
TV, every person in the room
is drop-jaw speechless.

"What?" It comes out a snarl,
and I don't know why and I
don't know what is going on

with me. Nothing has changed
except I just got asked out,
even if it was by Chet Burgess

and not Blake Mayberry, and
I've never been asked out before,
and it sounds like a really fun day,

so why do I just want to cry?
My eyes sting and my face
crumples and that makes Dad

and the boys uncomfortable,
so they go back to *Idol* without
a word and Mom says,

> *Lisa, will you please join me
> in the kitchen?* And when I
> hesitate, she adds, *Right now.*

I SENSE A LECTURE

Awaits me in the other room.
Mom's not usually the lecture
type, but I probably deserve one.
Oh, well. At least I can unload.

> Mom waits impatiently
> at the table, fingertips galloping
> against the faux oak. *Do you mind*
> *telling me what that was all about?*

The whole story spews from
my mouth, starting at Jumping
Java and ending with overwrought
editorializing about koala bears.

> Mom allows me to finish, takes
> a deep breath. *It's best not to judge*
> *a book by its cover, Lisa. This Chet*
> *may be a very nice young man,*
>
> *but how will you know unless you*
> *give him a chance? Anyway, it's*
> *only a date, not a commitment.*
> *Call him. Say you'd love to go.*

Why does she always have to be
so reasonable? Everything she
said is true. But Chet Burgess?
"I'll have to think about it."

MOM SHAKES HER HEAD

And I know what she's thinking:
How can you be so shallow?
(And maybe something like:
You wouldn't want people
to judge *you* by *your* cover.)

That makes me remember
the numerous times others
have judged me by my
looks. Shunned me
because of them, even.

Still, I'd like another opinion.
Mom has rejoined the *Idol*
crew. I ignore them, slip
down the hall to my room,
speed-dial my friend Stacy.

"Hey, girl, it's me. Something
happened today . . ." I repeat
the story, start to finish, wait
for her to laugh or tell me
I'd be a fool to date Chet.

Instead, the prolonged silence
on the other end of the line
indicates she's thinking.
Finally, she clears her
throat. *Ask me, I vote "go."*

STACY AND I

Have been friends since fifth
grade. We tell each other pretty
much everything. I can't dismiss
her advice nearly as easily as
I can reject my mother's. A loud
sigh escapes me. "You really think so?"

> I can almost hear her shrug.
> *Absolutely. Look, Lisa, your*
> *mom is right. It's just a date,*
> *and you don't exactly have 'em*
> *lining up to go out with you.*
> *Anyway, Blake will be there, too.*

Yeah, swapping spit (and
hopefully no other bodily fluids)
with Marissa Scott. But hey,
maybe I could learn a thing
or two. Resignation weights
my shoulders. "Okay. I'll go."

> *Good decision*, she underlines.
> *How often does a girl get to go*
> *Jet Skiing with Blake Mayberry?*
> *And if I were you, I'd make it*
> *clear to Cassie and Miranda*
> *that's where you'll be Saturday.*

SEE WHY I LOVE STACY?

Everyone should have
a friend who gets them,
one who insists on giving

an opinion, take it or
leave it, like it or not.

I'm still not sure I agree
with her opinion, but an
afternoon on Arrowhead

soaking up sunshine and
chilling in cold alpine water

doesn't sound half bad.
I say goodbye to Stacy,
promise to let her know

how it goes. Where did
I put Chet's number? Oh,

man, I left it on the end
table. Now that I've made
my decision, anxiety begins

to gnaw and I hurry to the
living room. *Idol*'s wrapping

up, everyone getting ready to
call that 888 number and cast
a vote. I scramble to find

Chet's number before the dash
to the phone, but it isn't where

I left it. I search all around
the table and underneath it and
the chair beside it. When I bring

myself upright again, Mom
is standing next to me.

> She holds out her hand.
> *Looking for this? I thought*
> *I should keep it safe for you.*

Everyone should have
a mom like my mom, too.

"Thanks," I say, and for
the first time I notice how
my heart pumps excitement.

Brian and I start for the phone
at the same time. He's got a lead

and would definitely beat me
to it, only to be stuck on hold
for an hour, but Mom stops him.

> *In a minute. Lisa has to*
> *make an important call.*

I CALL CHET

Who seems genuinely pleased
that I've accepted his invitation.

> *Radical. Don't forget sunscreen.*
> *If you're like me, you'll toast.*

Radical, okay. What a picture—
Chet, all crimson and peeling.

> *Is there any kind of food you don't*
> *like? We were thinking Mexican . . .*

"I'm not picky." Wait. I don't want
him to think that. "About food, that is."

> *Cool. Or whatever. 'Cause I mean,*
> *we can go steakhouse instead.*

Is he nervous? Hey, am I his first
date, too? "Whatever you want."

> *Long pause. Very long. Too long.*
> *Really? Like whatever I want?*

Joke, right? I ignore the double entendre.
"Whatever food you choose is fine."

> *Awesome. Blake's driving. We'll pick*
> *you up around nine-thirty, okay?*

"Sounds great, Chet. I'll be ready.
Bye for now." What have I done?

I GO TO THE BOOKSHELVES

Locate my yearbooks. Thumb
through, searching for anything
Chet. As I suspected, he's not
really
the jock type, although he did
run cross-country his sophomore
year. Weird thing is, he kind of
looks cute in shorts. Oh, brother.
What
am I thinking? Honor roll, every
semester. Spanish Club. Ah-ha.
There it is: Chess Club. And,
better: editor, yearbook and
school newspaper. I should
have
remembered. He interviewed
me one time after a choir
performance. So, okay, he's not
a total loser. Oh, key piece of
information. Chet tutors.
I
bet Blake has a hard time
maintaining the GPA to stay
on the swim team. Wonder how
much of his homework Chet has
done.
No wonder they're tight.
There I go again. Thinking
the worst. Where does this ever-
present sarcasm come from?

TWO DAYS

Since I told Chet I'd go.
Two days till Saturday
and the big event, which
I agreed to without thinking
I might have to work. I had
to trade time with Miranda.

> *Maybe,* she said when I asked.
> *You have a good reason?*

I'll always remember her
reaction when I told her
I'd been invited to go Jet
Skiing with Blake Mayberry.

> *No effing way!* She launched
> a volley of disbelief—in Spanish.

I did mumble "and Chet
Burgess and Marissa Scott,"
which softened her shock
a little. Still, it was a highly
satisfying moment or two,
something completely new.

> *Okay*, she finally agreed. *I'll*
> *trade. But take a camera, okay?*

THAT WAS YESTERDAY

And right now I'm working
her shift. The crowd trickles
in steadily all morning. About
eleven, I look up to take an order.
Chet. For some silly reason, I smile.

> He smiles back, and I notice
> how straight and white his teeth
> are. *Hey. I thought you might*
> *like to have lunch so we can*
> *get to know each other a little.*

I glance at Cassie, who's pouring
a tall iced coffee. She shrugs,
points at Marvin, who has just come
in to work swing shift. I tell Chet,
"Good idea. Give me a minute, okay?"

He takes a table by the door
as I go to hang up my JuJa apron,
swing into the bathroom for
a quick mirror check. Same ole
Lisa. I run a brush over my hair,

spritz a shot of decent perfume,
pop a couple of breath mints.
Sorry, Chet, this is as good as it
gets. And why do I suddenly
feel inferior to a koala bear?

CHET CHANGES

That almost immediately.
   He's open. Laughs easily.
In fact, he makes me feel like
   I'm the wittiest woman alive.
Apparently he likes sarcasm.

   The temperature creeps up,
relentless, but there's a sweet
   little coffee shop nearby. We
walk slowly, hugging shade.
   Our bodies almost touch.

I don't want to check him
   out, at least not overtly,
so I make it a point to look
   directly at him when he talks.
Covert checking out. I spy.

   I spy decent clothes, clean
and wrinkle-free. Nice hair.
   Wavy, but controlled. My
nose spies, too—good soap,
   not too perfumed. Deodorant,

working hard to do its job.
   Designer shampoo. Laundry
detergent. Chet Burgess
   just might be the cleanest
guy alive. Not a bad thing.

NOT, THAT IS

Unless it's a symptom of OCD,
and obsessive compulsive disorder
is something I consider as I watch
Chet rearrange the silverware,

moving every fork, knife, and spoon
on the table until they're spaced
equally (almost certainly—I don't
have a ruler, but they look perfectly

equidistant to me). Finally, Chet
notices me noticing. *Sorry*, he says.
*I bus at Le Vallauris. Anything
less would not be tolerated.*

Le Vallauris. One of the desert's
five-star restaurants. Anything less,
I'm sure, would not be tolerated.
"Wow. Great job. Connections?"

He smiles. *Of course. My dad
is a sous chef. I could take you
there some time if you like.
The food really is incredible.*

He could take me to Le Vallauris?
Without a single worry about his
probable OCD, I spurt, "Any time!
I've always wanted to eat there."

OUR TWO-STAR WAITRESS

Arrives to take our order.
Caught up watching Chet's

silverware shuffle, I've barely
even glanced at the menu.

"I . . . uh . . . hmmm . . ." I try not
to look at the waitress, whose

impatience is written clear
across her makeup overdose.

Mind if I make a suggestion?
asks Chet, in a tone that says

I shouldn't mind. Unsure how
to respond, I say, "Uh, okay."

*I was thinking beer-battered cod
and garlic fries. Sound good?*

I would never have ordered it.
But somehow it does sound good.

I nod and off goes Lorraine. We
watch her snarl our order to the cook,

then stalk over to the next table.
"Think she could work at Le Vallauris?"

*Absolutely. They're not picky about
who scrubs the toilets and floors.*

OKAY, THAT WAS MEAN

But it was also funny and hey,
she deserved it. I can't help but
crack up, and once the laughter
subsides, a wide smile remains.

> Wearing his own grin, Chet
> says, *I like when you smile.*
> *It shows me the Lisa inside.*

Instant, furious blush. I have
zero idea how to respond,
and even if I knew, my mouth
wouldn't let me do it right.

> Chet to the rescue. *Oh, hey. Here*
> *comes lunch. Should I suggest*
> *she apply at Le Vallauris?*

We both bust up and poor
Lorraine doesn't have a clue why.
She sets down our plates, twists
her head toward Chet, back to me.

> *May we have some ketchup, please?*
> asks Chet. *And maybe some ranch*
> *dressing. Anything else, Lisa?*

Nice. He really is the gentleman.
"I think that will do." Lorraine goes
off in search of condiments as I taste
my first ever garlic fry. Heaven!

I COME AWAY

From lunch totally stuffed
and feeling a whole lot better

> about Saturday. Chet walks
> me back to Jumping Java.

"Thanks for lunch," I say, rather
reluctantly reaching for the door.

> *Hey. No problem at all.*
> *I had a really great time.*

"Me too." And the funny
thing is, I mean it. Go figure.

> *I'm glad. So . . . is it okay*
> *if I call you later?*

"Well, of course. Why
wouldn't it be okay?"

> *I don't know. It's just,*
> *well, last night you were . . .*

A little cool. "Sorry. It gets
crazy at home sometimes."

> He looks not exactly sold,
> but says, *Long as you're sure.*

Last night, I wouldn't have
thought it possible, but "I'm sure."

ON MY WAY HOME

I stop by Stacy's, still tasting
vivid reminders of garlic fries.
OMG. They were worth every
darn burp, at least to me.
> *Eeewooo,* comments Stacy,
> grinning. *Let me guess what you*
> *had for lunch. So, okay, cough*
> *it up. And I don't mean garlic.*

So I tell her about Chet,
lunch, the silverware shuffle.
As I talk, I realize it was the
most fun I've had in a while.
> Her expression grows serious.
> *Rearranging the table is kind*
> *of strange, Lisa. And did he*
> *really order for you?*

"Well . . . yeah, but I said it
was okay. I wasn't ready,
and our waitress . . ." I tell
about Lorraine, Le Vallauris.
> Tension falls from her face
> as concern turns to eagerness.
> *Le Vallauris? Really? If you*
> *go, can we, like, double date?*

STACY IS GOING OUT

With Zach Riordan. It's kind of a new
thing, and my best guess is
it's doomed, not that I'd say so.

> *Hey, did I tell you Zach is starting*
> *this year? First-string running back.*
> *We have to go to every game, okay?*

"Stacy, you know I hate football . . ."
Her smile fades and I hurry to add,
". . . but I'll def go to every one! Promise."

> She lights back up immediately.
> *I love you, Lisa. Not as much as Zach,*
> *of course. By the way, we almost . . . you know.*

"No way! Stacy, tell me you didn't . . .
you won't . . . not wi—" Can't say *not*
with Zach. She'll take it all wrong.

> Her head tilts, signaling uncertainty.
> But she only says, *Don't worry.*
> *We didn't. I really wanted to, but . . .*

But what? She came to her senses,
knowing he'd dump her instantaneously
once she gave in? "But what?"

> *Well, I keep meaning to get on the pill,*
> *but thinking about the . . . exam . . . makes*
> *me want to gag. So I haven't yet.*

Not exactly what I wanted to hear, but
whatever works. "Not many guys are worth
that," I agree. "Especially not Chet."

Stacy laughs. *I told you before, and
I'll repeat, never say never. We can
always go in for those exams together.*

I THINK ABOUT THAT

As I drive on home.
I can't imagine a trip
to Planned Parenthood,
with or without Stacy.
How humiliating,

sitting in the waiting
room, everyone else
wondering if I'm
there for the pill or
maybe an abortion.

And after that lovely
experience, going into
a room, putting my
feet into stirrups for
some mangy ole doc

to take a really long
look at my personal
parts, jabbing and
scraping and finally
nodding an okay.

Beyond that heart–
warming hour,
consider going to the
pharmacy with a
prescription for birth

control, hoping no one
I know is around to even
suspect my purpose.
Doing any of that would
require an overdose of love.

SATURDAY MORNING

I'm up early. Considering how
torn I first felt about today, I can't
believe how excited I am.

And it has nothing to do with
Blake Mayberry. It's all about Chet
Burgess, my favorite koala.

He has dropped by Jumping
Java both days since our lunch, called
every night. He's funny. Sweet.

We relate really well, on so
many levels. He makes me feel
special. That means a lot.

I don't know what to wear.
Not a swimming suit. Don't dare.
But all my shorts are ratty.

I should have bought some new
ones. Too late now. So I guess it will be
the least nasty pair, a pink tee.

The top is in perfect condition.
Pink? Rarely a color I wear. My mom,
of course, bought it for me.

Who knows? she said. *One
day you just might want to go girly.*
Girly. Today I want to go girly.

NINE-THIRTY COMES AND GOES

Nine-forty. Forty-five. Fifty.
Just about the time I think
I should trade the pink tee
for something less girly,
the doorbell rings. Surprise!

Here comes the family, who
have stashed themselves until
this very moment. One by one,
they file into the front hall,
wait for me to open the door.

> As I do, I hear Brian whisper
> to Paul, *Can you believe*
> *Lisa's wearing* pink? *Weird.*
> Paul whispers back, *Who even*
> *knew our sister was a girl?*

Chet ignores the comments,
which he in no way could
have missed. He comes
inside long enough to shake
Dad's hand and greet Mom.

> *A pleasure to meet both of you.*
> *Lisa says great things about*
> *you.* Then he turns to me.
> *Sorry we're late. We had to*
> *wait on Marissa like forever.*

Marissa. Of course. High
maintenance, no doubt. And
who could have guessed (okay,
I might have suspected) that Chet
was such an amazing butt kisser?

> The trend continues, as he
> turns back to Mom and Dad.
> *Don't worry about Lisa. I'll take*
> *good care of her. We should be*
> *back around nine, if that's okay.*

What can my parents do but
nod mutual agreement? I offer
a quick, "Bye, Mom. Bye, Dad.
Bye, *boys*," the last word heavily
accented for maximum oomph.

IT'S A NINETY-MINUTE DRIVE

Give or take. Chet and I sit on
opposite sides in the back seat

    of Blake's Audi Quattro. Nice ride.
    Comfy leather seats, critically smooth.

        Up front, Marissa is so close to Blake,
        they look conjoined at the shoulder.

            Other than the briefest wave hello,
            neither has said a single word to us.

        Which means not a thing to Chet,
        who serves as unofficial tour guide,

    narrating area history and fast facts
    about the transforming landscape.

If the others can hear a word beyond
Blake's ear splitting hip-hop radio,

        they don't acknowledge it. I try
        to make up for their rudeness,

        stroking Chet's ego by asking,
        "How did you ever learn so much?"

            He reaches across the seat, takes
            my hand. *Books, darlin'. Books.*

I expect him to give my hand back.
Instead, his fingers gently lace mine.

Something trembles inside me, a flicker
like dragonfly wings on a breeze.

I fight my initial urge to pull away,
turn away, get away. Run away.

Run from the foreign sensations
percolating under my skin, my flesh.

But I don't run. Don't pull away.
I let my hand stay right there, cradled

in his. Chet acts like it's no big deal,
segueing his fabulous monologue

to rock formations and their
geological relevance. Phew!

In the front seat, Blake takes
curves way too fast and Marissa

hisses, *Would you please slow
down? I don't want to die today.*

And I think if I died today, at least
I got to experience dragonfly wings.

THE DAY HOLDS REVELATIONS

Like, for instance, the Jet Skis?
Seems we're not renting them.
We're stopping by the Mayberrys'

Arrowhead cabin to pick up
the family Yamahas. Marissa
and I stretch our legs as Blake

and Chet hitch up the trailer.
I attempt small talk. "Have
you Jet Skied before?"

> She looks like she just bit
> into a lemon. *Sure. Lots of*
> *times. Why? Haven't you?*

I try nice. "Nope. This will
be my first time. Is it hard?
What do you do if you fall?"

> Lemon mixed with bleach.
> *If you fall, you swim. And*
> *it's like riding a motorcycle.*

Okay, guess we're not going
to be friends. "I've never
ridden a motorcycle, either."

> If her eyes rolled any harder,
> they'd pop right out of her head.
> *Somehow that doesn't surprise me.*

Thankfully Chet interrupts.
*Okay. All ready to go. You
two getting along okay?*

"Absolutely!" I stifle a laugh,
which comes out a snort. "Just
like an old divorced couple."

Marissa stalks off. Chet
grins, slides an arm around
my waist, guides me toward

the Quattro. He puts his mouth
against my ear, whispers, *No
worries. She doesn't like anyone.*

I put my mouth against
his ear, again note the cool
of his shampoo. "I know."

JET SKIING

Is really fun, except it's really loud.

And also except we're not exactly

Jet Skiing. We're wave running.

You sit on runners. These are tandems.

I'm balanced close behind Chet,

who seems to know what he's doing.

Thank goodness one of us does.

It's kind of nice, leaning against him,

arms tight around his rib cage,

heart racing, relinquishing control.

That is something I very rarely do.

Maintaining control over the areas

of my life that are controllable

has always seemed so vital to me.

Suddenly everything is different.

I wonder if it's better this way.

WHEN WE FINISH

Shredding water, Blake and Marissa
stretch out on towels to catch some rays.

Chet and I dry off, and he suggests we
take a walk. *I'm not the "lie out" type.*

"That makes two of us." We start
down the beach. Chet takes my hand.

We walk silently for a while, listening
to the soft break of water, the scrunch

of our feet on the sand. Finally Chet
says, *I've never had a girlfriend before.*

Wait. Wait. This is not a commitment,
only a date. Right? "Is that what I am?"

He stops, turns to face me, looks into
my eyes. *If that's what you want to be.*

And now he pulls me into his arms,
looks down at me with those crazy

koala eyes, and I think he's going to
kiss me and I don't know what to do

because I have no idea how to kiss
a guy and something panicky rises

up into my throat and suddenly it just
doesn't matter because we're kissing.

OUR FIRST KISS

Is totally tentative—clumsy
exploration, lips bumping teeth,
accommodating. Adjusting.

> In wordless agreement, we pull
> apart, trade embarrassed smiles.
> *Sorry,* he says. *I hate to admit it,*
> *but I've never kissed a girl before . . .*
> When my grin widens, he hurries
> to add, *Never kissed a guy, either.*

He's so cute! I've never seen
a face quite so red—almost cranberry.
"It's my first time, too. And they say
practice makes perfect." Our second
kiss is a whole lot closer to right.

We keep our teeth to ourselves.
His lips are warm, just wet enough
to easily wander the perimeters
of my mouth. Tiny lightning
bolts spark through my body.

This is all so incredibly new.
It's like something has come alive
inside me. A being. An entity.
Maybe a whole different person.

Someone hungry. Okay, maybe
even horny. Wow. There's a word
I've never before associated with me.

FAIRLY QUICKLY, HOWEVER

I'm coming to associate it
    with Chet. Someone seems
        to have come alive inside

him, too. Someone assertive.
    Aggressive. Maybe even
        intimidating. And whoever

that someone is, he is most
    definitely . . . uh . . . stimulated.
        R-rated action, in the flesh.

His kiss becomes erratic.
    Demanding. Ravenous.
        Tongue and spit and fangs.

But when I draw back,
    demand softens to plea,
        and I am kissing Chet again.

AT THE ROIL OF EMOTION

Just plain Lisa screams silently, "Run!"
Just-hatched Lisa wants to know more.

Wants to know why that sudden sizzle
of fear felt exciting, if not exactly right.

Wants to know if every kiss leads to
such electric desire, zapping through

veins with each escalated heartbeat.
Wants to know how a merge of lips

can influence other body parts; why
scent of warm skin makes you want

to taste it; how a slow trace of fingertips
down one arm can raise goose bumps in

other places. Wants to understand how
all this makes me just want to melt into

a puddle right here on the toasty sand.
Needs to know if she's kissing Chet the

koala or Chet the grizzly bear and most
of all needs to know just exactly who's

kissing him: the regular Lisa I've been
all my life or a new (improved?) model.

FINALLY, IN MUTUAL WORDLESS CONSENT

Chet and I come up for air.
I look into his eyes, manage
a not-so-brilliant "Wow."

> He smiles. *Exactly. And*
> *definitely worth repeating.*
> So we do. And this time

it's even better than the last.
Practice makes perfect,
I guess. "Double wow."

> He laughs, takes my hand.
> *Maybe we should see what*
> *Blake and Marissa are up to.*

We wander back and from
fifty yards away can see them
screaming at each other.

> Chet stops abruptly. *Those two*
> *are like ammonia and chlorine—*
> *a dangerous combination.*

The shouting match escalates
until Marissa stalks off. "So
why are they together, then?"

> Chet shrugs. *For some people*
> *looking good together is more*
> *important than being good together.*

I PONDER THAT

Off and on the rest of the day.
Turns out the argument was about
Blake checking out some girl
with, as Marissa so bluntly puts it,

> *massive, obnoxious boobs,*
> *obviously not the real thing.*
> *I mean, no one who hasn't*
> *had babies could have . . .*

Her eyes fall to the rounded
protrusions beneath my pink
tee and the guys' eyes follow.
I really have to defend myself.

"Sorry. Never had babies.
And these are totally mine.
If it makes you feel any better,
bra shopping is a bitch."

> The guys bust up and Marissa
> sputters, *S—s—sorry. I didn't*
> *Mean . . . Of course those are γ—*
> the rest sticks like hot gum.

Saved by the restaurant.
Blake pulls into the parking
lot and before he can shift into
"P," Marissa bolts from the car.

BLAKE JUMPS OUT

In hot pursuit. I start to open
the door, but Chet stops me.

> *Give them a second. Anyway,*
> *I wanted to do this . . .*

He kisses me. All gentle,
sweet, no hint of grizzly.

> He pauses, smiles. *Great way*
> *to work up an appetite.*

"I'm not hungry yet." This
time New Lisa kisses Chet.

> Blake's knock on the window
> interrupts. *Come on already.*

> We stop kissing and Chet pierces
> my eyes with his. *So . . . hungry yet?*

"Getting hungrier all the time."
Who said that? Surely not me.

IF NOT FOR CHET

Dinner would be a quiet affair.

> Marissa sits in embarrassed
> silence, trying not to stare at
> my massive obnoxious boobs.

> Blake stares off into space,
> barely saying two words since
> the waiter took our order.

The two are on different planets.

> But Chet seems immune to
> their discomfort. He chatters
> away like a happy chipmunk.

> I try to stay tuned in, but my
> thoughts churn slowly, cream
> that has not quite become butter.

"Venus and Mars"? Understatement.

> I look at Marissa, sculpted
> nose tilted skyward. Def not
> Ms. Congeniality, but Blake's

> not exactly Mr. Friendly, either.
> Whatever her bra size, Marissa
> is an absolute head-turner.

Why isn't that enough for Blake?

SOMEWHERE BETWEEN

Dessert and the car, Marissa
and Blake find a way to make up.
Maybe it was the hot fudge sundae
he ordered. She couldn't resist sharing.
I guess I'm glad. Don't know why.

The drive home is totally different,
at least here in the back seat. This
time when Marissa scrunches against
Blake, kissing his neck, licking his ear,
it initiates similar action behind her.

I have no idea what serious bad
sense has overtaken me, but when
Chet reaches to unbuckle my seat belt,
pull me onto his lap, not only do I let him,
but I wonder what took him so long.

We're kissing. Touching. His hand
is up under my pink tee and I don't
say no. I close my eyes, give myself
to the sensation and barely worry at all
as Blake swerves to make the curves.

Beneath my ratty shorts and Chet's
swim trunks, the grizzly stirs. I'm not
ready to go there. Not even. But Chet
doesn't make the request. He only
kisses me harder. And I kiss him back.

HOME SAFE

Despite all the kissing, front
seat and back, Chet walks me
to the door. He wants a good-

night kiss, but I shake my head.
"Someone's watching."

He snatches a glance toward
the window. Grins. *You know,
or you're just guessing?*

I smile back. "Both. I had
a great time. Thanks, Chet."

*Does that mean we can go
out again? Like soon?* He tries
to ignore Blake's short honk.

"Sure. But maybe without"—I nod
toward the car—"all the drama?"

He takes my hand and, in a most
chivalrous gesture, brings it to his
lips. *Your wish is my command.*

I watch his retreat, take two
deep breaths, and go inside.

AS I SUSPECTED

Mom and Dad hover near
the living room window.

> Dad pounces, teasing, *Not*
> *even a little peck good night?*

Mom puts a finger to her lips.
So tell us. How did it go?

I can't help but smile. "You
were right. I had a fun time."

> Dad feigns fatherly horror.
> *Not too, too fun, I hope.*

Mom pokes him in the ribs.
Come on. Tell us about your day.

We sit for a while and I tell
them everything. Well, almost.

> Finally Dad yawns. *Bedtime.*
> *Sunday's my best day, you know.*

Be right there. Mom watches
him go. *Now tell me the rest.*

OMG. Does it really show? I share
all but the embarrassing details.

Mom stands, touches my cheek.
Everything is different now.

EVERYTHING FEELS DIFFERENT

I
       go into the bathroom,
       and for once I don't avoid
       the mirror. I stop. Stare.
       Weird, but I think I even
look

       different. My nose isn't any
       straighter, and my smile still
       reveals too much gum above
       my teeth. But there's something
       more confident—or
at

       least less apologetic—about
       my posture, and a strange
       sparkle highlights my eyes.
       I'm def not in love, but I am
       in like, and that has given me
a

       glow of some kind. I guess
       this must be what the books
       talk about, although I always
       found that concept ridiculous.
       Mom's right. Everything's
different.
       Who knows if that's good
       or bad? At the moment
       it feels on the right side
       of wrong, and I'm much too
       tired for further
reflection.

THREE WEEKS DIFFERENT

I know for sure that nothing
can ever be the same. Like
has moved well toward love,
and it shows in all I do.

Work is not so tedious, thanks
to regular visits from Chet.
And even when he's not
hanging out, he feels close.

If we can't see each other,
we talk or text. That's right,
I broke down and bought
myself a cell phone. No use

storing money in the bank
if it can be put to better use,
and as Chet said, what better
use than staying connected?

He has no idea how much
money I've managed to save
in seventeen years, but the truth
is, it's a decent amount.

I plan on community college
to start work on a nursing degree.
A cell phone won't cut into
tuition enough to worry about.

Anyway, I've got a whole year
of high school, and that costs
exactly zero. Before that, I've
got to get through this summer.

Not that I want to hurry through,
not now. Not at all. So far, it's
been a great summer. The best
of my life. Thanks to Chet.

We do movies. Bowling. Drives
in the mountains. Dinners out.
Sometimes at night, when it
finally cools off enough to be

outside, we take walks on the golf
course behind Chet's house.
They water the turf at sunset,
and when it's dark, the moist

grass creates an incredible
cool carpet for our bare feet.
Sometimes we get really stupid
and play in the sand traps

or roll down the man-made
slopes. Sometimes we get too
serious and lie together, coming
dangerously close to doing it.

SO FAR

I've managed   to hold on to
   my virginity,   that sacred
      possession I   just can't give
         away cheaply.   I know it's
            old-fashioned. Maybe
            even stupid, but I
               feel like that's

   all that's left of   the Lisa who
      used to be me.   Tell the truth,
         I always kind   of liked her,
            not that I so   dislike the
               girl who replaced her.
               It's just that she's
               still a stranger.

   A stranger who   really likes the
      way her body   reacts to Chet's
         touch, clumsy   as it was at first,
            and a lot more   practiced now.
               We have discovered much
               together. But there's
               more to know.

I HAVE NOT GIVEN IN

To Chet on that, no matter
how tempted I have been.

But I have acquiesced on
something else, something

I never thought I would.
It's not a big deal, not really.

It started after an early morning
bike ride, when a little spore

blew under my glasses, into
my eye, causing a tear eruption.

When we stopped to remedy
the situation, Chet took off

my glasses, found the tiny
intruder, used his shirt to dry

my face. *Wow. I never noticed
how beautiful your eyes are before,*

*with all those little gold flecks.
Have you ever considered contacts?*

I PICKED UP MY NEW CONTACTS

On my way to work this morning.
I chose a color that would accentuate
the little gold flecks in my eyes,
which, as I always feared, feel
assaulted. My optometrist says
that will lessen with time.

JuJa is busy when I arrive, and
Cassie is on vacation. Miranda
and Marv hustle back and forth,
taking orders and frothing drinks.
Miranda barely glances my way,
but Marv takes immediate interest.

                    Hey. You look different, he says,
                    appraising. *Must be the new blouse.*

Brilliant. Okay, I am wearing
a new blouse. And yes, that means
I'm spending my retirement on
more than just a cell phone. But
that's beside the point. "Actually,
I think it might be the contacts."

                    His face goes from ecru to crimson
                    in ten seconds flat. *Oh . . . yeah . . .*

Poor guy. "Hey, it's okay. I just
got them this morning. I'm not
used to them yet myself." He nods
and goes to pour an iced chai. Funny,
I never noticed it before, but he's
kind of cute, in a puppy dog way.

WHAT IS IT WITH ME

Comparing guys to animals?
Maybe instead of nursing
I should consider a career
as a vet. Better yet, zookeeper.

My favorite koala comes
in around two to take me
to lunch. It's been busy all
day and I feel kind of guilty

about leaving Miranda
and Marv, not that Miranda
didn't take lunch and a
half-dozen smoke breaks already.

Chet marches right up to
the counter and gives me
a major once-over. *"Wow"*
is all I've got to say. Ready?

I like being "wowed" and I'm
def ready for food. Still, I look
over at Marv. "Do you mind
if I go to lunch? We'll hurry."

Marv shrugs okay. But for some
reason, the exchange irritates
Chet, who snaps, *Do you need*
permission to go to lunch?

He's never been testy with
me before, and I'm not sure
how to react. "No, I don't need
permission. I'm just being polite."

Chet backs off immediately.
Sorry. Must be the heat.
Still, as we start out the door,
he glares in Marv's direction.

Maybe it *is* the heat, but it
kind of looks like jealousy
to me. And the really bad
thing is, I think I like it.

WE TRUDGE ALONG

Toward the coffee
shop, both mired
in some strange
mental bayou.

Finally, Chet clears
his throat. *Man,
that was really
kind of weird.*

His apology-filled
voice lures my hand
into his. I pull him
to a stop. "What was?"

*I'm not the jealous
type.* His eyes find
mine. *I don't want
to lose you. Ever.*

That should feel good.
But it makes me mad.
"I didn't do anything
to make you think . . ."

He pulls me against
his sweaty chest. *I
know. I've just never
cared so much before.*

NO SIGN OF NASTINESS

Over lunch, I drop the defensive
attitude and enjoy Chet's company.

You really look great, he says
around bites of cheeseburger.

My face flares. No one has ever
said that to me before. "Thanks."

*You know what would set your eyes
off even better?* Munch–munch.

I shake my head, search for an
answer. "Um . . . a face transplant?"

Chet grins. *Nothing that drastic.
I was thinking about your hair.*

"A hair transplant? I thought
those were for bald people."

He laughs. *Stop. I meant color. You'd
be a knockout as a redhead.*

Me, a knockout? Whatever. "Hair
dye causes brain cancer, you know."

*Old wives' tale. And anyway, you could
use henna. That's what Char uses.*

Charlotte is his older sister. I met her
once, and I did admire her auburn hair.

> *Your hair has reddish tints anyway.*
> *And Char says henna is good for it.*

Sheesh. One major change at a time.
But I smile. "I'll think about it, okay?"

> *Okay. But remember, real henna is*
> *all natural. It's made from . . .*

He goes on to give an entire tutorial—
what to watch out for, where to buy

> the "real" stuff without additives
> that could hurt my hair. By the time

he finishes, I feel like I just sat through
chem class. Never did like chemistry.

HENNA STINKS

It's supposed to smell
like hay. But if hay smells like this,
no horse in its right mind

would eat it. Yecch. Not
only that, but henna is green. How
can anything so green make

your hair turn red? You
mix the powder with hot water.
It's pasty. Messy. Stinky.

Despite all that, I leave it
on extra long. If I'm going to suffer,
it had better make a difference.

IT DOES

It takes forever
to wash out all
the green clumps.
Next, shampoo
and conditioner
specially made
to enhance red
highlights. As
my hair dries, I
can def feel that it's
thicker, but I can't
see red anything.
To hurry the process,
I use the blow dryer
for the first time
in five or six
years, and now
I can see all kinds
of red in my hair.
No more packrat
brown! It has a
mahogany sheen,
and copper glints
in the summer
sunlight. So, okay,
it was most def
worth the mess
and the stench.
It's really different.
I hope Chet likes it.

I'LL HAVE TO WAIT

Until later to find that out,
but in the meantime my family
is kind of freaking out. When I made
my grand entrance, breakfast conversation
braked to a complete halt. Everyone stared.

　　　After two or three minutes,
　　　everyone is still staring. Finally,
　　　Dad whistles. *Lisa? Is that really you?*
　　　Brian chimes in, *Nope. No way is that Lisa.*
　　　Paul stutters, *Wha . . . what happened to your hair?*

I try a move I've only seen
in the movies, twisting my neck
right to left, making my hair swing
side to side. Wonder if it looks like it's
supposed to. "I experimented a little. Like it?"

　　　The phrase "met with a stone
　　　wall of silence" seems to apply.
　　　The look on my face makes everyone
　　　react at once. Dad: *Great.* Brian: *Not bad.*
　　　Paul: *Uh, it's okay.* Mom: *You look lovely, Lisa.*

　　　Then she adds, *Will you come
　　　into the other room for a minute,
　　　please?* I follow like a rebuked puppy.
　　　Once out of earshot, she turns to me. *I do like
　　　your hair. But did you color it for you? Or for Chet?*

HOW DOES SHE ALWAYS KNOW?

She has this eerie sixth sense.
It makes me totally uncomfortable

and I have to confess, "Well . . .
actually . . . it was Chet's idea first . . ."

Mom doesn't have to say a word.
She clamps her lips into a thin,

tight line—tight enough to keep all
comments stashed behind them.

I press on. "But I think it's pretty,
and I used henna, not color, and it's . . ."

I repeat Chet's chem lesson, watching
her half listen, understanding what that means.

When I finish, she clears her throat.
Honey, I'm happy that you've decided

to do some positive things for yourself.
Just, please, do them for the right reasons.

HER MESSAGE

Comes through loud
and clear. I wish I could
ease her worries. But the truth
is, I'm not positive

                    why

these changes seem necessary.
Despite an admittedly flawed
exterior, I have always kind
of liked who I

                    am

inside, and so felt comfy
in my skin. The real issue
isn't superficial alterations—
hair or skin care or contacts.

                    I

can always undo those.
But they are manifestations
of the amazing, incredible,
even frightening way I'm

                    changing

inside my head. And if I am
brutally honest with myself,
I have to admit it was Chet

                    who

jump-started the evolution.
No amount of henna can
make me beautiful. But trying
it liberates me. Does it
really matter who I'm liberating

                    for?

MARV DOESN'T CARE

About the "who," but he def
notices the "what" as soon
as I walk through the door.

> *Holy guacamole, Lisa!*
> *You look like Patty Scialfa.*

His tone says it's a compliment,
but I have no idea who he's
comparing me to. I smile. "Who?"

> *You know. The singer? Plays*
> *guitar for Springsteen?*

Never heard of her. Still I don't
want to seem dense. I nod. "Oh
yeah, her. Well, thanks."

> *You're welcome,* he says, then
> adds, *You really like him, huh?*

I'm racking my brain, searching
for a mental photo of Patty Scialfa.
Really like who? "Bruce Springsteen?"

> Apparently I missed a subject
> change. *No,* says Marv. *I meant Chet.*

OMG!

Has he been conversing
with my mom? And what business
is it of his, anyway? I mean,

it's not like ole Marvin and I
have ever meant a thing to each
other. I hardly even know him.

Well, I sort of know him, from
work and school. He'll be a senior,
too. We're both 4.0 honor roll,

and once we were in the same
play, but it's not like we've ever
spent quality time together.

In fact, before a couple of
weeks ago, we'd hardly exchanged
complete sentences. All that

changed when . . . Chet came along.
Chet takes an interest, so Marv does,
too? Should that make me mad?

I don't know, so I take the high
road, absorbing Marv's expectant
expression. "Yes. I guess I do."

The look on his face changes,
morphs into something unexpected.
Something like disappointment.

AROUND THREE

Chet drops by. I glance
toward Marv, who grimaces
before turning his back.

> *Oooh la frigging la,* offers
> Chet. *Four cheers for henna!*

He sure has a way with
warped clichés. I smile.
"Does that mean you like it?"

> *It rocks. Iced coffee, please.*
> *Come talk to me when you can.*

Chet sets himself up at
a table in back. It's slow,
so I take my p.m. break.

> *I knew red was your color.* He
> reaches across, touches my hair.

I so like how that feels.
Still, I have to razz him.
"Henna smells, you know."

> *Did I forget to mention that?*
> *Sorry. Do you forgive me?*

I pretend to be annoyed,
but not for long. "I could
forgive you almost anything."

CHET'S ATTENTION SHIFTS

To whoever just came in the door.
I turn to follow his gaze. Stacy!

    She looks around uncertainly,
    goes to the counter, talks to Marv,

        who points toward our table.
        Stacy does a triple take, hustles

            over. *Hey, you. Oh, wow. Your hair*
            is fabulous. Did you do it yourself?

        When she bends to give me a hug,
        I can't help but notice how Chet's

    eyes fall to the scoop—a very low
    scoop—of her magenta tank top.

So it's more than a little irritating
when he answers for me. *It's henna.*

Wonder if either of them sees the little
green monster bloat real big inside me.

I'M NOT THE JEALOUS TYPE

In fact, I've never felt like this
before. I know Stacy would never
do anything to hurt me. And Chet
is so not on her radar. Checking

out cleavage is the all-American-
male pastime, isn't it? So why
this sharp-toothed bite of jealousy?

Suddenly I realize they're both
looking at me. Waiting for me to . . .
what? Oh. I suppose I could introduce
them. "Sorry. Guess my brain is clogged

with henna. Chet, this is Stacy, my
best friend." Way to go, Lisa. Toss
him a bone of guilt, hope he gnaws.

Totally oblivious, Stacy goes on
on and on about Zach: how they got
into a major tiff but kissed and made
up and now everything is just perfect.

We should celebrate. She looks at Chet.
Hey. What's up with Le Vallauris?
Are we all going or what?

BOTH OF THEM STARE AT ME

Me to Chet: "I mentioned you might
have an in at Le Vallauris."

Me to Stacy: "We haven't really
discussed going to dinner there."

Stacy to me: *Oh. Sorry. Didn't
mean to sound pushy or anything.*

Stacy to Chet: *Sorry. Didn't mean
to put you on the spot or anything.*

Chet to Stacy: *Hey. No problem.
It would be fun to double with you.*

Chet to me: *Tell you what. If your
friend will show you how she does*

*her makeup, I'll see what I can do.
I've been meaning to show you off.*

Stacy to Chet: *Really? I've always
wanted to go there. You rock!*

Stacy to me: *Come over after work
and we'll do Makeup 101.*

After a furious blush, me to Stacy:
"I might have to baby-sit. I'll call you."

As Stacy exits, me to Chet: "I have
to get back to work. I'll call you."

IT'S NOT

That I don't want to do Le Vallauris,
and going with Stacy and Zach
would be great. But I've never bothered
with makeup and I'm not sure I want to.

I mean, maybe I do. Makeup could
def cover up my skin imperfections,
and a little mascara might show off
the glints of gold behind my contacts.

But Mom's words keep echoing
in my head . . . *for the right reasons.*
Would I sit through Makeup 101
if Chet hadn't asked me to?

Marv brushes by me, and now
his words repeat in my brain:
You really like him, huh?
And the fact is, I really, really do.

THE FACT IS

More and more when we're alone together I think I more than like him. I think I've fallen in love with Chet.

That's good and bad. Good, 'cause it makes every day worth waking up for. Bad, because love makes me think about doing things I've never considered doing.

Things like going further than hot making out. A lot further. Only love could make me contemplate lust and what giving in to it might mean. The last time we took a walk, tumbled into the grass, knotted together, hearts *thump-thump*ing in unison, it almost happened. Maybe even would have, except a golf course security guy caught us, exposed. He asked if he could watch. When we said no, he made us leave.

OVE

or

UST?

MAKEUP 101

Is really kind of fun. Stacy
has enough stuff to supply
a whole troupe of showgirls.

> *Let's start with some basics.*
> *Foundation, light for you.*
> *Just enough to cover the freckles . . .*

"Not to mention the zits!" But
a glance in the mirror reveals
the AccuClear is working.

> *No, your skin looks great,*
> affirms Stacy. *Whatever you've*
> *been doing, keep doing it!*

A thin dusting of blush, and
then the eyes. I look at Stacy's.
"Nothing too dramatic, okay?"

> *No worries. I got some great*
> *tips from the Learning Channel.*
> *We'll use shadow to line them . . .*

"Just don't make me look like
a pole dancer, not that Chet
wouldn't like that, I suppose."

> Stacy laughs. *Him and Zach*
> *both.* A glide of lip gloss and she
> finishes with a satisfied *Voilá!*

WHO KNEW

Makeup could make such a difference?
    The person in the mirror (me, I guess)
looks polished. Almost chic. She still

    isn't what you could call pretty. But
neither is she plain. "I'm not sure I like
    the blue shadow. Let's try something else."

Stacy is game. We play with jade.
    Goldenrod. Raspberry. We experiment
with the "smoky eyes" look. Holy moley!

    Chet will melt. Or maybe he'll steam up,
and that will melt me. Stacy's yakking
    about Zach again, how sweet he's been

since their argument, how she broke
    down and told him she loved him. That
piques my interest. "What did he say?"

        She smiles weakly. *He said, "Me too."*
    Isn't that what every guy says? I keep
        waiting for more, but so far, no good.

Guilt rumbles. It's been too long since
    Stacy and I have had a real heart-to-heart.
Too bad guys get in the way of friendship.

ALL SMOKY-EYED

I think about calling Chet.
Decide against it. Reconsider.
Why do I suddenly feel torn
about seeing him? Is it

    the jealousy issue?

    the Lisa-revamp issue?

    the guys-vs.-friendship issue?

    the seriously-considering-sex issue?

Does everyone think and
rethink these things, or is
it just me, smoky-eyed Lisa,
worrying about silly stuff like

    maybe getting dumped.

    maybe turning into a stranger.

    maybe losing my best friend to a guy.

    maybe offering a gift I'm not ready to give.

BUT IT WOULD BE A SHAME

To let these fabulous eyes go
to waste. I might not ever

be able to recreate them.
So I do the obvious thing.

"Hey, Chet," I babble into my cell.
"Finished the mascara tutorial."

> *Come over. I want to see.*

"I should probably go home
and have dinner first."

> *Nah. Eat here. I'll cook.*

"You can cook?" And why
should that surprise me?

> *Hell yeah. It's in the genes.*

That's right. His dad's a top-
flight chef. "Well, maybe . . ."

> *C'mon. I'm here all alone . . .*

Invitation? Plea? It is both,
and more. Chet's is the voice

of temptation, the serpent's *please.*
And I am a smoky-eyed Eve.

MEANING . . .

Despite knowing exactly
what he's got on his mind,
I'm on my way over, still
undecided about how to
react when he tries to act.

Life sure has become complicated.

I mean, BC (before Chet),
things were completely
straightforward. I knew
where I stood on premarital
sex, and it was nowhere near

where I'm loitering now—on the brink

of saying, "Okay. Let's do it."
I love everything else about
what he does to me. Kissing.
Touching. Caressing those
intimate places I never knew

could respond in such amazing ways.

I don't think what's stopped
me is morality or even fear
of pregnancy. But the one
requirement I've always had
for sex is to fall in love first.

I think I love Chet. But does he love me?

I'D LIKE TO THINK SO

But truth is,
neither of us
has ever said
a single word
to the other
about love.

    As I amble
    up the walk
    toward his front
    door, I decide
    to keep my
    mouth shut.

        What if I
        dare confess
        I love him
        and he can't
        bring himself
        to say those
        three special
        words to me?

OVERANALYZING

May not be a bad thing for a nurse,
but it's probably not the best thing
when it comes to relationships.
I ring the doorbell, chewing on that.

>   Chet must be in the kitchen.
>   It's a couple of minutes before
>   he opens the door. When he does
>   his jaw literally drops. *OMG!*

I smile and bat my smoky eyes.
"Is that OMG good or OMG
bad?" Assuming the former,
I lean toward him for a kiss hello.

>   He totally obliges and his kiss
>   says a lot more than hello. *You*
>   *look like a whole different person.*
>   *Stacy has a real talent for makeup.*

I'm not exactly sure if those
are compliments or not. But I
might as well take them that way
as find reasons to feel hurt.

DINNER

Is a tolerable chicken Alfredo,
with Caesar salad and fresh
breadsticks. "Wow. You'll make
a fine husband for some very
lucky woman," I comment.

Chet grins. *Are you proposing?*

My turn to smile. "I don't know.
Personally, I always kind of
thought a husband might get in
the way of a good time. But how
good are you at changing diapers?"

His smile slips a little. *What's
a diaper? Oh, forget it. Let's
talk about that good time.*

He takes my hand, pulls me
right up against him, and this
time his kiss is hungry. Starved.
Starvation must be infectious.
I kiss back like I'm eating him.

He stops suddenly. *Come on.
Let's go to my bedroom.*

WRONG, WRONG

I know it's all wrong.
Shouldn't do it.

                          Can't

do it. But, of course,
I let him steer me
down the hall to
his room, knowing it

                          won't

be easy to stop if I
follow him through
that door. Am I really,
truly planning to

                          do this?

What if someone
finds out? What
happens to my
spotless reputation?

                          What if

my parents find
out? Will my mom
think I've been
coerced? Do

                          I want

her to think
otherwise? And
even if no one
ever finds out,
am I really prepared

                          to say yes?

PREPARED OR NOT

I don't say no as Chet pushes
me gently down on his messy
bed. He is wise enough to go
slowly, knowing any hint
of demand will persuade me
to change my mind. Still, I have
to protest mildly, "I'm not sure . . ."

> *Shh. It's okay. You can stop*
> *me anytime.* And he kisses me
> so sweetly that I believe him.

His hands are slow, warm,
persuasive, as they move over
my body, doing all the right
things, touching all the right places.
I close my eyes, give myself
to sensations unimagined.
"You've done this before," I whisper.

> Chet kisses me softly. *Never.*
> *But I've thought about doing*
> *this with you a whole lot.*

Buttons come unbuttoned.
Zippers come unzipped.
Skin touches skin and suddenly
I'm not one bit sure about any
of this. In fact, I'm not really
sure why I've gone this far, and
if that's not enough to stop me . . .

STACY'S WORDS

Tumble into my brain, echoing:
     . . . get on the pill . . . the pill . . .

"Wait!" I try to sit up, but I'm
    totally pinned. "Please, Chet . . ."

      What? He tries kissing away
         my unvoiced complaint, and

the heat of his kiss is alluring,
    almost enough to make me give in,

        until I imagine Stacy again,
          . . . thinking about the exam . . .

      When I stiffen, cement, he stops,
        looks down into my eyes. *What?*

"I can't . . . I didn't . . ." Throw it in
    his court. "Do you have a condom?"

      A condom? He rolls off me, onto
        his back. *You aren't on the pill?*

I could mention the exam thing.
    But I just ask, "Why would I be?"

      He stares at the ceiling. *I thought*
        you wanted to make love to me.

I HAVE NO ILLUSIONS

That making love has anything
to do with being in love. Still,
Chet saying the word *love*
is a pleasant surprise. "I do."

He rolls over to face me.
So why aren't you on the pill?
The unadulterated anger in
his voice is instantly contagious.

For someone who rarely gets
mad, I'm bordering on furious.
"It's a hell of a lot easier to buy
condoms than it is to get on the pill."

Did I just say *hell*? Maybe
I'll say it again. "I don't know who
in the hell you think you are,
but I deserve more respect."

Tears assault and I let them fall
as I yank on my clothes. Before
I'm even all the way buttoned,
I slam my way out his door.

CRYING ISN'T GOOD

For contacts
        (which float into uncomfortable places).

Or makeup
        (which drips like melted candle wax).

But it's a superb
        release for bottled-up unhappiness.

I haven't cried
        in years, not since Broomhilda the cat died.

But here I've
        popped the cork on those bottled tears

over Chet Burgess.
        (Who knew koalas were poisonous?)

I can't believe
        I thought I was falling in love with the clod.

I can't believe
        I almost gave in and gave him my body.

I can't believe
        I'm crying over any of that. But I am.

FOUR DAYS

Since my little blowup with Chet,
four days of alternating anger
and hurt, of silent rage and tearful
confusion. I keep waiting for him

to phone or come in. But not a single
word. Yes, I could call him. But
I need to know what happened
means something to him. Guess not.

No texts, no visits. No apologies.
I've pretty much written him off.
So when the flowers—two dozen
yellow roses—arrive, I wonder

whose birthday it is. Imagine
my surprise when the delivery
guy asks for me. My birthday
isn't for a couple of months.

> Marv, who I'm pretty sure has
> correctly assessed the situation,
> just stares. But Cassie can hardly
> contain herself. *Read the card!*

It says: *You were right and I was
insensitive. Please forgive me
and let me make it up to you.
Le Vallauris Friday night?*

> > > *Luv, Chet*

FORGIVE HIM?

Don't forgive him?
Do I really have a choice?

I never in my heart
wrote him off completely.

I kept looking for him,
kept waiting to hear his voice.

Each day that passed
without him cut a little deeper.

I love Chet Burgess.
. And now he sends a card

that says
he luvs me.

FRIDAY NIGHT

Stacy and I take a long time
getting ready for Le Vallauris.
Yes, I'm wearing makeup,
but the delay isn't choosing
the right shade of shadow.
It's picking the right outfit.

Okay, it's easy for Stacy,
who looks great in size-seven
everything. But I didn't want
to settle for Jackie Smith,
so I bought a few things in
size thirteen (yes, over

the summer, I made myself
drop a whole size, just for Chet)
but now nothing looks as good
as when I tried it on in the store.
"That's it. I'm not going."

> Stacy just laughs. *Yes, you
> are. Wear the gold blouse
> with the black and gold skirt.
> It looks great on you. And
> quit stressing. It will be fun.*

I try them on—again—and
well, they don't look great,
but they look okay. "All
right, I guess I'll go." And
I guess I will, but I wonder if
I'm going for me or for her.

I HAVEN'T SEEN CHET

In almost a week, and I'm still
torn in two about our argument.
Half of me needs to forgive him.
The other half wants to punish him.
Neither is sold on sex with him.

Yet when he rings the doorbell,
and I see him standing there, all
turned out in a dark blue suit, both
halves are really happy to see him.
Extremely happy to kiss him.

> It's a long kiss and finally
> Stacy taps my shoulder. *Ahem.*
> *Six-thirty reservation, and it's*
> *after six. We should go.* She
> hustles off to join Zach in his car.

Chet turns to watch her size-seven
behind, which I try to ignore.
I put one hand on each of his cheeks,
rotate his face toward mine. "Hey.
I missed you. Thanks for tonight."

> He bends for another quick kiss.
> *I missed you, too. Tonight will*
> *be fun. I told them it was a special*
> *celebration.* He closes the door behind
> us, slips his arm around my waist.

LE VALLAURIS IS STUNNING

Richly appointed, softly lit,
the definition of *romantic*. And
with Chet's connections,

we are treated like celebrities,
or at least like very big money.
Zach seems uncomfortable,

and I can't really blame
him, considering the hefty price
tag on every menu item

and the fact that we're *not*
big money. But Stacy is having
the time of her life, ordering

escargot (which taste
like chewy, garlicky boogers)
and roast duck in cherry

sauce. Chet insists I sample
the foie gras (which tastes worse
than escargot). I want stuffed

quail, but he says the rack
of lamb is better. When I acquiesce,
Stacy gives me a scathing look.

But I like lamb, so I shrug
her off and savor every moment
the evening has to offer.

ENTRÉE DISHES CLEARED

Our waiter brings the dessert
menu. A vibrant discussion
begins: soufflé versus crème brûlée,

ice cream meringue cake versus
bread pudding with dried fruits.
"I'll have the chocolate soufflé,"

I tell Chet, before excusing myself
to go to the restroom. When I return,
Stacy is shaking her head in disgust.

"What?" I ask. Did I forget to wipe
something off my face? I know
I washed my hands!

> *Ask him!* she says, pointing
> to Chet, who seems genuinely
> surprised at her reaction.

I wait for Chet to explain,
I guess she didn't like what
I ordered for your dessert.

My turn for surprise. "You don't
like chocolate soufflé?" I ask Stacy,
who is still shaking her head.

I ordered you the berries, says
Chet. *Thought you should skip*
the soufflé. It's calorific.

MY FACE FLUSHES

And from how hot it feels,
    I know it must be almost
        as purple as the berries
           that arrive at this
    exact moment, along
with Stacy's crème brûlée,
Zach's meringue cake, and

    Chet's bread pudding. At
      least he didn't order the
        soufflé for himself. He
          offers me a taste,
      which I decline around
    a bite of quite delicious
berries, the color of my face.

Stacy keeps shooting me
    sympathetic glances. She
      picks at her dessert while
        the guys polish theirs
      off, not noticing my plum-
    faced discomfort at all, or
pretending not to anyway.

    I finish the berries, eyes
      on the beautiful china,
        wondering why I lost
          a dress size for a guy
      who not only hasn't
    noticed, but also thinks
I'm still too fat for soufflé.

I GUESS MAYBE

Chet did notice, because as we
walk toward the car, he draws

> me off to one side. *Didn't mean*
> *to embarrass you. It's just I saw*
>
> *that you've slimmed down and*
> *didn't want you to spoil your diet.*

All the right words. Instantly
forgiven. "It's okay. And thanks."

> *Are we all good then? Because*
> *I really am sorry about the other*
>
> *night. Everything kind of happened*
> *so fast, and I wasn't thinking.*

Major understatement. But Chet
is Chet, right? "We're all good."

> He pulls me in to him, holds me
> close, pets my hair. *I'm glad.*
>
> *Hey, Blake's having a party*
> *tomorrow night. Wanna go?*

Beneath the cool of his silk
shirt, Chet's skin is warm. "Sure."

BLAKE LIVES

In Las Palmas, the poshest
part of the city. The houses
here are huge. Architectural
behemoths, with tile roofs
and sculptured yards, every
one with a swimming pool.

Blake's is no exception.
In fact, it takes posh to
extremes, with marble
floors and colonnades
and pricey works of art.

Not that anyone at this
party cares. Everyone's
half smashed by the time
Chet and I arrive. I'm
guessing Blake's parents
are out of town tonight.

Maybe forty people are
milling around, drinks in
hand. Several, some naked,
some fully clothed, are in
the pool. Inside, metal plays
full throttle. Wonder if Blake's
neighbors are out of town, too.

CHET AND I GO INSIDE

An open bar spills all kinds
of booze and for some reason
I'm not surprised when Chet asks,

                    How about a drink?

I've tasted booze three times
in my life, at weddings. I should
def say no. "Um, I guess."

                    What would you like?

Beer? Wine? Vodka? Gin?
All I've had at weddings
is champagne. "I don't know."

                    You don't know?

I hate to sound like a total
neophyte (even if I am).
"Whatever you have is fine."

                    Jack and Coke it is.

I watch him pour two glasses,
mostly Jack Daniel's. "Easy
on the liquor, okay?"

                    I wanna loosen you up.

THAT MAKES ME UNEASY

Especially coupled with Stacy's
warning last night when I told
her about tonight: *Don't go.*
Blake's parties can get wild.

I decide to sip my drink slowly.
It's strong. Not sweet enough.
More Coke! I take a quick gulp
to make room for more soda.

So much for sipping slowly.
The swallow drops straight into
my mostly empty stomach.
In no time at all, I feel a buzz.

I hate to tell Chet I need food,
but I do. Anything to absorb
a little alcohol. "Think there's
something to eat somewhere?"

Chet gives me a hard look.
Measuring the fit of my jeans
or my condition? *Probably*
in the kitchen. You okay?

"Uh-huh. I didn't eat dinner
and I don't want to pass out
too early." Hopefully that
won't be an actual issue.

Chet laughs. *We definitely
do not want that. Come on.*
He tugs me down the long,
narrow hall to the kitchen.

The granite countertops are
loaded with goodies—mostly
chips, dips, and salsa. Chet's
watching. Better skip the chips.

I settle for a handful of crackers,
a couple of slices of cheddar,
which make my mouth taste
like old cheese. Yecch.

I chase the taste with my drink,
which doesn't really make
my breath any better, so I down
the rest, reach for breath mints.

Better? asks Chet, and when
I nod, he smiles. *Great. I'll go
make us another drink. Meet
me by the pool, okay?*

I def do not need another drink,
but just because he makes it
does not mean I have to swallow
it, right? "Guess so. Okay."

WHEN HE LEAVES THE ROOM

I quick treat myself to some
chips and salsa. Guacamole,
too. If I'm drinking more, I'd
better eat more, right? And why
do I care if he sees, anyway?
Which reminds me of the rest
of Stacy's words of wisdom:

> *Lisa, you know I love you and
> I want you to be happy. But I'm
> not sure Chet's the right guy
> for you. He's so controlling!*

Which led to a lukewarm
exchange between us.
Lukewarm rather than heated,
because both of us knew she
was right. "I know. Sometimes
he is. But usually, he's sweet.
And I think he really cares . . ."

> She shot me a cannonball
> look. *That doesn't mean he
> won't hurt you. Most stalkers
> start out by "caring."*

That made me laugh. "Chet
is so not a stalker!" I didn't
mention my bigger dilemmas—
that I might not ever get another
boyfriend. And worse, that I'm
pretty sure I'm in love with him.

ALL THAT REPLAYS

As I head off in search of the bathroom,
where I can rinse the guacamole and chips
out of my mouth before finding Chet.

I wander down the hallway, opening doors,
hoping one of them leads to a sink. Every
now and again, I open one to find people

behind it doing interesting things. Things
I've never actually witnessed before, not
that I hang around watching for long now.

About the fourth try, I turn the knob
and hear a familiar voice behind the door.
It's Zach. With a girl. Def not Stacy.

Our eyes meet for the two seconds it takes me
to back away, shut the door, and hurry off, filled
with hurt for my friend. Forget the bathroom.

If Chet doesn't like the guacamole, up his.
Wait. Did I just think that? Yeah, I did.
What is it with guys, anyway? And now

what do I do? Keep quiet? Tell Stacy?
Let her keep believing everything is okay
between her and Zach, when . . .

I go outside, locate Chet. The second
drink is stronger than the first. Good.
No worries about sipping it slowly.

FEELING VERY LITTLE PAIN

And most of the hurt I'm holding
    for Stacy stashed behind a Jack
        Daniel's fog, I'm almost tempted to
            join the inebriated crowd in the pool.

But that would mean stripping
    down to my underwear or jumping
        in wearing jeans and a thin T-shirt.
            Either way, too much exposure.

Too much public exposure,
    that is. And when Chet suggests
        a bit of private exposure, I'm
            in just the right space to agree.

I might be approaching drunk.
    I don't know for sure, because
        I've never been there before,
            but I think I'm well on my way.

My tongue feels thick and
    my balance is off and my
        brain is blurred with too
            many jumbled thoughts.

Can you get this messed
    up from only two drinks?
        Who cares, anyway? Why
            worry about that right now?

CHET HALF CARRIES ME

To a distant corner of the yard, helps me
down on a cool grass carpet beneath

a breeze-teased palm tree. It's dark here,
and the laughter and voices seem far off.

I feel like I'm floating on a chill green sea,
head spinning like going around in circles.

Chet props himself above me, looks
down at me. *How are you feeling?*

"Like I want you to kiss me." I close my
eyes, push away stray thoughts of Zach,

Stacy, guacamole, and chocolate soufflé.
This kiss is different than all the others

that have gone before—practiced, yes,
but that's not it. Laced with passion,

yes, but that's nothing new. What's new
is how utterly helpless I feel right now,

like I'm on a rocket ride into space,
with no way to change my mind, no

way to turn around, head back home
to Earth, and safely touch down.

THRILLED, SCARED

A little of everything
in between, unable to
retreat, I push ahead
instead, give myself
to the sensual swirl.

Good. Bad. Wrong.
Right. Tonight there
is no black and white.
Everything is silver.
Shiny. Soft. Malleable.

Desire churns in my
core, lava, seeking
release. All it will take
is saying yes, please,
this very minute,

and I'm so ready to do
that. I know Chet has
come prepared, so I'll
have no excuse to say no.
The words *yes, please*

are right there, on
the tip of my alcohol-
thickened tongue. I open
my mouth to say them
and what spills out is

"I love you."

CHET'S REACTION

Is not to react at all. He doesn't
respond, barely even slows down,
and I have to ask, "Did you hear me?"

> He rolls to one side, slides
> out of his jeans, reaches into
> a pocket, extracts a foil pouch.

> > As he fumbles to open it,
> > he finally manages to say,
> > *I heard. Uh . . . thank you.*

> The five words sink slowly
> through the swamp in my brain.
> *Thank you?* Not even a *me too?*

Despite the whiskey numb, his
words sting. Tears are imminent.
"Is that all you have to say?"

> The tone of my voice slows his
> condom fumbling, which was
> retarded enough to begin with.

> > Finally, he gives up, tosses
> > the unused latex into a bush.
> > *What did you expect me to say?*

FAIR ENOUGH QUESTION

One I can't really answer.
I guess I didn't expect him
to say he loved me too.
But I guess I hoped he would.

I hate being semi-drunk . . . or
maybe totally drunk, I don't know.
All I know is, I feel like dirt
because of Chet Burgess.

"I'm not sure what I expected
you to say. But even a lie would
have been better." I sit up, straighten
my clothes. "Why are you with me?"

> Across the short space between
> us, I can see callousness in his
> eyes. *I always liked you, Lisa.*
> *You're okay. But you were practice.*

"Practice?" Oh my God, what's
he saying? That I'm like a tackling
dummy? How could I be so stupid?
"What are you talking about?"

> He looks up at me from his lair
> in the grass, carefully constructs
> his reply. Starts to say something.
> Changes his mind. *You were my first.*

"You told me that before . . ." This
makes no sense. "You were my first,
too, but I don't understand. What
does that have to do with 'practice'?"

> *Look, Lisa, asking you out was like
> a tryout.* His voice is honest. Mean.
> *I needed to play Single A before
> trying out for the majors, you know?*

My first thought is *Single A*
is better than a tackling dummy.
Which just goes to show how
totally messed up I still am.

This is all so unbelievable, like
trying to jerk myself out of a nightmare. My voice drops to a whisper.
"So why did you bother to change me?"

> He shrugs. Pulls on his pants,
> stands to zip them. *I did you
> a favor. Now, since I'm guessing
> we're not having sex, I'll take you home.*

Stunned, I shake my head. "Get
the hell away from me. I'll find
my own ride." I fall back into
the grass as he returns to the party.

WHAT JUST HAPPENED?

All I did was say "I love you"
and everything I've lately lived
for exploded in my face.

Across the large stretch of lawn,
the party continues. People still
laugh, still splash in the pool.

Nothing has changed for them.
Why has my world disintegrated?
All I did was say "I love you."

I feel like I just crawled from a car
wreck. Tears fall, and I know my
face wears smears of eye shadow,

mascara, blush. Good. I want
to be ugly again. Just plain Lisa.
Not Chet's Lisa. Not someone

created to make him feel better
about single-A hooking up. Favor?
He thinks he did me a favor,

changing me and controlling me
and turning me into someone
all new because I thought he cared?

If I'm Single A, he's third-string
Little League. What just happened?
All I did was say "I love you."

LIFE IS SEMI-NORMAL

By the time school starts again.
Okay, *normal* is a little different
from how it was before summer
vacation. My hair is reddish,
I wear contacts, and, yes,
I bother with a little makeup.

I decided I kind of like myself this way.

The night I left Blake's party, I stood
waiting for a cab. Zach came up,
more drunk than contrite, asked me
not to tell Stacy about him and Barbie.
I thought about that one for a long
time. I almost decided to keep quiet.

Then Stacy made an appointment for the exam.

At first she was mad at me, said
I'd only told her about Zach to make
myself feel better. Once she thought
things over, she apologized. I'm glad
I told. Stacy is def major league.
Zach only thinks he is.

I'm pretty sure he's boinking Barbie.

Dad and the boys showed mild
interest when Chet quit coming over.
So, okay, Paul and Brian teased me

a little about breaking up, singing
that old song about it. I knew it was all
in good fun, but I told them to shut up.

I wasn't quite ready for such humor.

Mom has been an angel.
The first few days, when all
I could do, alone in my room,
was cry and rant to myself, she
offered her shoulder if I needed
it but mostly kept her distance.

Then she told me her own breaking-up stories.

The stupidest thing was, despite
how deeply Chet's words had cut
me, for a couple of weeks I kept
waiting for him to call. He didn't.
Marv would happily step in, if I'd
let him. I'm thinking about it.

But if he decides to move on, I'll be okay.

IT'S THE SECOND WEEK OF SCHOOL

And my face is in my locker
when I hear a too familiar voice.
I peek around the door.

Chet is a couple of lockers down,
back toward me, talking to Katie
Clarke, who I know from history class.

Katie is a little cuter than I am, and
guess what color her hair is. But she's
a ditz. Chet has changed strategy.

          I can't help but listen in as he
          asks her to the football game.
          Great. It will be fun.

          Then he reaches out, touches
          her hair gently. *You know, it*
          will be my first real date . . .

My first instinct is to slam
my locker, shout out, "Liar!"
I take a deep breath, rethink

my own strategy. I close my
locker door quietly, turn, and
over Chet's shoulder say,

"If he asks you out to Le Vallauris,
he expects sex for dessert. And
he's not real good with condoms."

THINK I SHOULD HAVE

Kept my mouth shut?
Not so long ago, I would
have. But not today.

Not

anymore. The ironic thing
is, I have Chet to thank for
that. Before last summer,
the old Lisa was just

so

passive, so willing to let
life's good stuff pass her
by. I'll still never make
the cheerleading squad,
but no longer do I feel

plain

when I look into a mirror.
Mom says you reveal
how you feel about yourself
in the way you present
yourself. I think she's right.

My name is Lisa. And
I'm def not so plain

anymore.

Party Foul

BY LYNDA SANDOVAL

CHAPTER ONE

"Hey, babe, it's me," I said into Paige's voice mail—again. I swallowed back the shakiness, the screech I could hear as an unwelcome subtext to my words. I didn't want to sound like I felt, which was sweaty-palmed, coiled tight with worry.

Desperate.

No one likes a desperate girlfriend, right? There's a whole genre of Hollywood movies about them, and none are the least bit flattering.

I cleared my throat and tried for the whole casual vibe. "Um, I've been trying to get you all day so we can figure out tonight. When you check this, will you call me?" Awkward pause. "Okay, so . . ." I hesitated, hating myself for doing so. Should I say IT? Should I not? Was I the only one saying IT lately, or had my imagination kicked into obsession overdrive? Eh, screw it. I was being stupid. "I love you," I said, choking on the last word—*natch*.

I pressed "end" on my cell and tossed it onto the bed next to me, then leaned my throbbing skull against my headboard and closed my eyes. A sense of foreboding that I couldn't explain bubbled up inside me, dark and oily. So, she wasn't calling back immediately like she usually did. It didn't *mean* anything, right?

How could it? Paige had approached *me* all those months ago.

She'd made it clear what she wanted from me at a pool party just after the last school year ended, and heck yeah, I took the bait. *Hello,* what self-respecting gay girl wouldn't? Paige Knox—popular, beautiful, glowing, sweet, fun. Oh, and wicked hot—have I mentioned that?

W-I-C-K-E-D. Only in my dreams would a girl like her ever be interested in me. Not that I'm chopped liver, but Paige is . . .

Well, *straight,* for one thing.

At least, I'd thought she was until she'd made it abundantly clear she wasn't when she followed me from the pool into the girls' bathroom that day, grabbing the front of my T-shirt in her fist and pulling me toward her. It was all hushed words and quick kisses back then, the promise of it all leaving me buzzing and breathless.

When we finally hooked up for real? Man . . . mind-blowing. I know that sounds clichéd. But trust me, we've dated all summer, and now I'm sure. There is nothing straight about allegedly straight Paige Knox. And being with another girl? It's not just a physical thing like so many people assume (although there is that). But it goes much deeper, on so many levels. She and I *get* each other, we finish each other's sentences. We laugh together. We've been inseparable since the moment we kissed—really kissed—and I've been happier than ever before. And, in case you're wondering, YES, I'm well aware that I'm her first girlfriend, okay? My friends never let me forget it. Whatever. The passion between us says what words can't: none of that matters. Paige and I are special. Different. Destined.

If it seems as though she's been pulling away lately, well, there has to be a logical explanation. I've given it a little—okay, a lot—of thought. She is so intense about school and all her extracurriculars—volleyball, student gov, and most of all the editor in chief position of *Creighton Caller,* which she's been coveting since ninth grade and *finally* landed. It's no wonder she's feeling the stress about starting our all-important senior year.

Starting it *together.*

So . . . maybe that's a teensy part of the stress, too.

See, we've kept things on the down low over the summer—Paige's choice—because this being-in-love-with-a-girl stuff is all new to her. I understand. I mean, shoot, I'm not completely out at school either—just out on a need-to-know basis, for no other reason than . . . I don't think it matters to the masses that I identify as lesbian. I'm just *me*. But Paige promised we'd present ourselves as a couple, no matter what, once school started. Together, Out and Proud, and anyone who didn't like it could—

I clenched my fists, and tears stung my eyes.

Damn it, Paige. You *promised*.

My cell phone busted out a ring tone from Pink's latest CD— Paige's special song—and my heart spasmed. She called back! Thank God. I blew out a week's worth of tension in one long breath. See? I'd been making something out of nothing, just as always. My mom claims I emerged from the womb worrying, and although I've always denied it, I was starting to believe her.

I clicked "on" and snuggled into my pillows, happy again. I never wanted to be one of those girls whose moods are dictated by the person they love, but oh well. Happy is a good thing. "Hey, babe. Where've you been?"

"Just . . . getting stuff ready for school. You know."

Distracted again, but at least my instincts about why had been right. My body only semirelaxed. Something still felt off. "That's what I figured."

Deafening silence. God. How could an absence of sound be so loud?

Blood pounded in my temples. "Are you okay?" I asked.

"I'm fine," she tossed off. "So, what's up? I'm kinda busy."

The niggling feather of worry returned, tickling the back of my throat. Why the rush? We used to talk on the phone for hours every night, about everything and nothing. About *us*. And this after having spent the evening together.

"Mia?"

"Sorry. Uh, just wondering if you wanted me to pick you up for the Lake Bash tonight or if you'd rather drive?"

"Oh." And then nothing.

Seriously.

It seemed so absurd, I laughed, but it sounded forced. "What does 'oh' mean?"

I heard Paige ease out a breath on the other end of the line. "Mimi, look. I'm really feeling overwhelmed about school. Getting ready for it, I mean," she added in a flurry. "Do you mind if we skip the Bash tonight?"

Shock shot through me. I opened my mouth, but nothing emerged. Back up. Replay. Paige wanted to skip it? Say *what?* Allow me to put this into perspective. In our town, the Bash is *the* event to tie summer off in a neat party bow before school starts, especially for incoming seniors. And Paige has been the nucleus of every social event since the infamous fifth-grade ice cream mixer when Larry Cummings porked out beyond his means (dudes, I swear) and subsequently tossed his cookies (and cream) on the student teacher's chest. Larry's social faux pas could've stopped the festivities cold if not for Paige. She took the lead, managing to ease his embarrassment and keep the whole event hopping, just by being herself, and ever since then, she's been on the A-list for parties. Seriously, Paige skipping our pre-senior Lake Bash would be unpreceden—

"Mia?"

I gulped back my astonishment, trying to work up a supportive air. "Sorry, I'm here. I just didn't expect you to say . . . you seriously want to miss it?" I couldn't leach the bewilderment from that question.

"So you *do* mind," she said, sounding miffed.

"No, I don't. I'm just surprised." *White lie.* "I could come over and help you get ready instead. Take some of the pressure off your back."

"My parents are here."

I pulled my chin back and frowned. Um . . . okay . . . *so?* I'd been around Mr. and Mrs. Knox tons of times. Why, all of a sudden—

Stop it, Mia.

Reaching for humor, I said, "Well, I wasn't planning on tearing your clothes off in front of them to out you, if that's what you're freaked about."

She didn't even snicker. "That's not funny. It's just, my mom's help-ing me. You know, her little girl starting senior year, all that."

"I don't mind if your mom's there—"

"Yeah, but, I want it to be . . . just us."

My insides warmed, and I smiled. "I want that, too. Just ask your mom if—"

"No. I meant, Mom and me, not you and me."

Her hard words stung like a backhand across the jaw line. With brass knuckles. *Spiked.* "Oh." I paused, flailing to absorb it all.

"I'll see you at school on Monday, 'kay?"

I blinked. Monday? What the hell? There was tonight and then a whole day before Monday. Our last day of summer, in fact. "What about tomorrow? Want to go for a chai or something?"

She uttered a frustrated sound. "Jesus, Mia, please—"

"I'm sorry. Listen, I'm not trying to compound your stress. I just want to see you. Is that a crime? It's been a few days." I softened my tone. "I miss you."

I waited for her to reciprocate the words. *Nada.*

"All right. Never mind. Monday it is," I said, as defeat wrapped around my shoulders like a cold, wet towel, dripping all over my dreams.

"Uh-huh."

"So . . . I'll let you go." I took a deep breath and blew it out. "But everything's okay? Really?"

"I'm fine," she said in a flat voice.

Yeah, but are we? I wanted more info. Elaboration. Some inkling as to why everything had done a one-eighty for no apparent reason.

Nada, part two.

"I love you," I said, partly to fill the chasm of excruciating silence and partly to try to get a clue as to her state of mind.

A beat passed. "Okay, thanks. See you." And she hung up.

"Thanks"? No "I love you, too." Not even our private little joke of "You're tolerable yourself, in small doses." *Nothing.* I seriously felt like I'd entered some altered-reality state.

I was frozen, still staring in mute disbelief at my phone, when my best friend, Allison, burst into my bedroom unceremoniously—typical Al—messenger bag slung across her body. She raised one multiply pierced eyebrow as she lifted her bag over her head and tossed it onto the end of my bed. "You do realize you have to actually push buttons on those things to make them work, right?"

"Funny. Not." I chucked the phone aside. Come to think of it, when was the last time Paige had told me she loved me? I searched my virtual memory . . .

File not found.

Never one for extraneous bullshit chatter, Al bounced onto the end of my bed, maneuvered herself into a lotus position, then began pawing through her bag. She extracted six bottles of nail polish and grabbed my foot, wedging this foam thing between my toes to separate them. "So, were you waiting for it to ring?"

"Huh?"

"Your cell."

I shook off the stupid. "No. Just hanging up."

"Ah." She started in on my previously arranged pedicure, and for several moments neither of us spoke. She stared at my toes, I stared at the arc of her short-trimmed, brightly dyed mohawk.

"So, who were you just hanging up with?" Al asked finally. "As if I don't know." She never lost concentration on her task: painting my toenails rainbow colors. Allison has this thing about naked toenails, which is hilarious to me because she's unquestionably the most butch of all my gay friends. Except when it comes to her toes. And mine. She insists we paint them if they are going to be seen in public. Naked toenails are out of the question. It probably has something to do with the fact that Al's mom is a girly-girl aesthetician who owns a day spa and salon. Probably seeped in through her DNA. I didn't care one way or the other, so here we were, stranded on Pedicure Island, smack in the middle of Misery Bay.

"Earth to Mia Salazar," she said. "Come in, Mia."

"Sorry." I schooled my voice so it didn't shake. "Yeah, it was Paige."

"Uh-huh. And?"

"She doesn't feel like going to the Lake Bash tonight."

"So it begins," murmured Allison, seeming totally unsurprised.

"What's that supposed to mean?" I demanded, instantly pissed. I wanted Allison to be as shocked and bewildered as I was. I didn't want her to act as if this awful moment was a foregone conclusion, you know? "She doesn't want to go—big deal. She's getting ready for school."

"On Lake Bash night?" Al asked in this über-skeptical tone. "*That* was her pathetic excuse? You've got to be kidding."

I bit my bottom lip. It's not like I didn't grasp Al's implications, but still. I already felt edgy and scared about Paige bailing at the last moment after she'd been so weird and distant lately. I didn't need Al's "I told you so" on top of it. "You know how she is about school."

"Yeah, I know how she is about a lot of things, thanks to her wrapping my best friend around her little finger"—she sucked in her cheeks—"or whatever it was she wrapped you around, and *no,* I don't want details."

"Like I'd give them." Kiss and tell? No, thanks.

"One thing I'm sure about, Mia. She wouldn't miss out on the last Lake Bash of her entire high school career unless she'd severed a femoral artery with an ax or lapsed into a diagnosis-X coma after traveling to a Third World country or—"

"I get it, okay?"

"Then, come *on,*" Al said, her tone dubious. "I say this with love, but pop your head out. Toss the rose-colored glasses. Wake up and smell the coffee."

"Geez. Cliché much?" I managed to sound flippant but couldn't quite hold back my gulp. She had a point. One I was unprepared to see.

"Paige canceling is about more than some obsessive-compulsive need to color coordinate her spiral notebooks, and you darn well know it." She sniffed, and her tiny diamond nose stud glimmered. "Odd how things are changing, now that school's about to start, don'tcha think?"

I tossed my newly hip, choppy (thanks to Al's mom's wizardry with the shears) black hair over my shoulder and rolled my eyes. "Whatever, Al. Who cares about Lake Bash anyway?" Uh, I did. That's who. And Allison knew it.

"No sweat. We'll go together."

"You don't even *attend* Creighton High."

"So freakin' what? You aren't allowed to bring guests? I know Creighton's a snob school and I go to Last Chance High, but—"

"Don't call it that, Al." Allison went to—and loved—the Alternative High School on the edge of town. "Your school is cool—"

"Preaching to the choir, babe."

"Okay, then! I just don't want to go to the Bash," I said.

Allison scoffed. "Oh, come on. Don't turn all lovesick on me. You've talked about this beach-blanket bonanza for weeks."

I pouted. "It won't be the same without her."

"Hello! What the hell am I? The freakin' plague?"

"You know what I mean."

Al spread her arms wide, purple polish bottle in one hand, cap with the little brush in the other. "I'm not trying to bag on you, Mia, but it has to be said. You should've known this day was coming from the get. Hook up with a straight chick, and it only leads to heartbreak—"

"Not this again, Al. Seriously." I squeezed the bridge of my nose.

"No. It's tough love. You need to hear it. I told you that at the beginning, and I'll tell you now, tomorrow, and for the rest of our lives. They don't call it the 'Straight Date Curse' for nothing—"

"Yeah, yeah—"

"And the SDC is as bad as, or worse than, an STD. Straight girl gets her kicks, gay girl falls in love and gets kicked under the bus."

"Blah-blah."

She aimed the nail polish brush at me. "Happens every time."

"Not *every* time. Besides, Paige. Isn't. Straight."

"Keep telling yourself that." Allison rolled her eyes, then moved on to the blue metallic OPI.

My insides went cold and shaky. I tried to maintain my calmness, but I couldn't deny a flicker of fear mingled with stunned denial.

Paige was *not* dumping me. Impossible.

Please, God.

How could we be so hot for each other one minute, so in sync, and the next minute—*poof*—over? Fury rose up inside me. "I hate to state the obvious, Al, but almost everyone thinks they're straight until they *don't* anymore," I snapped, crossing my arms over my chest. "It's called mainstream socialization. Duh."

"Generally true. But still, *Paige Knox?*" Allison pulled a skeptical face.

My stomach contracted automatically. If I closed my eyes, I could smell the fresh clover scent of her long blond hair, could feel the softness of her lips against my neck, the warmth of her breath on me. All our private jokes, our intimate glances. Our songs.

Al was wrong. Big time. She just . . . had to be.

"So she's Paige Knox." I made those annoying air quotes with my fingers. "Why do you say it like that? Like she's not an individual?"

Allison gave me The Look. "Dude, your woman completely oozes the *straight-girl-experimenting* vibe, and you know it."

"Don't tell me what I *know.* She'd never use me like that." Al hadn't been with us when we were . . . just us. She didn't understand the soul-deep connection we shared. It wasn't a gay or straight thing, it was an *us* thing. I leaned forward. "You know, by saying that, you're basically implying that she's not into me and never has been." My heart actually cramped at the thought, shutting off the blood flow in my body until I saw stars. I teetered on the verge of full-blown hysteria, so I just kept talking. "Like, our whole relationship has been a joke, which is a pretty shitty thing for a best friend to say."

"A shitty thing would be for a best friend to lie."

"So you *do* think it was a joke?"

"I never said joke. I said Straight. Girl. Experimenting. Period."

Panic, panic, panic. I forced myself to remember our sleepover the other night, when Paige's parents were out of town. Falling asleep wrapped around her, waking up with her wrapped around me. Laughter and warmth and vanilla ice cream kisses. I shivered. "Trust me. No matter what you think of Paige, this thing between her and me? It's real."

Al didn't acknowledge my argument. "Question."

"Go for it." As if I could stop her.

"Has she told anyone the two of you have been dating all summer?" she asked quietly, moving on to green nail polish. "Does *she* identify you to people as *her* girlfriend?"

A beat passed. I felt dirty and clandestine from the question alone, and I hated that. "Not yet, but I don't care—"

"I'm not done. Has she gone with you to the Alley? Even once?" she asked, referring to the GLBTQ youth center, where I'd actually met Allison. We'd both just turned thirteen and had come out to our parents around the same time. Rainbow Alley was like a whole new world of overwhelming awesomeness for us back then. Eventually it just became a home away from home.

I hiked my chin. "If you have something to say, spit it out."

Allison angled her head to the side and drilled me with a stare. "Fine. If the girl was truly a lesbian, Mia, or bi, or even *questioning,* she'd want to at least go check it out. That's all. You and I both know it's the place to be."

"Not for everybody. Maybe she's shy about—"

"Right! Like Paige has a shy bone in her body, and that doesn't matter anyway." Al scoffed. "We couldn't wait to get there. And we were babies."

My jaw tightened. "Yeah, but that's not fair. She isn't out to her parents."

"So? She's a big girl. She doesn't have to tell them where she's going."

"News flash: some people don't like to lie to their parents."

Al's eyes widened. "Dude. If she isn't out to them and she truly *is* gay, isn't she lying already?"

Silence.

Point score: Allison. Lie of omission, maybe, but still.

Frustration bubbled inside me. "Just because you and I have had it easy with our families doesn't mean we can judge Paige for the way she's handling her own life. Her parents are different. Not so accepting."

"How does she know that if she hasn't told them?"

I clenched my fists. "Paige isn't *us*. She's not ready to be out."

"Being out isn't even the *point!* God!" Al's face reddened with frustration. "It's a freakin' youth center. No one gives a shit. She can tell everyone she's straight if it's that big of a deal."

"It's *not*. And she *isn't*."

"Yeah?" Al narrowed her eyes. "Well, movie night rolls around every Saturday. How hard could it be to show up for pizza and a flick in a place where she can openly cozy up to her secret girlfriend if she wants to?"

I didn't have an answer, so I stared down at my hands lying helplessly in my lap. I tried not to picture them touching Paige. I tried even harder not to picture them never touching Paige again. UGH.

"*You* haven't gone to the Alley with me once since she entered the scene," Al said, in a gentler tone, but laced tightly with a hurt that surprised me. "Your whole life totally changed to comply with her stupid, closety restrictions."

I glanced up, pierced through with guilt. I was a crappy friend.

Her big blue eyes pleaded with me. "Everyone asks me where you are. Constantly. Drag night just isn't the same without you lip-synching Hanson in that stupid-ass blond wig my mom gave you."

I snickered, in spite of myself. *MMMBop.* Those *were* good times.

Al pressed her lips together. "They miss you at the Alley, Mia. *I* miss you."

Without warning, I was slammed with an intense longing for my Alley friends, for not having to hide and pretend, for being around people who felt like I did and weren't afraid to show it. And then I immediately felt disloyal to Paige. Exhausted by the emotional pendulum, I wanted to cry, but I choked it back. "Okay, fine. We'll go to the Lake Bash together. But if it sucks—"

She grinned. "We'll bounce and head to the Alley. Cool? Everyone will be so stoked to see you."

I nodded, wishing I could manage a smile, but I wasn't even close.

"Tonight'll be awesome, just like old times. Promise." Allison gave my foot a squeeze. "You'll get through this, Mama Mia. And, no matter what, you'll always have your friends."

I didn't know what "getting through this" meant.

Pretty sure I didn't want to.

CHAPTER TWO

The Bash was in full swing by the time Al and I jolted over the rutted dirt road toward the weed-choked field designated for parking. Every possible genre of music thumped out from various tailgates, and kids stood around drinking everything from iced coffee to Red Bull to smuggled beer and liquor. A campfire licked orange into the star-strewn indigo sky, and beyond it, the moon led a silvery path across the rippling water of Creighton Lake. Perfect setting for hanging out with your girl.

My stomach soured.

"Hey, let me off here so I don't have to walk as far with the cooler," Al said.

"Slug," I deadpanned, lurching to a stop. "Meet me at the edge of the parking field, though, or I'll never find you," I added as she threw open the door of my Prius, drawing the woodsy, lakey, smoky smell into the car.

"Okay." She wedged the small cooler of sodas and snacks from my back seat, then strode off, confident and cool as ever in her long board shorts, tank top, flip-flops, and—of course—newly painted toenails.

Alone, I indulged in a few moments of quiver-chinned self-pity before maneuvering my microcar into an open spot near the back of the field. I ran fingers through my hair and flipped down the visor mirror to check my slightly Goth makeup job—which reflected my bleak mood—before getting out of the car. I'd only made it to the back bumper before Al ran up to me, huffing and serious-faced and still carrying the cooler. She set it on the ground, then rested her palms on her knees and bent over to catch her breath.

I blinked at her with confusion. "What are you doing?"

Peering up, sucking wind, she said, "You know what"—*gasp, gasp*—"I checked it out and this blows." *Gasp, cough.* "Let's just leave."

I stared at her for a moment, dumbstruck. Beyond the laughter and music, I could hear the water lapping against the shoreline. The hot day had cooled down to a perfect temperature, and the festivities sure didn't seem lame from where I stood. "Are you high? We're talking Lake Bash, Al. You dragged my ass here, and we're staying. At least for a little while." I edged around her, and she grabbed my arm.

"Don't go."

I spun back toward her, not liking the gravity in her voice. Every nerve ending in my body prickled. "Why not?"

Silence.

Right then, it hit me. My insides collapsed like an imploding high-rise building, and I felt dizzy, ice cold. "She's here, isn't she?"

"Wait—"

For a moment, my stupid, hopeful heart lifted. "Did she have a change of plans? I wonder why she didn't call my cell."

"She didn't have a change of plans," Al said in a monotone.

For several long seconds, we just searched each other's eyes.

"You're saying she freakin' lied to me? Why would she do that?" I started to bolt toward the throngs of kids.

Al did her best to hold me there, her hands wrapped around my biceps. Her voice grew more urgent. "Seriously, dude, we should just—"

I wrenched away, all adrenaline bursts, desperation, and blind need. "Where is she? Tell me!" I yelled.

Al's chest still heaved from the exertion of running with the cooler, and her eyes were round, troubled. She said nothing for a moment, then whispered, "Don't do this, Mia. Trust me."

No! No!

I turned and started running, stumbling over the uneven ground, my legs weak with both the truth of what was happening and my abject denial of it. When I reached the crowd, I scanned the fire-lit faces like a panicked mom searching for her missing toddler. A few people called out friendly hellos to me, but I couldn't risk opening my mouth to reply. A scream had lodged in my throat, ready to explode at any moment. I staggered through the bodies, not caring that I drew stares and whispers. If Paige had lied to me, that could only mean—

That's when I saw her.

Shock burst through me, leaving my hands tremoring and my heart in shards.

She stood cradled between the muscular legs of Marcos Antonopolous as he leaned back against his SUV. Her arms wound around his neck, and his big hands cradled both sides of her rib cage. *My* girlfriend and the current It-guy of Creighton High were making out like nobody's business.

So many disparate emotions avalanched over the moment, I didn't know which to grasp on to before they all buried and suffocated me. Rage, fear, sadness, love, jealousy, pain. The urge to puke. Before I even knew what had happened, my hand was on Paige's shoulder, wrenching her out of Marcos's clutches.

Startled, she whipped around to face me, and my gaze immediately dropped to her lips, moist and swollen from kissing. From kissing *him*. Her chest was flushed and a little blotchy like it always got when she was turned on. But how could she be turned on by Marcos? She was *gay*. She was *mine*.

"Jesus, what are you doing?" I yelled, raking all ten fingers into my hair.

Just then, Al caught up with me and laid a hand on my shoulder. "Mia, let's go before this turns into a scene."

Too late. Already a scene. Shrugging Al off, I moved closer to Paige as tears spilled down my cheeks. I felt like I was splitting apart from the inside out, like I couldn't catch a breath and wasn't sure I wanted to. Ever. Again. "What in the hell is going on, Paige? Tell me!" I'd been in limbo for too long. I wanted answers.

For the first time ever, I saw stark fear move across Paige's pretty face, which had reddened because, of course, I'd drawn a crowd with my outburst. Her neck tightened in a swallow as her eyes darted around at the onlookers.

"Mia, just go with Allison," she said, her voice low. "Please."

"No. Hell no! You are *my*—!" I flicked an arm toward Marcos, who looked both confused and—UGH!—aroused. "And you're here, where you weren't supposed to be, with your tongue jammed down his throat?"

Murmurs of astonishment and curiosity rippled through the crowd.

"What's she talking about, babe?" Marcos asked drunkenly.

I clenched my fists at my sides and wheeled on him, my entire body trembling. "Don't call her that!"

Al stepped up again, this time tugging at my arm. "*Now,* Salazar. She's not worth this, trust me—"

"Don't worry," Paige said to Marcos with a private smile. But beneath it, I sensed her quaking anxiety from the way her voice tightened, the beat-beat-beat of the pulse I could see in the side of her neck. "It's a misunderstanding."

"A *misunderstanding?*" I yelled. "You said you weren't coming to the Bash. Is that what you call a misunderstanding? Because I call it a fucking lie."

"Stop. *Please,*" Paige said, more wobbly by the moment. Tension and anxiety radiated off her skin in waves.

"Was our whole"—I sputtered, choosing my words, hating and resenting that I had to—"our whole thing a damned *misunderstanding?*"

I saw the exact moment when terror seized her. "We don't have a *thing,* freak!" Paige yelled, loud enough for everyone to hear. The crowd went dead silent.

All I could hear was the blood rushing in my ears.

All I could see was Paige. Killing me.

Freak. Oh, God. My beautiful, funny, passionate Paige had called me a freak in front of the whole school. I'd never felt so much crushing pain in my life. I started to sob, and that seemed to embolden her. She'd broken me, gained the upper hand—at least that's how I read it. She stood a little straighter and moved back toward the socially acceptable safety of Marcos.

"You might have some weird obsession with me, Mia," she said, her voice raised for all to hear, "but I am not a lesbian like you, okay? Let it go!"

The crowd crackled to life again, the occasional "Dude!" or "What?" or "Did she say *lesbian?*" rising above the murmurs to assault my ears. So much for being out on a need-to-know basis at Creighton High. Not that I cared what any of them thought of me. I'd never intended to hide in the first place. It was all Paige.

"You freakin' bitch!" Allison spat toward Paige in a low rasp, wrapping a protective arm around my shoulders. And then to me, "Let's get out of here."

I stepped forward one last time and softened my teary tone so that only she'd hear. "I love you, Paige Knox. And you love me. Deny it all you want, screw every guy in this crowd if you need to prove something to yourself." I paused, sucking back sobs. "But you and I know the truth. And you're the one who has to live with the lie. Or would that be the *misunderstanding?*"

Her chin betrayed her bravado with the slightest quiver before she regained control and tossed her blond hair. "Whatever."

And then she turned and entwined her body with Marcos's again.

Devastated. Dismissed.

Dissed.

I cried the entire way back to the car—eyes swelling, nose running—only slightly aware of the hundreds of people witnessing my walk of shame, of the words being whispered behind curved hands and plastic beer cups. I didn't care about the gossip. Frankly, it was a relief that I wouldn't have to come out to anyone else. But I did care that they'd believe Paige's version of "*Deluded, Obsessed Lesbian,*

Starring Mia Salazar," because it wasn't fair and couldn't be further from the truth. Then again, I no longer had my girl, so WHAT DID ANY OF IT MATTER?

At the tail end of the Prius, I wrestled my keys out of my pocket and lobbed them over the car to Allison, who palmed them without comment. She loaded the cooler into the back, then slipped behind the wheel and blazed out of there. Once we reached the street, she rolled down all the windows and simply let me sob, the night air blowing my tears backward into my ears, until the Denver skyline twinkled into view on the horizon.

Allison exhaled. "God, Mia—"

"Don't say it! I don't want any of your I-told-you-so crap."

After a long pause, Al said, "That's not *at all* what I was going to say."

I sob-hiccuped more, sniffled a little, then wiped my eyes with my wrists, undoubtedly smearing my makeup. Not that I cared. "What then?" I asked finally.

"You didn't deserve it, is all."

I glanced over to see my best friend shaking her head slowly. Her eyes glistened almost as if she'd been crying, too. "That was some cold-ass—"

"I never outed her, Al," I said, wavery and wet. "I never would've."

"I know. *She* outed *you*. Total party foul."

I flicked my hand. "But why did she hook up with Marcos?"

"All the better to show the world she's straight, I guess. Bag the biggest guy-ho in the whole school—every straight chick's fantasy."

My tears returned in earnest, and I curled into myself, wrapping my arms around a middle that felt hollow, scraped raw with a knife. "How could she do that to me? After everything we've been through, all the promises?"

"Fear. That's all. You could smell it on her."

"Fear of *what?* Someone who gets her? Who loves her? Who'd never hurt her?" I huffed and hiccuped at the same time, sick to my stomach. "Besides"—I shuddered—"all I could smell on her was *him*." Tacky cologne. Testosterone.

Allison clicked her tongue. "I know I haven't been her biggest fan throughout this whole . . . thing, but I never thought she'd pull something like that." She banged her fist on the steering wheel. "Damn, if I could've done anything to prevent it—"

"S'okay. You tried." I reached over and squeezed her forearm.

"Still. I'm . . . so sorry, Mama Mia."

"I had to see it for myself or I never would've believed it." The horrible picture that was now forever emblazoned on my brain. *That* was the problem. "Let's just go to the Alley. I need some serious chill time."

We drove in silence for a few minutes, then Al asked, "What are you going to do on Monday?"

I hiked one shoulder in a listless half shrug. "Go to school. What other choice do I have?"

• • •

Retreating into the fold at Rainbow Alley on Hell Night was just what I'd needed, but on Sunday it felt a bit like a Band-Aid over a stab wound in the whole scheme of things. No more Mia and Paige. Unfathomable. I spent all Sunday in bed, mostly sleeping, sometimes crying. Mom thought I was sick until I told her what had gone down. After that, she insisted I keep my strength up, whatever that means. Strength for what? She attempted to entice me with healthy stuff, which I blew off (duh), but then—wise woman—she resorted to junk food.

That worked. Double cheeseburgers *do* have a certain magic.

I finally lapsed into a fitful sleep and dreamed about—what else?— Paige.

At the crack of dawn, tension popped my eyelids open and kept them that way despite a haze of exhaustion.

The first day of school. Crap. Welcome to my nightmare.

I lay there for a few minutes trying (and failing) not to think about facing Paige and Marcos and the hordes of kids who would no doubt be all up in my business about the Lake Bash fiasco. I am not the Paris Hilton type—not even close. I don't *want* notoriety. Life as a wallflower is A-OK with me.

When I couldn't take my racing thoughts anymore, I pulled on track pants and a T-shirt, clapped a baseball cap over my bed head, dashed off a quick note to my mom so she wouldn't freak out and call the cops if she found me missing, then slipped out of the house. Hands stuffed in my pockets, I traipsed through the dewy, pink-tinged morning to a nearby coffee shop and nabbed a gigantic latte with an extra shot of espresso. Fortification for the day.

I drank it on the route back, planning my survival strategy. Although my deepest desire was to head to school in the exact outfit I had on, no shower or anything, I decided to take extra care with my hair and clothes. Paige might have dumped me in front of the whole freakin' school, but I was going to make sure she got one look at me and regretted the hell out of it. Allison's mom always said, "Looking hot is the best revenge," and today was the perfect time to test her theory.

I wore the low-slung, superexpensive Paige Premium jeans I'd saved for two months to buy. Paige loved them for obvious narcissistic reasons. I paired them with a V-necked, body-hugging shirt in BMW red—the color she thought was most flattering with my dark hair and olive skin. I made a point of wearing the heart choker she'd given me on July 4, as we watched the fireworks, and I spent way more time on my hair than any sane person who wasn't prepping for a pageant ever should. But I rocked the do, if I must say so myself, and I managed to look like I hadn't tried too hard. Al's mom would be proud.

By the time I pulled into the senior parking lot, though, my heart pounded so rapidly, I couldn't breathe. Had I been one of those inhaler-sucking asthma kids, I'd be dialing 911 right about then. I turned off the engine and sat there, toying with the idea of turning right around and heading home. Mom would call me in sick. But as I watched everyone funneling toward the front doors, laughing, talking, brand-new back-packs slung over their shoulders, I knew I'd have to face this sooner or later. Might as well get it over with.

Goal number one: I needed to zip from here to—I pawed through the stack of papers the school had sent home a week or so ago—lock-er number 411 in the senior pod as quickly as possible, making eye contact with no one. I broke down the land-mine trek into mental segments: car to flagpole; flagpole to doors; doors to locker.

The halls swarmed with kids—squealing, hugging girls, wide-eyed freshmen clutching oversize binders to themselves like body armor, and the omnipresent jocks, banging chests and knocking fists. The air was rife with competing scents of fresh paint, excessive cologne, and floor wax. All of it—the noise, the place, the stench? — familiar, generally comforting stuff. Not today. I stared straight down, counting the polished floor tiles beneath my feet . . . 26, 27, 28, 29—

"Hey, Salazar," said one of the aforementioned fist knockers, Dalton Prescott, falling into step with me, standing too close. The thick-bodied, thick-headed football lineman was a bully from way back. He'd never been a friend of mine.

"What do you want?"

"Wow, that's some way to greet a person on the first day of school."

"Whatever." I made it to locker 411 and spun the combination lock, ignoring Dalton as best I could. Mr. Annoying leaned his shoul-der against the locker next to mine and continued to invade my per-sonal space. A few of his stupid goons gathered behind him, all wide-eyed and leering. I braced myself for the hit.

"So, is it true?" Dalton asked.

Go time.

"That this is the first day of school?" I asked without looking up. "Yes."

"Ha-ha. I'm talking about you being a muff diver."

My hand froze on the lock and anger pulsed through me. Why did people like Dalton always have to make it about *sex?* It was so much more than that. After a moment of counting in my head so I didn't punch the guy (because I was sure he could punch back harder), I glared at him. "You're an idiot. If that's your ignorant way of asking me if I'm gay, the answer is yes." I raked a glance up and down his beefy body. "And if I wasn't, standing this close to you would make me want to be."

His friends hooted and shoved each other. God, they acted like such children. I hated that pack mentality.

"Ah, so you're a *man-hater* lesbo?" he persisted, not smiling so much, now that I'd out-dissed him. The shine in his eyes was more of a knife glint. I'd insulted his masculinity, and bullies don't like that, now do they?

"I don't see a man around here. I'm a person who's tired of this stupid conversation." I finally wrenched my locker open, whacking him in the face with the door accidentally-on-purpose.

"Ow!"

"Sorry," I said, not meaning it.

"Hey," he said, rubbing his nose, "I've got nothing against dykes. It's hot. But did you honestly think a top-shelf babe like Paige Knox would go for that?"

My breathing shallowed, and I white-knuckled the edge of the door. I wanted to scream the truth, tell him everything, prove Paige a liar and a cheat and a coward. But despite all that she'd done, I loved her too much to hurt her like she'd hurt me. And let me tell you, right then taking the high road sucked. Burning him some major stink eye, I said, "Piss off, Prescott. Go slap some guy's ass in the locker room, you stupid hypocrite, and leave me alo—"

"You're done, Dalt. Hit the road," came a deep, calm voice from behind me. I spun to see one of Dalton's teammates—in fact, the football captain, Wade Janson—locking eyes with my tormentor. "It's not cool what you're doing."

Dalton stared at Wade in disbelief. "C'mon, Cap, whose side are you on?"

Wade held the stare and said nothing.

Red-faced, Dalton glanced over his shoulder at his group of supporters. "Hey, guys. What's the male version of a fag hag?"

"You know, we have harassment rules in this school," Wade continued, unfazed. "I assume you don't want to be benched for the first few games."

"Brah, I can't believe you'd go there," Dalton said.

"Believe it. *Brah.*"

Standoff. Wade crossed his arms and didn't move. After a few moments of jaw clenching, Dalton waved his hands in disgust and left.

I waited until the group of them had melted into the crowd, then rested my head against the cool metal door of the locker adjacent to mine, sucking in a deep breath, trying to ignore the tears stinging my eyes.

"You okay, Mia?"

I shot a glance over at Wade and tried . . . really *tried* . . . to smile, but the expression came out tremulous. "I'll live." I swallowed. "Thanks for that."

"He won't bother you anymore. I'll talk to Coach."

I rolled my eyes. "Like Coach will care."

"He will. Trust me. He's cool."

Reeeally. I shut my locker and turned toward him, curious. "So, are you—?"

"No." He chuckled. "I'm not gay. My older brother is, though, but that doesn't matter. You don't have to be gay to be a decent person."

I hiked an eyebrow. "You'd think someone might've mentioned that to Dalton along the way," I said ruefully. We headed toward our first-period classrooms in companionable silence—mostly because I didn't know what to say—until we reached the stairwell between the junior and senior locker pods.

Wade jabbed his thumb toward the steps. "This is my stop," he said.

"Oh. Okay."

"If any of the guys on the team give you trouble, come to me. Deal?"

I bit my lip and nodded, a weak part of me yearning to trail after him like some wimp so he could pick off my tormentors one by one.

He must have sensed it. Hand on the railing, he said, "Just remember, a lot of people are on your side."

I twisted my mouth with distaste and rested one foot on top of the other. "There aren't really . . . sides. It's just . . . a thing."

"You know what I mean. Some of us don't *care* who you're attracted to." He winked. "I like your hair that way, incidentally. And no, I'm not hitting on you."

I laughed—which felt foreign to me but not unwelcome—and rolled my eyes. "Thanks. And thanks again for . . . back there."

"Not a prob." Wade took the stairs three at a time.

Once he was out of sight, I thought maybe this day wouldn't wind up being so horrible after all.

Of course, I was wrong.

CHAPTER THREE

Top Six Things about the First Day of Senior Year That Sucked

1. Seeing Paige attached by the tongue to Marcos in five different locations throughout the day. (Um, get a room? Please.)
2. The fact that she didn't even seem to notice my efforts to look hot that day.
3. The icky Dalton/Wingmen confrontation.
4. Hearing every rude variation of the word *lesbian* whispered behind hands all day long by homophobic idiots and/or lemmings. (It shouldn't have bothered me—because who gives a rat's ass what they think?—but I'm human. It did.)
5. Feeling like the Dumped Lesbo Poster Child of Creighton High (which could be a variation of number four, but also applies directly to number six).
6. Being pressured to head up the formation of Creighton High's very first Gay-Straight Alliance.

Yeah. I know. Can you believe it?

Less than two days after the Biggest Trauma of My Life—at least so far—and they want me to form and run a freakin' *club*.

The thing is, I'm totally cool with having a GSA at our school. I mean, it's about damn time Creighton realized that—YO!—many of its students are gay, and we deserve the same treatment as the straight kids. But do I want to spearhead the thing? Hella no. Refer to number four above. How did I suddenly get branded an extrovert? A joiner? I've been in school with most of these kids for three-plus years, some of them since the fat-pencil days of kindergarten. You'd think they'd know I am a fade-into-the-woodwork kind of person. Just because I was (a) publicly outed in a cruelly global way and (b) dumped at the same time doesn't mean I want to go on some banner-carrying tirade within the confines of CHS's hallways.

So totally not.

But how to convey all that to this group of bright-eyed students gazing at me like I'm some sort of celebrity messiah who should lead them to the bucket of gold at the end of the Big Gay Rainbow?

Jen Willis, starting point guard on the basketball team, had been the one to lure me down to an open classroom after school, asking if we could talk privately. I always liked Jen, so I said sure. I figured she wanted to offer me her sympathy or something like that. Much to my surprise, about ten people were gathered for this "intervention" of sorts, including Wade Janson, who sprawled on the teacher's desk, legs dangling, taking it all in.

To be honest, I stuck around because of Wade. I was curious.

So, the Mia Supporters' Coalition presented their GSA bandwagon and were now waiting breathlessly for me to jump onto it, which wasn't going to happen even if they started throwing hundred-dollar bills. But at least these kids were being *nice* to me, unlike Dalton and others. I didn't just want to say "No way" and walk out.

I suck at disappointing people. Too bad Paige doesn't share that trait.

"It's a good idea," I said finally, hedging, rubbing the side of my hand against my jaw line. "But I'm not really up for being the head of a club right now. Sorry."

Larry Cummings (yes, puke boy from fifth grade who, incidentally, is now solidly emo and a gifted gloom-and-doom poetry writer) leaned forward, his thickly lined baby browns intense. "We understand it was hard, the Lake Bash—"

"Stop," I said, holding up a hand. "Rule number one. If you want me to stick around, leave that night out of the conversation permanently. Please." My stomach flopped. "I don't want to talk about it, now or ever."

Everyone nodded like I possessed some sort of clout, which was new for me.

I'd never had clout before. Doubt? Yes. Loads. But never clout.

Larry continued. "Okay. It's just that, Mia, a lot of us have gone through stuff like . . . that, which will remain unmentioned . . . but privately. Your story is all over the school. Sorry," he added, probably in response to my grimace. "But it is. And it's the perfect springboard to show the conservative faculty and school board we need a group like this, that we have rights, too."

"Yeah. I want to be able to take my girlfriend to homecoming," Jen said.

"I'd like to take a date, too," Larry said, rolling his eyes with an impressive amount of drama, "and not have to pretend we're two loser guys who couldn't get dates with girls."

I wondered briefly whom Larry was dating. "I understand that. But—"

"Mr. Horst offered to be our faculty sponsor," Jen interjected, her words filled with hope, "so we have all the pieces in place. It wouldn't be a difficult job."

Mr. Horst? I raised my eyebrows. The German teacher? "Is he . . . ?"

They all nodded as if this were common knowledge. Huh. Who knew? Guess my Gaydar had been thoroughly Paige-washed along with the rest of my life.

I shot a glance at Wade. He just shrugged, like, *whatev.* I liked that he truly didn't give a rip. I could definitely hang with Wade Janson.

Still, easy job or not, it was time to cut to the issue at hand. "Look, I'm all for the group, but I'm sorry, I don't want to lead."

"Why don't you do it, Jen?" Wade said.

All eyes turned his way. Jen seemed to perk up at the vote of confidence.

"You're great at that kind of stuff, and it's obvious Mia's not up for it." He gave me a private I-got-yer-back smile. "Although I have a suggestion."

"What's that?" Larry asked, staring worshipfully at Wade. He'd be bummed to find out that the football captain wasn't gay, only gay friendly. Bubbles were bursting all over this week, weren't they? *Yipp-freakin'-ee.*

"Instead of such a narrow focus," Wade said, "why don't we expand the mission of the group and call it an Acceptance Alliance—"

"Wait," I said, on the verge of truly laughing for the first time since Saturday night. "You want to call it AA?"

Wade's eyes widened for one startled second, then he smirked. "I hadn't really considered the acronym. Obviously. But sure, why not?"

I shrugged. Indeed, why not? "I guess it would be kind of funny."

"Yeah. Plus, that way, kids from all walks of life who don't feel like they . . . fit in, or whatever, can join. Outsiders." He looked around at each person in turn. "There are a lot of us, gay or not, who'd want a group like that."

"Even you?" Larry asked, looking mystified. "You're the captain of the football team. How could you possibly be an outsider?"

Wade shrugged. "See, that's just it. Assumptions. None of us really know each other. But we all have our presumptions. And our insecurities. Just because I play sports doesn't mean I fit into the jock group I'm *supposed* to mesh with. So, yeah, even me. That's why I'm here."

"Well, we'd love to have you," Larry said reverently.

I cocked an eyebrow at Wade.

He managed to ignore me. "If the gossip in the hallways today is any indication, I think AA could potentially draw a lot more members than a strictly defined GSA. It's pathetic, but some students will shy away from a GSA. With AA, we cast a wider net, accomplish the same goal, and we'll all get to know people out of our normal circles."

"That's actually a great idea. Wish I'd come up with it," Larry said thoughtfully, tugging at his scrappy soul patch. "I'm just so gay-focused, I guess, which could be as bad as being totally straight-focused. Almost," he said, a humorous glimmer in his eye. "But your idea is much better, more inclusive."

Everyone murmured his or her agreement.

"I'll get it going with Mr. Horst's help, then," Jen said, "if you're sure, Mia—"

"I'm one-hundred-percent sure."

"We'd love it if you'd be involved, though," Jen added.

What is a group without a poster girl? I thought in a moment of unprovoked snark. Pushing that from my mind, I made an *X* over my heart. "I'll come to the meetings, hang out, whatever. I don't have anything to hide. And I appreciate all of you thinking I'd be the go-to person. I'm just . . ."—I flailed about for the right words— "not up to being anything more than a member. I hereby pass the torch to you, Jen. Deal?"

"Deal," she said.

Nine grins and one thoughtful glance (Wade's) glowed at me.

And so it was that CHSAA (which I liked to think of as "Sha-zaa!") got its start—all from Little Nothing Me dating and getting dumped by one of the hottest straight girls in school. Who'da thunk?

• • •

One week later, after Jen had blanketed the hallways with information about the group, "Sha-zaa!" met for the first time. Twenty-two kids showed up, every shape, size, grade level, ethnicity, and—I'd assume—sexual identity, although for the most part, that was hard to discern, since (1) none of us sported a rainbow flag tattoo on our foreheads, and (2) we blended in with everyone else, of course.

In my pessimistic state of mind, I'd figured that only the original ten people would show, and one by one, people would drop like monkeys with the Ebola virus until it was me, Jen, Larry, and Wade sitting in a room staring at each other in glum silence. Not so much.

For the first time this year, I felt a little whip of enthusiasm. I had a place to belong, a purpose.

At the beginning of this inaugural meeting, we pushed all the desks against the walls of the designated classroom and sat in a circle. Mr. Horst decided we should all get to know each other by introducing ourselves and telling everyone what brought us to the group. He broke the ice by telling us that he had agreed to be the faculty advisor because he's gay, and he and his partner have been together since high school (!!!), where they faced more than their share of problems. Back in the day, there was no such thing as a GSA, but he and his partner, Manny, persevered.

Let me just say, I've never in a million years paired the words *Mr. Horst* and *romantic* in the same thought, but there you have it. Just knowing he'd fallen in love when he was our age and *it lasted* gave me this buoyant sense of hope, which, considering the current train wreck called "my life," was *huge*.

I yanked myself back to the matter at hand. Introductions.

I'd inadvertently tuned out a couple of the gay kids I already knew, but I caught "Felicity Holmes. Junior. I'm straight. But I'm joining the group because, well"—pretty Felicity, from the theater crowd, tucked her pixielike strawberry blond hair behind one ear, then lifted her chin—"because I believe in abstinence before marriage, and I've gotten a lot of grief lately. I've been dumped. A lot. All because I choose not to have premarital sex."

"Same here," came the deep, smoky voice of motorcycle-riding rebel Braxton Malony, alleged to have hooked up hundreds of times, and never with the same girl twice (except for a few standouts).

"Cut it out, Braxton. I'm serious," Felicity said, her cheeks pinkening.

"I'm serious, too," Braxton insisted. He turned his attention to the group. "Since I'm talking, I may as well go next. I'm Braxton. Senior. I know what you've all heard about me, but it's not true. I'm a virgin," he said, the conviction in his words silencing everyone. "And I intend to stay that way until I'm married. You can imagine how well that goes over in my crowd, hence the reputation." His gaze fell on me. "Anyway, I know what it's like to have people talk about you in the hallways, say stuff that isn't true. It sucks. That's why I'm here."

Felicity and Braxton shared a smile that, swear to God, should've come with a romantic soundtrack. *Never* would I have associated those two, but I predicted a celibate hookup before winter break.

Plus, okay, color me shocked. Not just because Braxton Malony was a virgin *or* because he'd used the word *hence* properly in spoken language (I'd misjudged him—shame on me). Rather, because it looked like CHSAA was a hit with all kinds of kids. Yay, us. Well, yay, Jen.

"Welcome, Felicity and Braxton," Jen said. "Thanks for sharing." She peered expectantly at Wade.

He cleared his throat. "Wade Janson. Senior. My brother is gay. I hate hearing homophobic crap talk, and I confront people who do it. Always have, always will." He shrugged. "Let's just say it hasn't made me the most popular football captain in Creighton High history."

Everyone laughed.

"I'm glad you're here, Wade. Thanks," Jen said, and then she looked at me.

For a moment, I merely stared back. Eventually, I jolted and said, "Oh. My turn, huh?" I moistened my lips, then opened them to speak.

Just then the door swung wide, accidentally banging against one of the desks and yanking everyone's attention that way. Kellen Morales, Creighton High's answer to fame, came in. Her gaze widened and darted around the room. "Oops. Sorry. Sorry I'm late. I was just—never mind. Carry on."

Okay, *totally* unexpected.

Questions and theories rushed through my brain like swift water. Why would Kellen be here? Everyone likes her. I mean, when she's actually in school, everyone likes her. What's not to like? But she's been a professional ballet dancer since, like, fifth grade, and she's only at Creighton when she isn't cast in a production somewhere like New York or London or Hollywood. No exaggeration. She's an oddity, at least to me. Older-seeming, worldly. She has an established career, and I'm not talking the "would-you-like-fries-with-that" kind.

That had to be it. Yeah.

It makes sense that she'd feel like an outsider, considering she's never really fit into any particular group, even if it's only because she hasn't had the chance. But she's a nice girl, confident and beautiful. Elegant. Lean and muscular in that classic dancer way. I found myself studiously not looking at her because I *wanted* to look at her, if you get my drift. And I was *done* being attracted to straight girls.

Forever. Period. End of story.

"That's okay, dear," Mr. Horst said to Kellen, interrupting my racing thoughts. He moved a chair in for her. "We're just introducing ourselves. You can catch up on what you missed after the meeting."

Jen gave her a little wave. Once Kellen settled in, Jen said, "Go ahead, Mia."

"Okay, um, I'm Mia Salazar. Senior. I guess I don't have to tell you why I'm here. Let's just say I'm the tip of the CHSAA iceberg." Everyone laughed—with me, not at me. "Anyway, so . . . yep, gay. Happily so. I've been going to a GLBTQ youth center in Denver since I was, um, thirteen. It's a pretty cool place, if that's something you're looking for, and you can meet kids from all over." I hiked my chin toward the desk where Wade was sitting. "I brought brochures and calendars of the center's events that you can take. Oh, and you don't have to be gay to go there."

"Thanks, Mia," Jen said, smiling.

We continued around the circle. There were a few Goths and

emos from Larry's crowd—some gay, some straight, some gender-fluid. A couple of fiscally disadvantaged foster kids who felt out of place in Creighton—one of the wealthier schools in the area. Our resident supergenius, Jean-Paul St. Germain, who basically doesn't fit in with anyone because he has more brainpower than all of us clumped together and he always spouts off with random, esoteric data at the weirdest times. Three Sunni Islamic kids who'd felt unfairly targeted by some (ignorant—my aside) students. And, of course, a whole slew of gay and bisexual kids from every clique imaginable—more than I knew about, actually.

Finally, Jen turned to Kellen. "Last but not least," she said.

I cut my glance to the floor tiles. Still gleaming, but give it a month and they'd be scuffed and dull despite Custodian Craig's best efforts. Poor guy.

"Hi. I'm Kellen Morales. Senior. I'm not here at school much because I'm a professional dancer. I, uh, study with a private tutor when I'm on the road."

Just as I suspected.

"But that's not why I came," Kellen said. "I'm a lesbian, too."

My gaze shot up from the floor to her face. *What?*

"And I just broke up with my girlfriend after two years." Kellen's eyes filled with tears, but she waved them off. "Sorry. Anyway, it sucks. Getting dumped . . . sucks. I don't know how to put it any better."

"*Sucks* sizes it up pretty darn well," Larry interjected.

Kellen nodded. "I miss her, but I'm angry. Sad, too." She looked straight toward me. "I think it'll help to be around people who . . . get it."

Everyone murmured his or her sympathies, and then, with all intros completed, Jen and Mr. Horst launched into a discussion of how they were trying to get approval for same-sex couples to openly attend homecoming together—a first for the tight-ass Creighton school board—but, forgive me for being shallow, all I could think was, KELLEN MORALES IS FREAKIN' GAY?! Score one for our team.

Tacky. I know. But it went through my head. Hey, at least I'm honest.

• • •

After the meeting, we reassembled in the room, then I bolted like prey. My brain buzzed. I needed to be alone to soak it all in.

Twenty-two kids?

Kellen Morales, a lesbian?

Creighton has a GSA—well, an AA?

Unbelievable, all of it.

I'd just heaved an elbow against the door bar at the front of the school when I heard "Mia! Wait up!"

I turned. Reluctantly at first, but I straightened up (no pun intended) immediately when I saw who'd called my name. What can I say? I'm susceptible to cute, classy girly-girls.

Kellen Morales even jogged gracefully. With her long neck and honed muscles, she looked like a gazelle. She wasn't the least bit winded when she caught up to me. "Hi."

"Hey." I wasn't sure why she'd sought me out, so I just waited. I hated feeling so guarded, but how else was I supposed to act after the Paige thing?

We stood there for several long, awkward seconds, then Kellen said, "So. Want to go get some tea and bitch about our evil ex-girlfriends?"

So not what I expected. I blurted out a laugh and then couldn't stop. Kellen joined in. I'm not sure what prompted my slap-happiness. Probably relief that she didn't want to pick through the bones of my roadkill romance like the rest of the universe. Rather, she'd been smashed on the same stretch of pavement, which was sick but oddly comforting. "Sure," I said, my desire for alone time dissipating. "Any place in particular you want to go?"

Kellen pursed her lips, thinking. "If you don't mind driving, we can head to Denver and go to Common Grounds." She shrugged with apology. "I have a bazillion frequent-flier miles, but no driver's license. Go figure."

"Common Grounds it is," I said, holding the door. "I've never been there."

"You'll dig it." Kellen passed through, smiling her thanks. We were halfway through the parking lot when she asked, "So . . . your girl-friend was straight?"

I huffed. "Well, not when we were making out."

Kellen threw her head back and laughed, then did some pirouette thingie in the parking lot. "You are exactly the kind of person I need around me right now," she said, holding up her palm.

I smacked mine against hers.

"High-five for the Piss and Moan Posse," she said.

I smiled. "PAMP," I said, trying it out on my tongue. I beeped my car doors open, and we both threw our stuff in the back. "It's perfect. Well, almost."

"Almost?"

I fired up the engine as Kellen clicked her seat belt into place. "It would have been funnier if our acronym could've been PIMP instead." We roared off into the afternoon, goofing and carefree—or at least faking it, trying to figure out some way to call ourselves PIMPs (never found one). I felt better than I had in weeks.

CHAPTER FOUR

Kellen and I slipped into a comfortable, companionable mode with astonishing ease, probably because we both inhabited the same circle of hell, relationship-wise. Or maybe simply because she was cool. Then again, it could be the PAMP/PIMP thing, which was a crack-up, at least to us, and right then, no one else mattered. But I'd had enough loss lately. I didn't want to get hooked to a new friend and then have her blaze for parts unknown within weeks, leaving me behind. I had to know. "How long will you be here this time?" I asked as casually as I could manage, after we'd sat down with our tea—hers Earl Grey, mine chai.

"All year."

I had a mouthful of spicy, hot chai, so I raised my eyebrows at her in pleasant surprise rather than speaking. Or splattering, which is so not a date getter (not that I'm trying to get a date, mind you).

She nodded. "Yeah, I know. Unprecedented."

I swallowed. "So, what's the deal?"

"Call me selfish." She quirked her lips to one side. "I wanted one full school year of feeling like a normal teenager, and since we're seniors—"

"I get that. Very cool," I told her. A sense of relief I couldn't explain spread through me. "How do your parents feel?"

"Oh, they're great. It's my management who's giving me fits."

Management. Her *management*. Groove on *that*, peeps. Lame admission time: I was a bit starstruck. I wasn't ready for a new hookup (side note: whom was I trying to convince by repeating this in my mind over and over? Million-dollar question, that one), and clearly neither was Kellen, but I won't deny feeling an instinctive pull toward her, and not just because she was cool and sexy and here for the year. Or because she had "management." She just seemed so down-to-earth, so comfortable in her skin. So NOT Paige.

I couldn't be happier that she'd *be* here. Meaning Kellen, not Paige.

"Plus, Bianca—that's my ex," Kellen continued, "is choreographing the ballet I'd auditioned for, which would've taken me to New York for most of this year." She toyed with a sugar packet listlessly. "I got a part, but I'm not ready to face her. So I backed out."

"That explains the management freakout?"

"Yep."

I could so understand that. On both sides. "Is Bianca older?"

"Yeah, but not creepily or criminally so."

"I have an idea. You stay here and face Paige every day, and I'll go deal with Bianca." I kicked my feet up onto one of the unoccupied chairs at our four top. "Of course, there's that little issue about me not being able to dance."

"That might pose a problem." Kellen smirked. "I have a better idea. We'll both stay here, hang out, avoid unattainable girls, and ignore Paige and Marcos."

I smiled, but it quickly morphed into a grimace punctuated by a sigh. If I were a superhero, I'd no doubt be dubbed Pathetico-Girl or the Bionic Wuss-ball. "I won't lie, it's hard to ignore her when she and Marcos are groping each other in the halls every single day and the whole school is drowning in gossip about my business."

"Screw the gossips." She winged aside the sugar packet and sat back. "People gossip because your life is more interesting than theirs."

I tilted my head to the side. "I never thought of it that way."

"It's true. Gossip in the world of dance? Rampant. You should have seen the shit storm when I hooked up with Bianca." She rolled one shoulder and propped her feet up next to mine. "But look at it this way. You're totally out now at Creighton, so you stole their power. They have nothing to hold over your head. Pretty soon a new scandal will erupt, and you and your infinite gayness," she said with a smirk, "will be like last week's issue of *People* magazine. Bo-o-oring."

"Excellent point," I said, lighter all of a sudden.

"If you want my opinion on the Paige thing"—she held up a palm—"which I'm sure you probably don't, but oh well, I'm opinionated, so you're getting it anyway. She's trying too hard to show the world just how *into guys* she is," Kellen said.

"You think?" I pulled my bottom lip between my teeth and clutched my mug with both hands. I wanted it to be true. At least, I thought I wanted it to be true.

Of course I did. I still loved Paige, despite everything.

But could we ever repair what had been damaged? Highly unlikely.

"Definitely. It's like macho boys who flaunt how much they dig chicks because, deep down, they're attracted to guys and it scares the crap out of them."

My gaze drifted across the room to the exposed brick wall behind the barista station. Food for thought. Unfortunately, I didn't want to think. "You could be right. Still, it sure seems like she enjoys kissing *him*."

"I don't know. Scared people will suffer through anything."

Was Paige scared? Did I care? "Okay, enough Paige talk. I'm so over that." I held up a hand. "I mean, if you want to talk about Bianca—"

"Not."

"All righty, then. Moving the heck on. Tell me what it's like." At her quizzical expression, I added, "Your life, I mean. It sounds so exotic."

Kellen crinkled her nose. "Really? You won't be bored?"

"Bored? I've spent my life in Creighton, Colorado. Need I say more?"

Kellen giggled. "You asked for it." She regaled me with tales from the big stage through another chai and two shortbread cookies each. As we left Common Grounds, I realized an ally like her was just what I needed to battle my way through the mean halls of CHS (to be overly dramatic about it). I had Allison, of course, but she wasn't there to bolster me throughout the hellish school hours, and I couldn't trail after Wade like some puppy, expecting him to fight my battles. Kellen could be my daytime Allison, my sidekick, my wing woman. Speaking of that—

"Hey! You should come to Rainbow Alley with my best friend, Allison, and me this Friday," I told Kellen. "It's drag night, but that just means people perform however they want to. You could even dance if you wanted to."

"I'd love to go. But I'll probably just watch this time."

"That's cool, too." We drove without talking for a few minutes, instead cranking up Kelly Clarkson's "Never Again" and singing along with angry, effusive abandon, louder and louder until we were screaming more than singing.

After replay number six, Kellen lowered the volume. "Enough of that. My throat's starting to hurt."

"My ears are buzzing," I said.

"So, this Allison. Do I know her?"

"You might remember her. She went to elementary school with us, but she decided to go to Alternative rather than suffer through Creighton. Allison Wendall?"

Kellen's eyes brightened. "Oh! With the long curly red hair. I remember her."

"Well, she has a short blue-and-green mohawk now, but yes, that's my Al."

"A mohawk! Killer. I've always wanted to do something wild with my hair."

"Why don't you?"

She made a face. "Can't. They don't hire ballerinas with mohawks much."

I laughed, then said, "Well, your long hair is beautiful anyway. Al looks great all mohawked out, but it would be a shame if you shaved your head."

She peered at me shyly. "Thank you."

After we'd crossed into Creighton town limits, Kellen asked,

"Were you and Allison ever together as a couple?"

"What?" I bugged my eyes. "No. No way. She's my best bud. That would be like hooking up with my sister, if I had one. Ick."

"You're lucky," Kellen said, her expression winsome. "My life's so . . . unusual, I don't really have a best bud. All I had was Bianca."

I reached over and patted her leg. "Not to worry. You are more than welcome to hang with Al and me. There's always room for a third musketeer."

Kellen sighed, then relaxed her head back against the passenger seat. "I could get used to this normal teenager gig. I love my career, don't get me wrong, and I know a dancer's career is so short. I'm lucky to have started working so young, really. But sometimes you just want to chill, you know?"

"Totally." *And I'm going to love chilling with you*, I thought. But I kept that to myself. No way in hell was I going to put the moves on her (mention number three million and five in my head about being attracted to Kellen), but I was more than ready to hang out with a hot girl who wasn't afraid to be herself.

• • •

After dropping Kellen at her house with a promise to pick her up before school the next day, I sped over to True Colors, Al's mom's salon located in the great old Victorian house that used to belong to Al's grandma. I knew Al would be there. She helps her mom whenever she can. Have I mentioned how much I love their relationship? Ms. Wendall looks like a movie star from the red carpet—femme, glam, and gorgeous. Allison—just as adorable, mind you—would most likely be sporting an oversize Avalanche jersey, long baggy shorts, and Chuck Taylors when I arrived, not to mention the signature mohawk. But despite their vast superficial differences, they're tight like sisters, and Ms. Wendall never acts like she wants Allison to be anyone other than who she is. She's so cool that way.

If only Paige's parents were so accepting, maybe none of this drama-trauma would've happened. Then again, scratch that. She never even gave them the chance to accept or reject her, and if it's unfair to say that, too freakin' bad.

The bell over the door jangled when I entered the salon, which smelled of pungent hair dye mixed with the salon's signature lavender and lemongrass candles (made by Allison, the crafty little *chica*). A serenity fountain bubbled in one corner of the entry, and satellite radio piped a Gwen Stefani tune throughout the place. Ms. Wendall, who always asked me to call her Kimberly (but I couldn't make myself do it; that respect-for-your-elders thing was hammered into my psyche by my mom and my sweet *abuelita*—which is Spanish for "grandma," just FYI), glanced up from behind the front desk, where she appeared to be working on a giant stack of paperwork. "Mia! Honeybunch, what a nice surprise."

"Hi, Ms. W." I could tell she was scrutinizing my do. Hazards of the job. I have an uncle who's a dentist, and whenever you smile at him, you just know he's scoping out the pearly whites and assessing how often you floss. I'm just glad he's not a proctologist, and if you don't know what that is, look it up.

"You look gorgeous," she said as she made her way around the kidney-shaped distressed-wood counter. "The cut's holding up well." She fiddled with my hair. "What products did you use to style this morning?"

I dutifully rattled them off.

"I love a client who listens to my expert advice," she said with a sigh.

"I follow directions well," I said. If I didn't listen to her, I'd look like crap. What the hell did I know about hair?

"I heard about you and Paige, hon." Ms. W shook her head slowly. "How are you holding up?"

Ugh. *So* did not want to discuss this. "I'm fine," I lied, peering around the brightly painted salon. "Is Al here?"

"She is. Storeroom. Go on back." She squeezed my shoulder and lowered her tone to the sympathy range. "Just remember, as much as this hurts right now, there will be a lot of girls before you find Ms. Right."

"Uh, thank you," I said. BLEHHHH! I wheeled off toward the stock area, nodding and saying hello to the stylists at their stations as I traversed the epicenter of the salon as quickly as possible.

I stopped at the threshold of the stockroom, which appeared empty. "Al?" I said, scanning the area.

From her position on the floor, reloading the shelves, Al leaned back to peer around a shelf and smiled. "Hey, chickadee. How much did it suck today?"

She meant school. Duh. Probably didn't have to tell you that. "Same ol'," I told her, crossing into the room. "But we had our first CHSAA meeting this afternoon, and you'll never guess who showed up."

"Lay it on me."

"Kellen Morales."

Al scrambled to her feet and came toward me, eyes glittering. "Are you kidding me? Is she family?"

"Yep." I sat on a discarded swivel stool.

A Cheshire cat grin spread across Al's face. "Whoa! Score one for us."

Now you can see why Allison and I are besties. We aren't just on the same page, we *wrote* the same page. I smirked. "My feelings exactly. She and I just went out for tea. She's a recent dumpee, too, so we had a lot to talk about."

"Dang," Al said, joking. "A tea date right out of the chute. I suppose that means you've already got dibs on her?"

"Dude, she's not a freakin' eBay auction. You sound like a guy."

"I know. Just kidding."

I hooked my heels in the rungs of the stool. "But, anyway, yes."

"Huh?"

"Dibs." I knew my face had turned red, because it flamed.

From her expression, I could tell I'd managed to stun her. "Really?"

I held up both palms. "I'm not ready and she's not ready, but I really like her and she's totally hot. So if we're ever ready at the same time—"

"I get the picture." Al smiled. "You're probably more her type anyway. Besides," she added in a smug tone, bouncing slightly on her feet, "I met someone at school, too. She's coming to the Alley with us Friday night if that's okay."

I laughed. "Awesome! So's Kellen. I just invited her. It'll be like a double date that isn't. Details about the girl, please."

"Of course!" She glanced around. "Let me finish up here first."

"Can I help?" I asked, lifting my chin toward the storage shelf.

She shrugged. "I'm almost done, but sure."

We settled cross-legged next to each other on the hardwood floor. Al, who knew her stuff when it came to product, scanned the stock numbers on the shelf's edge, compared them with the shipping manifest, then requested various bottles and tubes of color. I—her clueless lackey—rooted through the jumbled crate and handed them over. "So, tell me about her while we work," I said, unable to wait.

"Three eighty-four, ash blond," she said, holding out her hand.

"That's an interesting name."

"Ha-ha."

I pawed through the bottles, then passed over the first of five I'd found.

"Her name is Chanel, actually."

"Hot."

"Yep. She came from one of the directionals," Al said, referring to either North, South, East, or West High Schools in Denver. "I can't remember which, but she's half Mexican, half Korean. Studies kickboxing. Tiny, tough, gorgeous."

"I can't wait to meet her."

Al grinned. "I told her all about you."

"I did the same with Kellen."

"Did she remember me? Three sixty-six, champagne blond."

"She did. She remembered your long, curly red hair," I teased as I riffled through my cache, and handed her a lone bottle.

Kellen ignored the hair reminder. "Anything new on the Paige front?"

"Status quo. Still sucking face with Ick-boy and avoiding me like herpes."

"Eh, her loss." Al straightened the bottles into a neat row. "Any more champagne blonds?"

I shook my head.

"The football captain bow out of your merry band of misfits yet?" she asked, running a finger down her stock sheet. "One fourteen, deep mahogany."

"No," I said, handing her the first of about twelve bottles. Apparently deep mahogany wasn't the popular shade for fall. Dissing the brunettes again. Typical. "Wade's really cool. You'd like him."

"So, invite him to the Alley, too."

I'd never thought of that. "Maybe I will. I bet he'd come. He doesn't seem to fit in with his clique at school very well."

"I hate cliques."

"Me, too. But they are what they are."

"That's what I love about Alternative. We're all one big clique of noncliquers. And, I gotta tell you, we all seem to click."

We laughed. After the last bottle of one fourteen had been shelved, Al brushed her hands together, stood, then reached out to yank me to my feet. "Okay, so Friday night at the Alley it is."

"I can't wait!"

"I know." She grinned. "I have a sneaking suspicion this year's going to turn out great after all."

A guarded sense of hopefulness came over me as I followed Al out in the main salon area, but I had the urge to knock on wood to guarantee she was right.

• • •

On Friday, I picked up Al first (as the best-friend credo dictates), then Kellen, and last Chanel, who lived closer to Rainbow Alley than we Creighton creeps. After introductions all around, we fell into that easy talk-over-each-other conversation that friends tend to engage in. Unexpectedly, in the middle of the conversation, a *missing-Paige* wave swept over me, but why? I was in a car filled with cool gay girls eager to head to the Alley. Why should I give a crap about Paige?

My anger flared like a bad match, white-hot for a second but fizzling quickly.

Thing is, maybe *she* could turn her romantic feelings on and off like a switch, but I couldn't. As much as she'd crushed me, I still loved her and didn't know when or how it would stop. Just call me Sap of the Year.

Allison and Chanel were in a heated debate about the Broncos season opener, and I'd fallen silent with my tumultuous thoughts. I hadn't meant to. Kellen reached over and briefly squeezed my shoulder. "It'll be okay."

I blinked with surprise initially, then flashed her a quick apologetic grimace. Weird how she could just read me, you know? "I'm sorry. It just sucks sometimes," I said in what was arguably one of the world's biggest understatements.

"You don't have to apologize. Believe me, I understand."

And she did. That was the best part about Kellen.

"How about this," she said. "Just for tonight, we won't think about anyone or anything that makes us sad."

"I can try."

She pursed her lips, thinking. "If I say I'll dance at the Alley, will that help?"

I did a double take. "Seriously? You will?"

She winked. "Anything to keep you smiling."

Glug! My stomach performed a round-off, back handspring, full-twisting layout combination and barely stuck the landing. *Dude.* Kellen-freakin'-Morales wanted to make me smile. Uh, believe me, I could think of about twenty different ways she could accomplish that goal, and dancing at drag night wasn't even in the top five. But I kept that to myself for now. "How about you and I lip-synch a duet instead? Kelly Clarkson?"

"'Never Again'?"

"That's what I'm thinking."

"Deal." She held out her fist, which I knocked with my own. "Nothing like a good 'fuck off' song to empower a couple of dumpees."

"What are you guys plotting up there?" Al said, leaning forward from the back seat. Not that she had to. I drove a compact hybrid, not a stretch limo, for God's sake. We were practically sitting on top of each other as it was.

"Our duet for drag. That's all."

"You're going to sing together?" Chanel asked. "So cool."

"You know what they say," Al said. "Lesbians who lip-synch together at the Alley lip-lock together later."

"Shut up, Al," I said, laughing, but I wondered if it was true. Hoped it was.

Wished, dreamed, prayed, *fantasized.*

I shot a quick glance at the girl in my passenger seat, and my stomach flopped. Oh, man. How could I have a thing for Kellen when I knew neither of us was ready? When I was still in love with Paige? When there was only one constant in my life: utter confusion?

Can you say "Glutton for punishment"?

CHAPTER FIVE

Top Six Reasons Things Were Finally Looking Up

1. As editor in chief of the *Creighton Caller*, Paige was basically ordered by the faculty advisor to run a front-page article about CHSAA. This required her to interview Mr. Horst, Jen, and a few other members, all of whom knew exactly how she'd treated me. Sweet vindication.

2. Kellen and I had become so inseparable in and out of school, people soon referred to us as Moralazar. Nice, because I've been called *much* worse (not to mention I liked being connected to Kellen in people's minds).

3. Allison and Chanel were a bona fide couple!! Yay, Al!

4. Being truly out at school proved utterly freeing. I felt powerful, fearless, light.

5. Thanks to my friends Kellen, Al, and Wade, the scab of Paige's cruelty had begun to heal. She'd made her choice, and I was having too much fun to focus on the past.

6. CHSAA was a huge success. And I wasn't in charge! HUZZAH!

It didn't take long for the whole school to start speculating about Kellen and me, which—I won't lie—rocked. Dalton and his idiot goons might think "a girl like Paige Knox" would never go for me, but I knew they were stung by the whole Kellen twist. It showed on their stupid faces. Ha! Call me shallow—whatever. I loved it. Paybacks are a bitch, as they say.

Luckily, Kel got swept up in the furor, too.

She and I decided to play it to the hilt, go the Bonnie Raitt route, and give 'em something to talk about. We strode through the halls holding hands, shoulders back, wearing our "Lesbians?! WHERE?!" T-shirts just so we could laugh about the waves of silence that trailed us like smoke. More and more, people just got used to us, which is how it *should* be. We weren't hurting anyone. And, as a side benefit, it got easier every day to ignore Paige and Marcos. But the most interesting and unexpected reaction was that Paige stopped ignoring *me*.

Yeah. I know. Go fig!

Whenever Kel and I passed by them, Paige would either break free of the face sucking to glance surreptitiously at us or continue making out but with her eyes open, so she could watch us over Marcos's shoulder as we passed. I moved from wondering what she was thinking to simply not giving a crap. Well . . . mostly. Much as I would have loved to do it, I couldn't seem to write off my first love that easily.

We were four weeks into the school year, four weeks away from homecoming, on our third CHSAA meeting and up to forty members. The meetings had become more like social events, with everyone laughing and interacting, all clique lines erased the moment we entered that room. Though a lot of our early lobbying seemed to center around equal rights for the GLBTQ students, we intended to provide something for everyone. For example, we were holding a massive bake sale to raise money, so the kids who couldn't otherwise afford to would be able to attend homecoming. And on the final day of Ramadan, the whole group agreed to fast with the Islamic kids from dawn until dusk, as a symbolic show of respect for their religious observance. We had equal opportunity coolness going on with "SHA-ZAA!"

That afternoon, Kellen and I were sitting with Wade waiting for the meeting to begin. We'd teamed up over the past week to find him— poor guy—the perfect nonheinous homecoming date, but the pickings were slim. So far we'd given the big negatory to his first six totally lame suggestions. Cute and cool as he is, Dude has *zero* skills when it comes to choosing worthy girls, I swear. (Not that I have room to talk.)

"How about Miranda Brae?" he asked, all hopeful, like a golden retriever.

"Ew!" Kellen and I both squealed.

"Come on, she's not that bad," Wade said, unsure. "Is she?"

"Fake hair," I said, lifting my index finger. "Fake boobs"—*middle finger*—"fake nails"—*ring finger*—"fake tan"—*pinky*—"FAKE"— *thumb*. Kellen and I smacked him playfully from either side.

"Yeah, but what are you trying to say?" Wade asked, laughing and curling into himself to deflect our blows.

"Cross her off the list!" Kellen said. "That's what."

Just then, the classroom door opened, and Jen bustled in followed by Mr. Horst. The back of my neck prickled; I don't know why. Something in their energy, the way excitement seemed to crackle from their smiles like electricity, settled the raucous group immediately. The unfortunate Miranda Brae and her infinite fakeness faded from our brains, thank God.

"Hey, kids," Mr. Horst said, rubbing his palms together. "Listen up."

Everyone slid into seats or settled cross-legged on the floor, and all attention arrowed toward him.

"What's going on?" asked Larry, sitting forward on his chair in his black pencil-leg pleather pants, a Boy George vintage T-shirt, and combat boots. He smelled of clove cigarettes and Jean Paul Gaultier fragrance.

Jen bounced on her feet, then grinned at Mr. Horst.

He stepped into the circle and opened his arms. I swear, it looked like he wanted to cry. "I am ecstatic to announce that, after a lot of hard work and research, mostly by Jen, the school board approved same-sex dates for homecoming."

The entire room erupted into cheers, and everyone leaped to their feet, high-fives and hugs all around. This was a massively progressive step for our conservative school, and it was so awesome that *all* the "Sha-zaa!" kids viewed it as a group victory, regardless of gender identity or sexual preference or the reason they had joined in the first place. I mean, can you grasp the implications?

Kellen and I smacked palms with Wade, then threw ourselves into each other's arms for a hug. She swung me around—damn, dancers are strong—then slid me down the front of her body to set me on my feet. I stumbled back. My legs were wobbly for some reason. Our eyes met and held, and then I knew.

The room was a motion-filled cacophony, but it all disappeared for me in that instant. My breathing shallowed and my gaze dropped to her lips. I couldn't help it. "Hey," I said softly, a sudden knowledge blossoming inside me.

"Hey," she whispered.

I wondered if she could hear my heart pounding.

We edged closer, hesitated. Moved closer again.

And then we kissed.

I had to convince myself it was a friendly, celebratory kiss, because I wasn't mentally prepared to hope for more, but, God, her lips felt so good against mine, and her warm breath tasted like strawberries. Friendly and celebratory or not, I wanted more. It hit me like a home-run swing of the bat.

When we broke apart, both of us seemed shocked by what had happened. Not in a bad way, at least not for me. I didn't know how she felt, but it'd sure seemed like she was as blown away by the kiss as I was. We sat closer for the rest of the meeting, listening to Mr. Horst lay out the details. Neither of us looked at the other. I, however, remained acutely aware of her nearness, of every breath she took, of each time she moved and her shoulder brushed mine. An uncharacteristic shyness overtook me. I only half listened to the rest of the meeting because my brain buzzed with questions about and feelings for Kellen, but I did catch that the various groups involved in CHSAA—the abstinence kids, the Muslim kids, and so on—received permission to hand out literature at the pep rally pre-homecoming. It was like this win-win-freakin'-win all the way around for our group.

But on my mind? Kellen.

I knew what I wanted, pretty much, but terror left me cold.

Then again, I didn't *want* to run scared.

Dilemma.

By the end of the meeting, I decided to get my brave on. As she and I walked out to my car close enough to hold hands (but not doing so), I peered at her out of the corner of my eye. "So . . . listen. I have a crazy idea."

"Lay it on me," she said, sounding utterly normal. "I'm all about crazy ideas."

For a brief moment, I worried I was the only one who'd felt the explosiveness of our kiss. The potential. She didn't seem to be suffering from internal freakout like I was. Still . . . *now or never, Mia.* I cleared my throat. "What if we go to homecoming together?"

She hesitated for, like, half a second, but long enough for me to doubt myself.

I freaked and added, "As friends, I mean," in a humiliated rush. "I know neither of us is ready for—"

"Some of us might be ready."

"W-what?"

"I said, some of us might be ready. To try, at least," she added shyly.

I lost my footing and stumbled to a stop. Kellen stopped, too, and faced me. For a long stretch, I simply stared at her. "Really?"

She moved closer and grabbed one of my hands. The fall air stirred up the crispy leaves around our feet, and above us, the clear sky was the bluest of blue. "If you aren't, I understand. Going as friends is okay, I promise."

"N-no. I just thought you might not . . ."

She tilted her head in a way that made her long hair tumble over one shoulder and twirl in the breeze. The mannerism was so unaffected. So *kill-me* sexy. Did she even realize?

"I can't read your mind. But when we kissed, Mia? I felt something."

"Me, too," I whispered.

"Yeah?" Her eyes glittered.

"Could've been a fluke, I guess."

"Maybe we should test it again."

I risked stepping even closer, though my legs were still shaky and my skin tingled all over. "I think that's a good idea. Just to be sure."

"Just to be sure," Kellen repeated, reaching up to cup my face with both hands. Her lips on mine felt soft, sweet, warm. A myriad of emotions set flight inside me. I deepened the kiss, pulling her toward me until our bodies touched, chest to knee. From somewhere off to our left, I heard a wolf whistle and some guys yelling out rude comments, but I didn't break away. Instead, I lifted a hand to flip off whoever it was and kept on kissing Kellen. I never wanted to stop kissing Kellen. Never, ever, ever. But we couldn't spend the rest of our lives lip-locked in the senior parking lot, so we eventually broke apart on a sigh.

"Yep, I'm sure," she said.

"Me, too. Way."

"So, homecoming as a real date?"

"Definitely," I said.

"What do you say we get out of here?" she asked, smoothing the backs of her fingers down the side of my face.

"Excellent plan." I threaded my hand into hers. "Where do you want to go?" As if it mattered. Right then, I'd follow her pretty much anywhere.

"Well . . . my parents won't be home for another two hours."

The implication stalled my breath. It took me a moment to regain my voice. "Sounds perfect."

She squeezed my hand and we headed toward my car. I glanced over out of sheer curiosity to see which pack of idiots had been hooting and hollering, fully expecting it to be Dalton and his wingmen. But it wasn't.

My stomach dropped to my feet. Marcos and his friends.

And, of course, Paige, whose face was that particular shade of beet red it always turned just before she started crying. Eyes wide, hands trembling slightly, she never moved. Our gazes locked for a brief second before I tore my attention away. *She made her choice, and I made mine*, I reminded myself.

So be it.

But why did it feel like I was cheating on her?

Once we'd slammed the car doors and clipped into our seat belts, I realized Kellen had witnessed the whole ugly moment, too, when she asked, "You okay?"

I flashed her a quick, hopefully nonchalant smile. "I'm great."

"Really?"

Something inside me tugged. "Yeah," I said in a half whisper. I kicked the engine over and started to back out.

"Mia, wait. We can be honest with each other, right?"

Hating that I'd ruined our first magical moment, I yanked up on the emergency brake, then covered my face with both hands. "God, Kel, I'm so sorry. That was just—"

"Don't apologize. It's okay to feel weird. If Bianca had been standing in that parking lot, I would've felt the same way, probably."

I uncovered my face and peered at her. "Really?"

She nodded, so sweet. So understanding. Too good to be true? Or just more mature than the rest of us? "Really. But that doesn't mean I'm not completely attracted to *you*. Bianca is *yesterday*. I'm looking for tomorrow."

Relief. "I feel the same. Still, I'm sorry. That was . . . awkward. It wigged me out."

"It's okay." She reached back and wound her long hair into a bun at her nape.

"You deserve better."

"Oh, please. We can take things slower if you want. Or forget it altogether—"

"No. Not that." I reached out and squeezed her leg. "I don't want to be with Paige. I want to be with you. It was weird, that's all, having her see us. She was my first serious girlfriend and"—I sighed—"I'm rambling. Just bear with me, if you can."

"Of course I can." She crinkled up her elegant nose. "Still want to come over?"

"Um . . ."

"I'll keep my hands to myself," she teased.

"Well, gee, where's the fun in that?" I said, my equilibrium easing its way back on track thanks to Kellen's carefree, trusting demeanor.

"How about a compromise then?"

"Like what?"

"From here on out, you're in the driver's seat, and I don't mean, like, in the car, because that would be a big duh."

I giggled, but then we both sobered.

"I mean, with us. Our relationship."

I wanted to cry, but in a happy way. "We have a relationship?"

"Friendships are relationships. And we can have more if we want to." She trailed her fingers down my arm. "Gotta start somewhere. Deal?"

"Deal," I said, leaning forward to cup her chin and kiss her quickly, then I laughed out loud.

"What's so funny?"

"Just a surreal moment." I reached behind her seat to look over my shoulder as I backed out. "I can't believe I kissed Kellen Morales. And in the middle of the senior parking lot, of all places."

"Give me a break," she said, shoving her hand against my shoulder playfully. "It's not like I'm Britney Spears."

"There's a relief."

We'd returned to our normal easy banter as we pulled away from school property, but I couldn't help stealing a sidelong glance over to where Paige and Marcos had been. Marcos still stood there, jaw jacking with his buddies, not a care in the world.

Paige, however, was gone.

• • •

Kellen and I hadn't done more than kiss a little (okay, a lot) and catch up on TiVo at her house, but by the time I left, I was officially head-over-heels. I'm a sap that way. That night before bed, I was in my standard nighttime wear, boxer shorts and a tank top, finishing my calculus homework, when my cell phone rang. Not an unusual occurrence; however, this was an oh-so-familiar Pink ring tone.

Paige's ring tone, to be exact. I hadn't heard that sound in so long.

My heart dropped like a sixty-pound boulder, and the tip of my pencil snapped against my notebook page. I toyed with the idea of ignoring the call. Then again, Paige and I hadn't spoken since the day of Lake Bash, and, well . . . maybe I'm weak. Or maybe I just wanted some sort of an explanation. Pick whatever rationalization you like, but in any case, curiosity grabbed me, so I clicked the phone on with shaking fingers and said nothing.

"Mia?" Paige asked, sounding vulnerable.

Whatever. She was truly the least vulnerable human being I'd ever known, but that didn't keep my heart from stuttering. A rogue wave of yearning crashed over me, and it came with one hell of a rip tide. You can't love someone like I loved Paige and not . . . drown in it all.

Still, I hardened my voice as best I could. "What do you want?"

She sighed. "So, are you seeing her?"

"What does it matter to you?" My breathing shallowed, and I hugged a pillow, scrunching my body up into my headboard, as small as possible.

"It matters," she said. "You know it matters."

I honestly didn't know what to say. I loved her, I hated her. I wanted to hear these words, I didn't. Everything twisted and warped inside me until I couldn't punch my way out of the darkness. Why was love so confusing?

"I miss you, Mimi," she said, sounding like the old Paige whom I'd loved so intensely. She used to call me on my cell after I left her just to whisper those words, even if we'd only been apart for ten minutes.

Oh, God. I squeezed my eyes shut, but a tear found its way out the corner anyway. Did she still love me? We could've had it all, but she'd ruined everything. And for what? *Marcos?* Acceptance in the Greater Hetero Universe? What was the damn point? "It sure doesn't seem like you miss me," I said finally. "You and Marcos are attached at the tonsils—"

"Mia."

Having voiced that, having *remembered* it, I regained a little of my emotional footing. Anger reared up inside me, which was good. Bring it the hell on. Clearly I needed the defense. "And—oh, wait—wasn't it you who called me a freak in front of, like, the whole school?"

Paige started crying—a pitiful, tormented sound. I'd always hated hearing her cry. "I'm sorry. I'm so sorry. I was scared and everyone was watching. It . . . slipped out."

Weak f-ing excuse. "Right. See, those words would *never* 'slip out' of my mouth because I wouldn't hurt you like that, Paige. Therein lies the difference between you and me."

"Please . . . you have to know how much I regret it."

"Well, gosh, that's great for you." Cold freakin' comfort. Once voiced, some things can't be taken back, and suddenly I just wanted to hang up, turn off my lights, and slip into oblivion. I'm not stupid. She could have called and apologized anytime in the past month, but no. She called tonight for one reason only: because she saw me and Kellen kissing. Paige didn't want me. She just didn't want anyone *else* to have me, which was so unfair. Difficult as it was, I knew what I needed to do.

God, this sucked.

I curled into my pillow. "Paige, if you're truly sorry, if you really care about me, then don't call me again." I ignored her sharp intake of breath. "I like Kellen. A lot. She and I deserve a chance."

"What about you and me?" she asked, her voice hoarse from crying. "Don't we deserve a chance?"

Everything inside me flipped and toppled again. Confusion. Regret. Sadness. Love. Anger, bitterness, *rage*. "What the hell are you talking about? Why don't you ask Marcos about our chances? All this happened because of *you*. You destroyed anything we might have had."

"That's not true. Love can overcome anything." She sniffled. "You said it yourself—we're meant for each other."

Her words kicked me in the chest. "Well, I was wrong. Does this mean you and tongue boy broke up?"

A beat passed in silence. That said it all.

"I have to go."

"Wait!"

Hang up, Mia. Just hang up. I couldn't. Why couldn't I?

"Can we at least be friends? Go for a chai?"

I pressed my lips together, warring with myself. Half of me yearned to see Paige again with an intensity that left me breathless, even though it made no sense. The other half felt desperate to avoid her. "I don't know if I'm ready for that. I may never be after what you did."

"Please," she said with a teary hiccup. "I'm confused."

"About what?"

"About *everything*. Me. You. Just . . . everything."

"Paige, you're not confused. You're *straight*. There's a difference."

"No, I'm—"

"Don't *even* try to tell me you're gay now or I'm hanging up." She sighed. "I'm just asking for . . . I need someone to talk to about all this stuff. Someone who really knows me."

I scoffed. "And you decided I was your best option?"

"Why wouldn't you be?"

"Because, apparently, I don't know you at all."

"Not true." Her voice lowered to a ravaged whisper. "I love you, Mimi. Please, you know what we have."

"*Had.*" Damn her. I wanted to say no. Really. I *told* myself not to get caught in her web again. But the codependent words that emerged from my mouth were "I'll think about it, okay?"

"Really?"

I hesitated. Panicked. "I have to go, Paige."

"Okay. I love you." Silence. After a moment, she added, "Mi? Did you hear me? I said—"

"I heard." Shaky, awash with shame and confusion, I whispered, "Me, too, you," then hung up, stunned.

Oh, God. I'd just told Paige I still loved her. What a pathetic idiot.

I mean, I *did* love her, in a way. It doesn't just go away. But I probably didn't have to let *her* know that. Ugh!

How was I going to explain this to Kellen? Or to Al, who would want to kill me, especially when I didn't even understand it myself? Paige Knox had hurt me more than any other person in the history of ever. She'd gouged straight into my soul, yet I couldn't seem to manage a clean break.

What did it all mean? That was the big question.

CHAPTER SIX

The morning after Paige's unexpected call, I'd awakened with a fresh perspective and renewed determination. Our unexpected conversation had thrown me. Absolutely. And I take full responsibility for having acted so wishy-washy. Telling her I still loved her? A huge mistake, one I steadfastly planned to avoid in the future. I'd told Paige I would think about being friends, and I had.

The answer was, it wouldn't work. Everything was still too fresh in my mind, and I didn't see the sense in ripping open those wounds. Therefore, I didn't feel the need to say anything about the whole situation to Kellen or Allison, because really, what had happened? Nothing.

Instead, I set my focus squarely on Kellen and homecoming and moving forward with my life. Paige continued calling over the next couple of weeks, but I never picked up. Voice mail, baby. It's a wonderful thing. She e-mailed; I read and deleted. She IM'ed, and I pretended I wasn't at the computer. I felt good about my avoidance decision as a whole, but I'd be a liar if I claimed ignoring her didn't bother me every now and then. It's weird how the brain can play tricks, blocking out bad memories, filling you with nostalgia and doubt about choices you know are sane and sound. Some days it felt like I was turning my back on a friend in need. But then I'd go for a long walk—my medicine of choice—and eventually regain my perspective.

Paige was my past.

And it didn't matter anyway, because I was with Kellen and totally happy, despite the fact that we spent an inordinate amount of time debating what we should wear to freakin' homecoming. Sheesh! You think one girl obsesses about homecoming clothes? Try throwing a second girl into the mix. Swear to God, the whole thing was out of control. I wondered if Larry and his date (some guy from a different school whom we were all dying to meet) were embroiled in the same fashion drama.

The sticking point? Kellen always wears frothy, floaty, girly-girl costumes for her productions, so she basically wanted to go the drag route and rent a tux. Ninety-nine percent of the time, I wear jeans or cargo pants, so I was leaning toward a dress, just to mix things up. Plus, the "lesbians wearing tuxedos" thing was so overdone it was almost clichéd, which made me not want to go there. If Kel wanted to rock the menswear, more power to her. She's the type of girl who looks hot and feminine no matter what. As for my outfit, I just wanted her jaw to drop when she saw me. In the end, we decided to surprise each other, which made it that much more fun anyway.

I was browsing funky boutiques in downtown Denver one day after school—alone, which is my favorite way to shop. You can look as long as you like, avoid stores you aren't interested in, and you don't have to take anyone else's viewpoint into consideration. I'd picked out five dresses at my best little store and carried them into the changing-room area, hoping a particular favorite would fit me. It was a black-and-white, shoulder-baring tuxedo dress, cut all the way down to my waist in the back. Ha! I knew Kellen would appreciate the irony of the tux angle. Plus, if she did end up wearing an actual tux, we'd look cool together.

I was almost afraid to try it on, in case it didn't fit like I hoped, so I tried on the other four first and immediately eliminated two. Finally, I slipped into the tuxedo dress, and it was perfect. A definite jaw dropper. The salesclerk had given me some black patent leather heels to try on (since I'd come in wearing clogs). I slid them onto my feet and felt instantly beautiful. But I needed to check out the butt view in the three-way mirror before it was a done deal.

The changing-room door creaked as I opened it, and I came face to face with Paige, who'd emerged from the room across from mine.

I froze. She froze. What are the odds?

We warily checked out each other's outfits. I hadn't been this close to her, alone, in almost two months. Awkward.

"Wow, Mimi. You look awesome," she said, as if this were utterly normal, like we'd been shopping together or something. At least it broke the ice.

"You think?" I moved toward the three-way mirror and turned

this way and that. Oh, yeah. This sucker was going home with me, along with the shoes.

"Definitely," she said.

I spun and eyed her fitted, army green halter dress. "Thanks. That color looks great with your hair." I shook my head around a little bit, realizing how weird this was. "Wait a sec. What are you *doing* here?"

"Same as you, probably. Getting a dress for homecoming."

"Yeah, but *here?*"

She hiked one shoulder. "You always talked about how great this boutique was, and I didn't feel like shopping at Creighton Crossing with everyone else. I hope you don't mind."

"Mind? N-no," I stammered. "It's not that. It's just . . ."

"What's the likelihood of us both showing at the same store, same time?"

"Yeah," I said, crossing my arms protectively over my body. And in some sick twist of fate, Pink was wailing out of the shop's sound system. I thought of all the calls, e-mails, and instant messages she'd sent me that I'd ignored, briefly considered offering an excuse about them, then decided I didn't owe her one. She'd no doubt gotten the hint from my silence.

"Well, I'm not stalking you if that's what you think."

"Please. Give me a break." I could be the bigger person here. I lifted my chin toward her dress. "So, is that the one?" My insides roiled with an odd mixture of apprehension and ease. On the one hand, being around her felt just . . . normal, which simultaneously felt unsettling and uncomfortable. I didn't like it one bit.

She glanced down, running her palms down the curves of her body. "Yeah, I think so. It fits." She twisted her mouth to the side. "And it's on sale. Whatever."

I nodded soberly. "I'm sure Marcos will like it."

"Oh," she said, as if that hadn't occurred to her. "Well . . . I guess. I don't care. I'm not dressing for anyone other than myself." She took her turn in the three-way mirror, holding her long, blond hair off her back so she could peer over her shoulder at the rear view.

For a few moments, I just stood there, open-mouthed and blinking. I thought of how much I wanted to wow Kellen with my own outfit. Paige's ambivalence saddened me. When I'd finally swallowed back my shock from her admission, I said, "It shouldn't be like that, Paige. If you're dating—"

"Eh." Her small smile seemed winsome as she released her hair, letting it float around her shoulders. "It doesn't really matter, does it?"

Yes! I wanted to yell. *You traded in a relationship with someone who cared about every detail of your life for that?* "Aren't you guys nominated for homecoming queen and king?" I asked, as if I didn't know. As if I didn't get ripped-angry every time I read the nominations that were plastered all over the school. Like what were the selection criteria? Being *examples* for the rest of the students?

"Yeah, but . . . whatever." She rolled her eyes, but I sensed a deep sadness behind the flippancy. "Anyway." Her hands sort of twirled, then dropped to her sides. "I'll let you get back to your shopping. The dress is great, though. You should definitely get it." She turned toward her dressing room.

"Paige, wait." My heart started thud-thud-thudding.

She stopped. I watched the rise and fall of her shoulder blades as she inhaled, then exhaled slowly. Finally, she turned around.

"Why?" I whispered, in a voice shaky with anger and sadness. I didn't have to explain the simple question.

Her lips trembled, and tears filled her eyes. "I freaked out."

I huffed a weird mixture of exasperation and defeat. My body exploded with heat. "That's it? You were scared? You destroyed my life because of your own fear?"

She nodded as a tear spilled over her cheek.

"So, are you straight or not?" I demanded, spreading my arms. Her mouth twisted to the side. "Not."

I sank down onto a bench in the mirror area and rested my forehead on my fingertips, breathing deeply, trying to contain all the dark emotions that I yearned to unleash on her.

"Mia?"

I leveled her with a stare. "What you're doing to Marcos? It isn't right."

"I know. But what's done is done. It's not like he cares."

My jaw tightened. "Is that what you thought about me, too?"

"No! Never."

"Then?" I spread my arms, searching her face for some reasonable explanation. "I don't get you at all. And I thought I knew you *so* well."

She shrugged helplessly, hiccuping back a sob. "Mia, I don't know what to say. Nothing I say will take it away."

I stood, straightening my back. "That's the first honest thing you've said in a long time. I have to go."

"Wait." She stepped toward me and reached out.

I stared down at her hand, and she pulled it back. "Please."

"What?"

"Is there . . . anything at all I can do to make it up to you? So that we could at least be friends again?"

Friends? I relived the agonizing moment at the Lake Bash, the desperate lows it had led to. I thought about Marcos, and how he'd feel knowing he was just being used. Finally, I heard Paige whispering, "Not," when I asked her if she was straight moments earlier. The whole thing was too overwhelmingly bad. I blew out a breath. "God, Paige. I don't . . . think so."

"I'm so sorry," she said, clasping her hands together, pressing them to her mouth.

"I know. So am I."

"But that's not good enough, is it?"

"No." I shrugged helplessly. "I don't hate you, if that's what you're worried about. It was just all so public and ugly. I didn't deserve that."

She nodded, and a fresh torrent of tears spilled down her cheeks. "I know."

This whole situation was dragging me down. I needed to escape, to call Kellen, to get back to my new reality. I turned toward my dressing room, but before I closed the door, she whispered, "I'm sorry."

I gripped the knob and faced her. Sorry just wasn't going to cut it. "You need to stop lying, Paige. To yourself. To everyone. You'll never be truly happy until you stop worrying about other people and start *thinking* about them instead."

• • •

So, the jaw-dropping thing? Yeah, times two. Kellen indeed wore a tuxedo, but it was a girl tuxedo. Black and white and killer hot all over. The top was just like a tuxedo vest, backless (and man, could she rock the backless), and it went so well with my dress, it looked like we had planned it. When she opened the door and we saw each other, it went like this: step one, *gape*; Step two, *laugh*. It was just too perfect.

We groaned through a round of photos at Kellen's house, then had to drive back to my house so my mom and dad could snap their own library of shots. After that, we met up with Allison and Chanel, who were attending homecoming at Alternative that night, and we all took pictures of each other and promised to meet after our separate festivities at the twenty-four-hour coffee shop Chanel had turned us on to. But it wasn't over yet. Once we arrived at school, the entire CHSAA group met for an historic photograph by the flagpole. Even local media had shown up.

Phew! No one was going to forget this night anytime soon.

Wade had eventually decided to work the stag angle, so we invited him to be our guy date. Larry's mysterious boyfriend, Micah, looked like an Abercrombie and Fitch model—I swear! As predicted, Braxton and Felicity had arrived hand in hand, and Mr. Horst and his partner looked supercute in their suits. It was the best night of my entire life.

Sure, Dalton Prescott and a few others lurked around in the

corners of the darkened, decorated gym cracking jokes at our expense, but, dude, we're "SHA-ZAA!" We're a force to be reckoned with, the school board had recognized us, and no one could chip through our armor anymore. I'd gotten a glimpse of Paige in her army green dress sort of loitering by the food table, and, strangely, it didn't hurt anymore. I just felt sorry for her.

Kel and I were dancing to a slow song, midway through the night, talking and laughing with Wade, who'd been dancing with a cute, normal (meaning, not fake) sophomore girl none of us knew named Cherie. Apparently she'd just transferred in from a school in New York City. Wade danced her around until her back faced us, then raised his eyebrows over her shoulder as though seeking our approval. Kellen and I gave him the thumbs-up, then snuggled in to finish out the song. I sighed. "This is awesome."

She nuzzled my neck. "I know. When I said I wanted a normal teenage experience, I did *not* expect you."

"Is that a good thing?"

She kissed me. "It's a great thing." She hesitated briefly. "I love you, Mia."

My heart opened up and I didn't even pause. "I love you, too."

The song ended, and the band got up for a break, probably wishing this gig was at a bar that served beer instead of a high school that served punch and cookies. The lights went up on the stage, and Vice Principal Marlene Moriarty click-clacked up to the microphone in her pumps and pencil skirt. "Welcome to homecoming, everyone. Are you having fun?"

Applause and whistles rose to the rafters.

"Excellent. It's the moment I'm sure some of you have been waiting for. The announcement of this year's king and queen."

A smattering of cheers and hollering rippled through the crowd. Kellen and I both scanned the crowd looking for Paige and Marcos. Paige wasn't by the food table anymore.

"Uh-oh," Kellen said.

I followed her glance. Paige and Marcos were clearly arguing in the far corner of the gym, not paying attention at all to the coronation ceremony, which rolled along.

"Trouble in paradise?" Kel asked, biting the corner of her lip.

"Looks like it." I'd told Kellen about my run-in with Paige at the boutique. "It was destined to happen."

"I know, but should we do something?"

"Do what?" I blinked.

"I don't know. Go over there and warn them? Make sure everything's—"

"And this year's homecoming king and queen are . . ."

The drummer had returned to the stage for a quick drumroll.

Kellen and I both held our breath and squeezed each other's hands.

"Marcos Antonopolous and Paige Knox!"

The arguing couple spun toward the stage upon hearing their names boom out over the speakers. Everyone other than us burst into applause.

"Oops," I said, just as Kellen whispered, "Shit."

After a moment, Paige headed for the stage, and Marcos headed for the front doors of the gym. Halfway through the crowd, Paige looked over her shoulder, paused a moment when she realized she was on her own, then pressed her lips together and forged ahead.

"This can't be good," Kellen whispered.

Paige accepted the crowns, but shook her head when they tried to place hers on her head. She leaned forward and said something into Mrs. Moriarty's ear. The VP looked confused, but lifted her arm toward the microphone and retreated. Paige stepped hesitantly toward the mike, the two crowns looped around her wrists like oversize handcuffs. She cleared her throat, and the mike squealed feedback. The whole gym fell silent.

"Um, hi. Thanks for this, I guess. I don't deserve it."

A wave of curious whispers rustled through the crowd.

"So, bear with me for a few minutes, because I have something to say." A beat passed. "A person I love and respect told me recently that I have to stop worrying about what other people think and start thinking about people other than myself instead." She paused, sought me out in the crowd, and braved a small smile. Everyone turned to look at me, and my face went hot.

"Well," Paige said. "She was right."

"Kill me now," I muttered.

"Shh," Kellen said. "Just listen."

"I guess I'll turn over that new leaf right now." She flapped her arms. "I just got dumped."

Gasps rose.

"No, don't be surprised. I'm not." She twisted her mouth to the side. "I had it coming, and Marcos deserves better than me. Everyone deserves someone who can love them for who they truly are." She stirred her hand, encompassing the group. "This whole moment? It's a bit of bad karma coming back to bite me in the ass." She flashed a look toward the veep. "Sorry."

I hadn't seen a group of teens so universally rapt since Lake Bash. Paige moistened her lips, a little bit of fear peeking through her veneer. I swear, we could all feel it. Larry and his hottie date moved closer. "What's this about?"

I shrugged and kept my eyes on the stage.

"So, did any of you go to this year's Lake Bash?"

"Crap," I wheezed out. "I have to sit down."

"Stay here," Kellen said. "Hold on to me."

I did. Clutched, really.

"I told a horrible lie that night and hurt someone I love very much. All because I was too weak and scared to be myself. I've been up nights racking my brain for a way to make it up to her. You know, come full circle." She hiked one shoulder. "Couldn't figure it out until Mrs. Moriarty called my name. Well, our names. So, here goes nothing." She sucked in a deep breath and blew it out. "I'm gay"—more gasps—"and

Mia Salazar was my first true love. We dated all summer, the best months of my life. But I wasn't as brave as all of you who formed CHSAA, so I lied about her, I lied to Marcos, and worst of all, I lied to myself."

I couldn't tear my eyes away from the stage because I felt a zillion pairs of eyes looking back and forth from the stage to me.

"What did it get me?" She held up one arm slightly. "A stupid crown. I lost Mia, as I deserved. She has a great new girlfriend who's worthy of her, and I'm not trying to sabotage that *at all*."

Kellen held me closer.

"I hurt Marcos," Paige said, "and I feel ashamed."

My heart spasmed. God, I knew how she felt. I wanted to cry for her, to whisk her off to safety like Al had done for me on Lake Bash night. I couldn't believe she was standing there in front of the whole school and—

"Anyway, this year's homecoming is about more than the so-called popular couple wearing crowns." She flicked the notion aside. "That's *so* last year."

Laughter.

"The school board made the historic decision to allow same-sex couples at our dance, and I think that needs to be acknowledged and commemorated. If I had been just a little bit braver, maybe I'd be here with my girlfriend, if I had one, and maybe I'd feel like I could stand before you proudly and wear this crown." She shook her head. "But I can't. So, I'd like to suggest we have a homecoming queen and queen this year. Mia and Kellen?"

"No," I said under my breath, digging in my heels. "No. I don't want to go up there, Kel."

"We have to," Kellen said, searching my face. "Don't you see? We cannot leave her hanging out to dry like she did to you after the Lake Bash."

"Yeah, are you *high?*" Larry asked, his eyes round. "I've wanted to be homecoming queen my whole *life*. You have to do this for us, Mia. For the group."

A brilliant idea struck me. "Come on." I grabbed Larry's hand and

Kellen's. Larry grabbed his date's hand, and we approached the stage. I looked up at Paige and shook my head. "Okay, okay," I said. "I heard you. Everyone heard you, so stop, please. You're killing me."

She looked like her old self, but more peaceful. "I need to make my point."

"Uh, you did. I swear."

"I swear, she swears," Kellen said.

I pushed Larry and Micah gently toward the stage. "But, as much as we appreciate the shout out, we don't want to be homecoming queens—"

"Ooh!" Larry said, lifting his arm. "We do."

The crowd started clapping to a rhythm and chanting, "LAR-RY! LAR-RY!" Honest to God, you've never seen an emo kid beam so brightly. Kellen and I shared a grin, then eased back from the stage and joined in on the chanting and clapping.

Larry and Micah skipped up the steps and gladly freed Paige from the shackle crowns on her wrists. She leaned in and spoke to them as they affixed the glittery things to their heads, then she stood between them and held each of their hands. "I'd like to present you with your homecoming king and king—"

Larry hip-checked her to the side and leaned into the microphone. "Um, homecoming *queens,* thank you very much."

The crowd hooted and laughed.

"Okay, then," Paige said, "to your homecoming queen and queen, Larry and Micah!" She lifted their arms like prizefighting boxers, and the entire gym erupted into applause.

Wade and Cherie moved up next to us. "This is the best friggin' dance I've ever been to," he said. "How awesome is it that Larry is homecoming queen?"

"No kidding!" Cherie said.

We all hugged and laughed as the music started up again. Larry moved through the crowd like the royalty he was. I caught a glimpse of Dalton Prescott staring at the spectacle in horrified disbelief, and that made me grin. I wondered if he'd *ever* grow up.

"Come on," Kellen said, tugging at my arm as I spoke to Wade and Cherie.

"Where?"

She lifted her chin toward Paige, who hovered at the edge of the stage, alone.

"I can't. Allison will kill me."

"No, she won't." Kel gave me another tug. "Allison loves you. All she wants for you is happiness. And for you to be peaceful. You need to jump this hurdle to get there, and you know it."

I looked at Paige, my first love and my first horrible breakup, and I felt free. Free to love Kellen, free of the pain Paige had caused me. Free to be her friend again, one small step at a time. She glanced over and saw us approaching, a tentative smile on her face.

For a second, we all stood staring at each other. Then I expelled a breath. "God, Paige, you might've been afraid to come out, but you ended up doing it in a big-ass way."

She and Kellen laughed, then Paige sobered. "I'm sorry, Mia. And I know sorry's not enough, like you said. Everything you told me about myself? True."

Kellen reached out and grabbed Paige's hand. "I think you can both move past that, though. Let it go."

I swear, Kel was the sweetest, most giving person in the world. How many girlfriends would say that to the proverbial evil ex?

"Can we, Mia?" Paige asked. "I could really use some friends."

I glanced at Kellen for reassurance, and she winked. "Yeah," I said, leaning in to kiss Kellen before glancing at Paige. "Friends."

The three of us embraced, my past and my future reaching out and connecting, leaving me happily whole in the present with my life.

And isn't that what it's all about?